# SAINT: AN AFRICAN AMERICAN URBAN STANDALONE

## LAKIA

*Lakia*Presents

❀ Created with Vellum

## JOIN AUTHOR LAKIA'S MAILING LIST!

To stay up to date on new releases, contests, and sneak peeks join my mailing list. Subscribers will enjoy the FIRST look at all content from Author Lakia plus exclusive short stories!
https://bit.ly/2RTP3EV

# PROLOGUE

## Saint Carmichael

*C*oach Chef flailed an aggressive "T" in the air using his right and left hand. The referee blew the whistle and yelled time-out. My chest heaved up and down as I bounced the ball in the refs' direction and jogged over to the team huddle.

"It's only fifteen seconds left and we gotta push this shit down the court! We tryin' to win this shit!" I clapped at them boys in a motivational manner.

My teammates clung to every word and I would forever love these boys, we got it out the mud together this year. We were so close to winning the state championship basketball finals. Win, lose, or draw, your boy was straight but this was a goal that I was so close to accomplishing. I secured a full ride scholarship to the top three schools on my vision board so I was out this bitch come August. For now, it was about my current team.

"Push them niggas, Saint! Bring the dub home! Them fuck niggas can't see you, Saint!" Bishop roared from the front row of the bleachers.

The gym was swanging, seemed like the entire city took that drive to see us play in the championship game. I nodded my head at Bishop who stood next to his girlfriend, Natalie, and blew a kiss at the love of my life, Mia. She caught the air kiss with her right hand and placed it over her heart. They were at every game, rocking my name and number on a custom shirt that Mia created with her lil cricket machine. Bishop used to pay to have custom shirts made but Mia's looked just as professional so he started paying her.

"Stay focused, nigga! Now ain't the time to be worried about pussy!" Bishop barked.

Natalie slapped fire from Bishop's ass and he rubbed the back of his neck before talking shit to her. I'm positive she was checking his ass for that mouth he never knew how to filter. The audience, location, or time didn't matter to my brother, he was going to talk his shit with no filter. He had been that way since I could remember, and everyone that knew Bishop was always shocked to learn that I was his younger brother. Although Bishop raised me by himself for the last eight years, I didn't inherit his brash demeanor and I never would. At eighteen years old, I was still lowkey with my shit, playing ball and accomplishing my goals were the only thing on the agenda.

The referee blew his whistle, signaling the end of the time out. As the point guard and team captain, it was my job to lead the team, orchestrate plays, and above all else, utilize my keen court vision to exploit any opportunities to create shots for myself or my teammates. I was only five ten so I didn't have the typical basketball player's height on my side, but my size allowed me to drive that lane quicker than the taller players.

Stepping in position, I shook all of the jitters off and got in my zone. Everything around me went silent once I gained possession of the leather sphere, we were hungry for this win and were determined to have it. I passed the ball to Asim and he faked the jit guarding him out and passed the ball back to me. Pushing that shit down the court, I saw the clock winding down but I didn't have a shot. The boys from Crystal Lake were on my ass hard. I knew they were expecting me to take the shit, leaving Asim open, so I passed the ball back to him and he posted up at the three point line. Watching in angst, I think I stopped breathing once the ball left his fingertips.

"Let's fucking goooooooooooooooooooo!" I erupted in celebration

2

as the fans from the stands, our teammates, and coaching staff rushed the floor.

"Come on, them pussy ass niggas wasn't ready!" Bishop's voice was heard over the crowd. I shook my head, but I wasn't at all shocked by Bishop's antics. The other parents have been giving that nigga dirty looks since I was in middle school, even back then, he was talking his shit in the stand to a bunch of middle school kids, but that was Bishop and he couldn't help it. He trolloped over to me, slapping my hand and pulling me in for a hug. "I've always been proud of the young man you've become, securing a scholarship, keeping your grades up and now this?! I'm proud *as fuck* that you my young nigga!"

"Thanks, Bishop," I fought off my emotions in his embrace.

Mia and Natalie approached after Bishop and I embraced my sister in-law in a church hug before focusing my attention on my girl. She was always in the stands, cheering me on and looking good as fuck. Her thighs were spilling out of her shorts and the black and red number twenty-eight always looked perfect on her. Lifting Mia off the ground, I spun her around as she clasped her soft hands over my face and pecked my lips. I couldn't fight the urge to swirl my tongue around her mouth so I did that shit.

"Come on man, nobody wanna see all that," Bishop voiced behind us.

"Let them be kids, Bishop," Natalie mumbled.

"Nah, he needs to go shake up with the other team and his team-mates and get changed so we can slide. I got big plans for the night."

"Yeah, let me go do my thing," I informed Mia.

She bit her bottom lip as I planted her on the floor. Bishop raised his left fist and I glided my right fist to meet his, they gently collided somewhere in the middle of the space between us. With one final glance at my family, I went to handle my business with the team. We talked shit, celebrated, and enjoyed our final moments with each other on the court before the trophy ceremony went down. Coach Chef took the microphone and his eyes swept across his team before he began.

"I want to take a quick moment to shout out my team. We aren't a big name prep school and they counted my boys out but **we did it!** We are taking home the 2023 Championship title! I'm proud of each and every player on the team and I can't wait to see what the future has in store for all of them. NBA talks for Asim and Saint, all of our seniors have full ride scholarships, and we are just blessed!" Coach Chef stated and we clapped it up.

We didn't clear out of the gym for another two hours. "This shit feels weird as fuck knowing this was the last time we will be hooping on the same team together."

"I know, it's the end of an era," I shook my head. "We had a good run and we ended that shit on a high note and you were behind that winning shot, jit. Man I was nervous as fuck."

"Shit, you were scared?" he exhaled. "Man, I was on the three point line like *don't fuck this shit up*. I couldn't go back to the hood if I fumbled that type of play, we set that shit up too sweet."

"Bishop is throwing a lil something back at the crib. You trying to slide?"

"Nah, my mama wanna go to dinner and shit. I'mma hit the groupchat because we gotta get the gang together and turn the fuck up without the adults in our business."

"Already," I shook it up with Asim as he jogged over to his family.

Bishop and the girls had already left. We only lived forty minutes away from the arena where the championship was held, perks of being a Tampa native. The parking lot was turnt the fuck up, family laughing and waiting for their champions to exit the arena. A few niggas pulled up to the entrance and had *Win* by Jeezy playing to the max. Bishop was usually the nigga pulling that type of stunt but he was in a rush to slide tonight.

I wasn't dumb though, if Bishop didn't stick around and rushed home, I was in for a real surprise tonight. Hopping in my Dodge Challenger, I turned on my Jimbo World playlist and hit I-4. Riding along the interstate with my music turned up was always therapeutic for me. Until those red and blue lights flashed behind me. Pulling into the grass, I barely made it out of Polk County before them boys were on my ass.

As Bishop always taught me, I rolled my windows down, placed my documentation on the dashboard, and placed my hands where they could see them. "Hey Siri, call Bishop," I requested and a few moments later, the ringing of his phone filled the car. Interacting with the police always brought on a different type of anxiety, that lil play anxiety I experienced during the basketball game was nothing compared to the manner in which my heart was thumping in my chest now.

"Sir, I noticed your car swerving back there and we received complaints of a car fitting your description driving recklessly on the interstate so I need you to step out of the car," he commanded, pulling on my door handle. When I put the car in park it automatically unlocked the doors and now I wish I would've locked them back. I didn't have time to rebuttal before I was exposed to the elements on the side of the interstate. Confident that I wasn't under the influence, I unbuckled my seatbelt and stepped out of the car.

"You have reached..." Bishop's voicemail picked up and it seemed like that moment was the catalyst for the events that changed the trajectory of my life.

"Hands up! Step away from the vehicle!" The officer shouted, panic lacing his voice.

"Yo chill, I'm..."

In the midst of me speaking, the officer kicked my legs from under me, sending me crashing into the cement. He fell onto my back, knee lodged into my spine as he cuffed me. "Hey, what's going on? I didn't do anything wrong, I stepped out of the car and followed your commands," I expressed, fighting to stay calm in this predicament that called for rage.

The officer didn't respond but leaned into my car and retrieved a gun.

"That's not mine!" I shouted, astounded by his retrieval. Although my brother was in the streets I wasn't that type, I didn't ride around with a gun on me or no shit like that. Bishop didn't even ride in my car dirty or let his people come around me unless they were clean as a whistle. My future was of the utmost importance to him so I had no idea how a weapon wound up in my vehicle.

"Yeah, I've heard that a million times. This same caliber of firearm was used in a home invasion in my neighborhood recently and you and your vehicle fit the description. I'll let the system figure it out," he boasted with a smile.

Clearly, this officer didn't give a fuck to hear me so I laid on the ground, praying that a car didn't accidentally run us over for the next hour while he did whatever the fuck cops do while they have a teenage boy handcuffed and face down on the side of the interstate. Throughout the duration of my time at the lowest point in my life, literally and figuratively, I came to terms with why Boosie screamed ***fuck the police*** so hard, it was *forever* fuck them.

# CHAPTER ONE

## Saint

### *Eight Years Later*

*S*taring up at the tattered ceiling, I counted the stains to help
ease my anxiety and hopefully fall asleep. After eight years in
prison, for a crime I didn't commit, I developed anxiety and this was
how I dealt with the shit. At barely eighteen years old, I was railroaded
by the criminal justice system, charged with possession of a firearm,
robbery, and assault with a deadly weapon. The gun was in fact used in
a home invasion where a neighbor was pistol whipped and an acci-
dental round was shot during the commission of the crime.

As soon as Bishop caught wind of my arrest, he hired the best
criminal defense attorney and we took that shit to trial. Unfortunately,
the police went at me hard as fuck when they learned I was the
younger brother of Bishop Carmichael. Hillsborough, Polk, and
Pinellas county officers formed a task force to go at Bishop and his
crew a few years prior to my arrest and failed miserably. In my honest
opinion, they threw the book at me as a consolation prize for fumbling
their shot at Bishop. It was clear that the prosecutor and crooked ass
judge were on a mission, overruling every objection my lawyer threw
out while sustaining all of the prosecutor's bullshit objections. The

victim of the crime got on the stand capping and fingered me confidently. That sealed my fate because my only alibi was my brother so that didn't help my case any. For some reason I couldn't stop that day from running through my head tonight.

*The group of seven white men and five white women shuffled into the jury box and my stomach was bubbling, palms were sweating, and it was taking all of my strength to hold my shit together. My future rested in their hands. All of my scholarship offers were rescinded, I'd been confined to the four walls of my home since Bishop bonded me out and my life would probably never be the same regardless of the outcome. Even though my dreams of becoming a starting point guard in the league were thwarted, I would be thankful for my freedom after this ordeal.*

*My breathing slowed and sweat dripped off my forehead in this cold ass courtroom as everyone took their position. Candace Valentine, my lawyer, squeezed my hand in an attempt to comfort me as the proceedings started. When the wrinkled ass white judge rendered the* **guilty** *verdict, I allowed my emotions to consume me. I burst into tears, an emotional ugly cry escaped me.*

*"Keep yo head up, Saint!" Bishop shouted, on his feet and reaching across the barrier to hug me. "Fuck these crackas, I'mma get you out!" The judge banged on his gavel, demanding order in the court. "Fuck you pussy!" Bishop shouted at him and was swiftly tackled by two bailiffs. Mia and Natalie were also enthralled with their emotions, hugging each other and screaming obscenities.*

I jumped out of my sleep, hearing Mia and Natalie's deafening cries. Running my hands down my face, if I was going to dream about that shit, I'd rather stay awake. Mia got ghost as soon as I was sentenced to eight years in prison and I couldn't blame her, baby girl had to live her life. Bishop rocked out with me, visiting me every other week, making sure my books had money on them and all that good shit until he was sent up the road himself two years ago. Getting released from prison while my brother had to sit down was definitely some bittersweet shit that I wasn't really prepared for. After everything I'd been through at the age of eighteen, I had grown accustomed to gearing up for life's curveballs.

"You up, Saint?" I heard Dylan's voice from the cell next to me. Unfortunately, the system devoured him whole at the age of eighteen and we wound up relating on a lot of things.

"Yeah man, can't sleep, ready to get out this bitch."

"Man, they about to open them gates for my boy," Dylan celebrated. "When you get out, don't let them fuck niggas trick you off the streets again like they did me. Make shit official with your shorty and rock out."

"That's the plan," I confirmed.

"I love you, bro."

"Love you too," I admitted.

The sun crept through the windows and I smiled thinking about Shalana, my girl for the last six months. When Dylan's baby mama came to visit him, I happened to be visiting with Bishop and noticed how fine she was. My eyes constantly drifted in their direction to the point that Dylan noticed and got her number for me. Shalana used to drive Dylan's baby mama up to see him anyways so we started chatting and shit. Next thing I knew, I'm asking her to be my girl. Shit been cool as fuck too, I was thankful for meeting her because her pretty face was standing on the opposite side of the fence when they finally opened them gates.

"Saint!" Shalana screeched, rushing in my direction. "They done freed my nigga!"

Dressed in my basketball shorts and black t-shirt I was arrested in, I almost wanted to kiss the ground now that I was on the opposite side of that gate. Once Shalana was within reach, I scooped her slim frame up into my arms and accepted her assault of kisses. Her legs wrapped around my waist and my dick grew in my basketball shorts. This was the most affection I'd received in years and it was more than welcomed.

"Come on, you're already excited," Shalana licked her lips.

I placed her on the ground and she grasped my hand, leading me to her car. Shalana drove a cute Nissan Altima and it was spacious as fuck on the inside. She pulled away from the prison and I didn't bother to take a look back. "I brought you a change of clothes and shoes. Plus a toiletry set, they are in the backseat."

"Word?" I questioned. My release date was moved up and I couldn't get in touch with Natalie to pick me up. Last I heard, Bishop caught thirty days in solitary so I couldn't have Natalie message him to set anything up. When I called Natalie she didn't answer the phone, probably sick of me and Bishop's prison bullshit. Thankfully, Shalana didn't hesitate to pick a nigga up and take me to the crib.

"Yeah," she bubbled.

"Pull over at the first truck stop so I can shower. My boys said there is a Pilot twenty minutes down the road on 301," I stated.

"Okay, look it up on the GPS," she requested, passing me the phone.

Phones changed since I was locked up but it wasn't unchartered territory, however it would take some getting used to. I opened the Maps App and set up the directions. Resting in the passenger seat, I couldn't believe the day finally arrived and I was a free man. I completed my full eight years, didn't want to get out early because then I'd have to confess to a crime I didn't commit and I didn't want to wind up like Dylan. He did all of that work to get out, just to end up with a parole officer that was on his ass and found himself right back in prison. I wanted to leave that bitch free and clear of the soul sucking system, no strings attached. The idea of *any* interaction with the police shoving me back in a cell didn't sit right with me.

Twenty minutes later, we pulled up to the rest stop and Shalana waited in the car while I washed the prison stench off of me and dressed in the Nike jogger set, a pair of Air Max 95s, and matching Nike socks. The early February air was cooler than usual in Florida but I loved this shit, we didn't experience it often. Tossing my clothes in the trash, I swaggered over to the Altima feeling like a new man. Dropping into the car, I noticed Shalana staring at me. "What?"

"You just so damn fine," she complimented, reaching over to massage my dick. I just got my shit to go down from the hug and I wasn't going to be able to remain a gentleman if she didn't move her hands. Gripping her neck, my shit fit all the way around her tiny neck and that shit turned me on even more. I pulled her face across the seat and devoured her lips. They were thick and luscious, the softest thing I'd encountered in years.

Without further coaching, Shalana climbed over to my side of the car and straddled my lap. "You was talking all that freaky shit on the phone, let me see if you about all that shit you were hollin' 'bout," I urged, pulling my joggers down.

Shalana's eyes widened as she viewed my shit, I wasn't lacking in the length or girth department. "Nah, don't get scared now," I encouraged. My dick was damn near touching the ceiling as she reached back and retrieved a condom from the glove compartment. I pulled her titties out the top of her dress and popped one in my mouth. For the first time I noticed her nipple piercings, the metal added to the erotic feeling of sucking her titties as she grinded into me. One thing Bishop always taught me was to bring your own condoms but I wasn't in a position to give a fuck about all of that at this moment. Shalana was moving all sexy and shit, prompting me to snatch the condom and roll it down over my dick. I gripped Shalana's waist and ripped her panties off before easing her onto my dick.

"Fuck Saint, baby, it hurt so good!" Shalana moaned out, and I planned to take shit easy on her when we fucked for the first time but I couldn't. Shit felt so unfamiliar. I promise a nigga was fighting not to bust fast but the eight year drought made me feel like a virgin all over again.

"Ride that shit, that's your favorite position right? Show me," I leaned back in the seat and encouraged her while thumbing her clit.

"Don't challenge me to a good time. I'mma show out every time." Shalana placed both feet on opposite sides of me and bounced on my dick like a pro.

"Show out on that dick." I pinched her nipples, praying the shit didn't hurt her because I never dealt with a chick who had her nipples pierced. Shalana moaned and planted her hands on my chest so it must've felt good. "I'm about to cum, Saint!" Shalana squealed.

I gripped Shalana's back and brought her in close to me, sucking her neck while controlling the pace, thrusting my dick into her from behind. Her words were music to my ears and the moment I took over, my dick spit. Shalana was right behind me, her body tensed up as she collapsed on my chest. Rubbing her back, I enjoyed this moment of intimacy, I hated that we were in a car. Guiding Shalana's dress back over her hips, I pulled my dick out of her and tapped her thigh. In the moment, I didn't give a fuck if somebody walked by and saw me dicking her down, but I was more respectful than this shit.

"Come on, Ion want nobody to walk by and see you like this," I informed her.

"I have on a dress," she stated groggily, pulling her breast back into her dress. "It's you that gotta hide that monster."

I shook my head and pulled my dick back into my joggers. Shalana nestled into my chest before emitting light snores. Easing from under her, I allowed Shalana to remain asleep. I knew she got straight off her eleven to seven shift and drove three hours to pick me up. Her car was lowkey and I should be fine to drive until I got my license straight. Exiting the car, I rounded the whip and claimed the driver's seat and backed out of the parking spot then hopped back on the interstate. The traffic was terrible and added another hour and a half to our drive. We arrived at the home Bishop raised me in at six o'clock.

Gently tapping Shalana's leg, she stirred from her sleep. Baby girl was a rider and I appreciated her for everything she'd done for me today. Throughout my time in prison I was able to use Bishop's connections to look out for her so it was refreshing to receive the same in return.

"This is y'all house?" Shalana gawked at the exterior of the home. The shit was nice as fuck with a lot of land and her response wasn't unusual for someone viewing the home for the first time. Bishop put a lot of work into the home, making it the most valuable in the neighborhood. He had a huge circular driveway paved in the front yard with an African sculpture planted in the middle. The three level home boasted six bedrooms and four bathrooms, way more room than we ever needed but after spending the last eight years in close proximity to so many other men, I was going to enjoy every inch of my room. *My room*. I thought to myself. I had no idea if they revamped it, turned it into something else or anything like that. My room was the last thing on my mind while in prison. I had to assimilate to survive, and those were my only concerns.

"Yeah, I have lived here since I was eleven," I confirmed. "I appreciate you for making that trip for me today. If you don't want to drive back to Tampa, you can crash here, I'll get some money and grab something to eat if big sis didn't cook."

"Can I get round two while I'm here?"

"Man bring yo freak ass on," I shook my head and exited the car.

"I'm just asking," she giggled. "I know you have a comfy bed, can't wait to cuddle up and do other things. I'm sure your brother left some nice shit for you."

"Yeah, I was just thinking I hope I still have a room because I hadn't asked," I admitted, knocking on the door.

"Who is it?" I heard a male's voice on the opposite end of the door.

"Saint," I faltered because that shit caught me off guard.

"Who the fuck is you?" Some tall, bald nigga answered the door looking like a black Mr. Clean.

"Naw, who the fuck are you?" I stepped up, prepared to knock his shit if I didn't like his response. No longer the non-confrontational eighteen year old he would've encountered prior to prison, present day Saint would bust his ass if he didn't respond in a manner which I appreciated.

"I got it, baby, these are my people. Go get Junior, he's upstairs crying," Natalie rushed towards the door in a robe and bonnet.

"Oh my bad y'all, I ain't know. Nat ain't say some of her people were pulling up," he waved at us before rushing up the stairs. Natalie stepped onto the porch and her eyes landed on her feet. Shaking my head, I already knew what was up, she ain't have to explain shit to me, I was a master at putting two and two together. Her robe slipped open and I noticed her shirt grew wetter while she was still eyeing her feet.

"That's breast milk?" I questioned, pointing at her shirt.

"Yes, Saint," she teared up. "I'm sorry. I got pregnant and decided to move on. I couldn't tell Bishop, that's why I kept starting shit with him last year. My belly was too big for him to not notice. I didn't realize that you were getting out because I would've answered the phone for you to save you the trip. You can't stay here and the money Bishop left me with is gone so I don't have anything for you except the truck Bishop bought you as a gift for winning the championship. That's why we rushed home so fast after the game. Bishop was going to give you the car on your graduation day but it arrived early and he wanted to put a bow on it before you got home. When you got locked up, he upgraded the truck every two years in hopes that you would come home early. It's in Bishop's name and parked at my grandma's house. I will call my grandma and inform her that you are on the way to grab the car. Let me go grab the keys for you."

Before I could process her bullshit, Natalie disappeared into the house. Shalana's tense energy filled the space and I hated that she was all in my family business now. A little barefoot boy with chocolate all over his face rushed outside and Shalana swooped in and grabbed his ass up midway through the driveway. If it wasn't for her quick reflexes he would've been as good as gone.

"Roman, what have we told you about running out of the door?" Natalie chastised him.

"I sowwy," the lil boy cried. I eyed his lil ass, wondering who the fuck he belonged to. He was too old to be a child she conceived since Bishop was sent up the road and to my knowledge, Natalie was never pregnant by my brother while I was in prison. Shalana carried the lil boy back over to Natalie and she accepted him into her arms.

"I can already see your wheels churning so let me clear this up, I only have one child who was conceived after Bishop was incarcerated. Roman isn't mine, this is my husband's son and we just have him for the week while his mom is out of town."

"Husband?" I scoffed, thoughts of the little boy now a distant memory.

This shit crushed me just as much as it would hurt Bishop because Natalie was my big sis, been around since before my mom died when I was ten. Natalie was my mother figure, she raised me alongside Bishop and played a major role in my life. Hell, Natalie was the reason I strived to treat women with the respect they deserved, it definitely wasn't Bishop's ass.

"Saint, I'm sorry but I was able to grab fifty dollars for you and the keys to the Chevy Tahoe. Don't forget that Carl has a job for you at Carl Hauls if you want to get right to work," Natalie passed the items to me while wrangling the bad ass boy in her arms. "I have to go, my baby is hungry."

Nodding my head, I couldn't speak because anything I uttered would've been disrespectful. Even prison couldn't remove that trait from the fabric of my personality, that's how deep rooted Natalie's teachings were in me. Turning away from Natalie as the little boy flailed in her arms, I marched back over to Shalana's car. I tossed her the keys and slid into the passenger seat. The high I was riding on wrecked out and I was struggling with my reality. No money, no home, no plan, just a lost soul out here. Taking a deep breath, I looked at Shalana as she sat idle in the driver's seat, wondering why she hadn't taken off.

"Look, it's been fun and all but this is too much for me. I thought you had things in order for when you got out, I wasn't expecting all of this. It's too much. I wasn't planning to take you in. I actually thought you would be able to help me out a lil seeing who your brother is but..." Stepping out of the car, I shook my head.

When I say I *helped this bitch out*, I mean that. Bishop met her at one of the visits and took a liking to her so when her lights were about to get cut off, he paid the shit on the strength of me and gave her some extra cash so she would be ahead, now she acted like a nigga wasn't shit. I shouldn't have been surprised, Bishop's name always drew attention, that's how I ended up in prison in the first place. No, it wasn't Bishop's gun but it was the prosecutor's thirst for his head on a silver platter that fueled their fixation on me, a first time offender who really ain't even do the shit they accused me of. Marching down the sidewalk, I observed my name in the cement outside of the house. When they repaved it I stuck my finger in and wrote my name. Bishop and Natalie were mad as hell that I had hardened cement on my finger when I finally came back in. Shaking my head, seeing that drove the knife of my reality further into my heart.

Shalana pulled up beside me and rolled the window down. "I can take you to her grandma's house so you can at least get around."

I wanted to tell her *fuck you* but that would've only hurt me because I needed that ride. Shoving my hands in my pockets, I jumped in the Altima and didn't say shit as she maneuvered through traffic. Racking my brain, I thought about Bishop's partners but I knew better than to reach out to any of them. Bishop let me know how niggas was moving funny with him out of the way now. Even though Carl was offering me a job, I didn't know the nigga like that to pop up at his house and ask for shelter. Since Bishop wanted better for me he kept me out of the way and didn't allow his associates close to me. At the time it was some noble shit, now it was a hindrance because I didn't have a soul out here now.

"Where does her grandma live?"

"In Nuccio," I grumbled, keying the address in her phone.

The rest of the ride was silent and I allowed myself to enjoy one of my favorite past times, driving on the interstate with the music up to the max. When we arrived at Natalie's grandma's crib, I jumped in the whip without addressing her people and peeled out of the yard, they never fucked with us like that anyways. With my fifty dollars in hand, I went to Walmart on Dale Mabry to buy a toothbrush, toothpaste, pack of boxers, socks, a bottle of water, and a sub from Subway. Most of my money was gone from that one trip to the store. It was eight o'clock once I got settled into the car again. I drove to the back of the parking lot, cracked my windows, and came to terms with the truck being my temporary home. Sadly, it was still better than the prison cell. I had space and privacy for the first time in a long time.

# CHAPTER TWO

## Saint

*I* woke up refreshed and ready to tackle the day. The comfort of the Tahoe wasn't my childhood bedroom but it beat prison, I had my freedom and that was the greatest feeling. My body had grown accustomed to waking up at the crack of dawn in prison so I was up before the sun. I drove to Carl Hauls in South Tampa because I knew the address but not the phone number. Although Bishop made sure I didn't want for shit, he still wanted to keep me grounded so I often helped Carl out when he was short staffed during the offseason. He told Bishop I had a job with him as soon as I got out because he knew I wasn't on none of that dumb shit I was accused of.

Parking in the second closest spot near the door, I allowed the air conditioner to fill the car as I listened to the radio. Around eight o'clock, Carl eased into the owner's parking spot and stepped out of a nice ass Range Rover. Killing my engine and exiting the car, I immediately sensed the irritation in his tone as he spoke into the big ass earpiece in his ear.

"Ion care that they are your nephews Bianca, the niggas are fired whenever they do pop up. I don't pay them that salary so they can pop pills, drink, and call in to work two or three times a week. I'm throwing their positions up on Indeed and hiring a whole new team." He paused for a moment, frustrated and fumbling with his keys when he sensed my presence. "Saint," Carl grinned, displaying his mouth full of permanent gold teeth before embracing me in a hug and leaning back to observe me in adult form. "Wassup man! I pray you here for that job offer because I sure need somebody reliable. Welcome home man!" He hugged me again for a brief second then returned to opening the front door.

"Shit, I'm ready to take whatever you offering," I remarked.

"I gotta go Bianca, I just hired them niggas' first replacement," Carl informed his wife before pressing a button on the side of his ear.

"Man, I'm so mufuckin' mad, I couldn't get the key in the hole," he admitted, finally opening the door. "I wasn't bullshitting, I got a job for you here. Full-time with benefits, time off, and a 401K plus I'm paying weekly."

Carl just didn't know he didn't have to sell me shit, I was desperate with no direction. I needed this blessing right now.

"Even if you can't take the position permanently, please help me out for today, and I'll pay you cash before you go home," he pleaded with his hands in the prayer position. "The three unreliable mofos I got on the payroll called in fifteen minutes ago and they are already supposed to be at the job site for the day. It ain't a big job, I'm only making a few hundred off this shit because she's pregnant and in need so I'm giving her a discount already, but Ion need her ass spraying my business in the reviews and in Facebook groups. She already called with a lil funky ass attitude so I know she is the type," he grumbled.

"I'm down for the job permanently but I'm fresh out so if you could pay me for today's job today, I'd appreciate that."

"I got you," he nodded. In a matter of seconds, Carl retrieved a shirt with his logo from the storage closet and unlocked a drawer that housed a slew of keys. "Let's roll," he commanded, tossing me the shirt.

I hit the locks on my truck before following Carl out of the backdoor. Business was clearly booming because he upgraded from his two pickup trucks to four box trucks wrapped in his *Carl Hauls* logo. Climbing into the truck, I realized I didn't know the pay, hours, or anything but I was down for whatever. We traveled to a home in South Tampa and the aforementioned chick with the funky attitude stood outside with her hands on her hips. Carl swerved against the curb and jumped out, leaving me to follow suit.

I expected to encounter a big bellied woman after Carl mentioned she was pregnant but that's not what I saw at all when I caught a glimpse of Ava. She couldn't be more than 5' 5" with a petite frame, handful of titties, slim waist, and a small ass to match. Ava had her hair pulled up in a messy bun, showing off her natural coils. Her cinnamon brown skin glistened underneath the sun and if she was pregnant, either she was super early in the process or her body was hiding that shit.

"Good morning, Ava, I apologize for being tardy. Our entire crew tested positive for covid but me and my assistant are going to get the job done," Carl assured her with a smile.

"I hope so," she sassed. "Everything is packed and I have to return the keys before the office closes at four o'clock, so I need this done," she ranted, rolling her neck with every word. The frustration was oozing out of her pores as she led the way into the house. It was a small one bedroom, one bathroom home and I observed the neatly stacked boxes lining the living room and hallway. Everything was labeled perfectly and I was actually shocked. From previous jobs I worked on with Carl, motha fuckas usually half packed shit which slowed us down tremendously.

"Oh yeah, we can definitely get this stuff moved by four o'clock," I assured her, hoping to ease her nerves.

She took a deep breath and exited the house without another word. *That fucked up attitude is probably why she's in this situation alone. Moving shit solo while pregnant.* I thought to myself while shaking my head. Following Carl's lead, we entered the bedroom and took down her queen size bed before moving all of her bedroom furniture onto the truck. Within a matter of those few minutes, I noticed Ms. Attitude sprint into the bathroom and puke her guts out. We kept shit moving, working on her office furniture next. Within the few hours we were there packing shit onto the truck, I worked up a sweat and an appetite and also noticed the lil chick run to the bathroom nine additional times to throw up.

"Damn she got it bad," Carl panted, passing me a bottle of water as we watched her rush inside for a tenth time.

"Are all pregnant women like that?"

"Ion know, my woman would throw up here and there but not all day back to back like that. What's that? Her sixth or seventh trip?" He questioned before guzzling the water.

"It's her tenth, I have unfortunately been keeping track," I leaned up against the truck to drink some of my water. The cool breeze that we had yesterday was non-existent now and the sun was beating down on us as we waited for her.

"She needs to come on though. When she set up the appointment, lil mama didn't have a definite moving location so Ion even know where we are supposed to transport her things."

Carl pulled a towel from the truck and wiped the sweat off his face. He was a big nigga so the sweat was covering him way worse than me. The woman exited the house and she was damn near pale, appearing depleted of all energy sources. "You straight?" I inquired, concerned about her health.

"I'm good," she huffed before turning to lock the front door and dropping her keys in her purse. "Can I ride with y'all to the storage location? We are going to leave the stuff there and I'll be in touch to set up a new appointment to move my things to my new place."

"I'm sorry, due to my insurance, I can't allow clients to ride in the truck with us," Carl informed her.

"It's okay," she nodded her head, fighting off tears as she dug around in her purse for her phone. "I'll call an Uber."

"Alright man..." Carl ran his hands down his face. "I'll let you ride with us, which storage do you want to go to?"

"I already secured a unit at the storage on South Dale Mabry Self Storage."

"That's not far, you sure you good?"

"I'm positive," she nodded. Carl gripped her hand and helped her into the truck. I eased in behind her and she was sandwiched between two sweaty men in the truck. "I'm not trying to be rude but can I sit near the door for the fresh air and just in case I have to throw up?"

Carl eyed me and I graciously opened the door to switch seats with her. Once she was comfortable in the truck, I prayed her ass didn't throw up on me during the short ride. Thankfully, her body waited until we arrived at the storage to expel her stomach contents again. Unfortunately, I was close enough to see that she ain't have shit else in her stomach to regurgitate, just yellow slimy shit.

"Baby girl, have a seat in the truck, we got this," Carl urged her, passing her a few napkins from the glove compartment.

We spent the next two hours organizing her storage unit then dropped her off somewhere downtown near the intersection of Seventh Avenue and Florida Avenue before making that trek back to South Tampa. A nigga felt exceptional when Carl hit me off with two hundred dollars for today's job.

"She paid two hundred for the job and I'm giving it all to you. That's how much I appreciate you for coming through. I got a cool fifty on me and I can cash app or Zelle you the balance."

"Ion have none of that yet," I admitted.

"I'll pay you the rest in cash tomorrow."

"Good looking," I accepted the fifty dollar bill, happy as fuck.

"We can handle all of that paperwork shit tomorrow because I'm tired as fuck. Ion know what we have scheduled for tomorrow yet so lock ya number in and I'll let you know what time to pull up," he passed me the phone.

"Ion have a number yet. I'mma cop a phone today, write your number down for me and I'll hit you as soon as I have a phone," I explained.

"The number is underneath the logo on my shit. Let me grab a few shirts for you. If you know anybody fresh out that's really trying to work or getting out soon, give them that number too. I'm about to rebuild my entire team so we are going to be a two man crew for the time being and that will come with a higher salary. If you're willing to take on a leadership role, I got you with thirty an hour," he offered.

I was damn near salivating at the offer and feeling like I could see light at the end of this dark tunnel I found myself in since Natalie fucked my world up yesterday. "I'm down," I slapped Carl up, excited as a motha fucka and not ashamed about displaying it.

"Make sure you hit me up," Carl called to me before hopping in his whip.

I slid into my truck and peeled out hungry as fuck. It was only three o'clock in the afternoon and I decided to stop in Walmart to purchase a prepaid phone, a pack of shirts, and two pairs of basketball shorts to wear to work over the next two days. This would be enough stuff to keep me presentable until payday on Friday.

"Your total is fifty nine dollars and ninety cents," the cashier read off the number. I only had sixty dollars and I still needed to eat tonight.

"Actually, can you take one of those basketball shorts off?"

"Yeah, give me a minute," she took a deep breath before clicking around on the register.

I waited patiently until she came back with a total that was almost six dollars cheaper. With the change in hand, I went to McDonalds and grabbed a Big Mac meal. Sitting in their lobby area, I used their free Wi-Fi to activate my prepaid phone. I was thankful as hell that Tracfone was having a deal on a free month with the purchase of the phone or I would've been assed out.

Hopping on the internet while I devoured my first meal of the day, I looked up shelters near me. A lot of the niggas told me about shelters really helping you get on your feet and I needed that shit until I could get in touch with Bishop. As soon as I could speak with my brother and locate the title to this truck, I'd have the cash I'd need to secure a spot and do my own thing. I'd rather have shelter than a whip. Unfortunately, I didn't know how long that nigga would be in confinement so I couldn't solely rely on that. My search led me to the Salvation Army shelter. It stated that it was a first come first serve type of deal and they offered case management to help you secure food stamps, Medicaid, and above all else food and free showers for the night. I didn't know a thing about applying for any public assistance so I could use the help for real. Gathering my shit, I exited the McDonalds and made my way across town to ensure I was one of the first people in line.

# CHAPTER THREE

## Ava Jamerson

*S*tanding in line for a bed at a homeless shelter at twenty-three years old was humbling as fuck and I couldn't believe that my life led me here, while pregnant nonetheless. I made the terrible mistake of putting my trust in a fuck nigga and allowing him to knock me up and now he was in the wind. Jermaine was my high school sweetheart. We'd been together since ninth grade and were engaged to be married after I delivered the baby.

Unfortunately, Jermaine didn't mature with age and told me that this family shit was too much for him to handle four months ago. His trifling ass wasn't even the reason I was temporarily homeless. I wasn't the sit around and wait on a nigga type but my job let me go due to my attendance. They listed performance issues in the paperwork but really, they were setting me up for this termination since I got sick from my pregnancy, they couldn't put that in the paperwork though. If firing me wasn't enough, these greedy ass hoes fought me tooth and nail about unemployment. I was just approved for unemployment payments but it wouldn't cover the cost of rent at my old place and I was behind on rent already so it didn't make sense to pay them off and still be evicted later down the line.

Thankfully, I was only in this situation for the next four days because I already put a deposit down on a one bedroom apartment and spent my last paying the deposit, having the utilities transferred, and securing the storage unit. Moving day was four days away, and I begged the landlord to let me know if I could move in any sooner, so I just had to thug it until then. I was already working with a program to pay my rent for six months and by then, I'd have the baby and found another job. My plan was foolproof, I just prayed that nothing went wrong.

Exhausted from the events of the day and my illness, I tried my best to fight off my urge to vomit but that was a battle I'd never win with HG rearing its ugly head. HG was short for *hyperemesis gravidarum*, a condition that affected a small percentage of women, and it's mainly characterized by nausea and *severe* vomiting during pregnancy. There were different levels to this shit and I was one of the unlucky women who had the severe variant. Whether I ate or not, my body was on one and I hadn't been able to keep anything down all week so I was weak as hell. I was frail and definitely looked sick, the only meat left on my bones were in the stomach region and even that wasn't much. I was down to the same weight I was in the ninth grade.

Today alone, I counted twenty vomiting sessions and my body rejected the saltines and ginger ale I ate and drank yesterday so I didn't have anything left in me, even the bile was depleted. Leaning over, I dry heaved for a few minutes then it finally came up. This time, there was more bile than I'd experienced the last time and it unexpectedly splashed on someone else in line.

"Yoooo bitch, what the fuck?" I heard the angry man in the black Air Forces shout. Looking up, he was stomping in my direction which scared the shit out of me. This was my first time staying in a shelter but I'd heard stories about how things could be. I really didn't want to subject myself to this bullshit but I didn't have a choice, the only other option I had was to sleep on a bench or something.

"I'm so sorry," I apologized, backing away from him. The fire in his eyes told me that my gender or barely protruding belly wouldn't stop him from putting his hands on me.

"Sorry? That ain't gone clean my fucking shoes, you need to take yo sick ass down the block to do that shit!"

"Aye man, chill," I heard a familiar voice then a male body stepped in front of me.

"Or what?"

**POP!**

Black Air Forces tumbled into the line of people behind him and they treated him like trash on the street, shoving him off of them until he collided with the pavement.

"Or you gone have to see me, nigga! Fuck wrong with you? Acting like you gone slide on a female," he barked unnecessarily because Black Air Forces was out cold. He turned to face me and I saw the recognition on his face.

"Th... th... thank you," I mustered up the strength to say before a dizzy spell consumed my sight and balance. My body tipped over and he caught me in his strong arms. I closed my eyes tightly, trying to fight this shit, as he yelled in my face, asking if I was okay. If his breath wasn't so minty, I'm positive that I would've thrown up all in his face.

"Shit, I'mma take you to the hospital."

I was too weak to speak, the only thing I could offer was a faint head nod and a silent prayer that he wasn't a creep. The motion from the kind stranger jogging with me clasped tightly in his arm forced me to jump up from the nausea. At that moment, I knew it was time for yet another hospital visit because I dry heaved in his arms and nothing came up. He placed me in the passenger seat of a vehicle and took a moment to buckle me in before rounding the car and climbing behind the wheel.

He sped through traffic until we arrived at the emergency room entrance. Tampa General was only eight minutes away from the shelter and I promise we probably made it there in five minutes. Then again, I was delusional as fuck so I couldn't say how long it took. The door swung open and he carried me through the entrance.

"Aye, I need some help. She's pregnant, has been throwing up all day. I'm talking back to back to back and then she almost passed out after the last time she threw up. Her body is all limp and shit."

"Okay, calm down, we are going to get her to the back. How far along is she?"

"I... I'm seven months."

25

The kind stranger peered down at me, probably surprised that my tiny baby bump was that far along. I got those looks every time I said I was seven months pregnant because I looked more like I was three or four months pregnant. But nah, I was almost at the finish line and I couldn't wait because this HG shit been kicking my little ass. My breathing suddenly changed to deeper longer breaths, he looked down at me, sensing the change. He was extremely attentive for a man I didn't even know for real, his eyes squinted at me, concern now more present than it was before. One of the nurses brought a wheelchair over to us and he gently placed me in the seat, eyes filled with sympathy and distress.

My chest heaved and I felt something about to come up. He snatched an emesis bag off the nurse's station and placed it up to my mouth. I vomited in the bag and hated every moment of it because the bile tasted disgusting. When I pulled my head away from the emesis bag, I felt a sliver of fluid on my face but I was too weak to do anything about it. However, my savior wasn't, he grabbed a napkin from the nurse's station and wiped my chin off.

"What's her name and date of birth?"

"Here," he stated, pulling my driver's license out of my purse that I didn't notice he was carrying until now. "Now help her, look at her, clearly she fucked up!" He seethed and clapped his hands in their faces.

"Sir, you need to calm down, we are about to take her to the back," the nurse stated before wheeling me away from the stranger. I looked at him, still incoherent, and pleading with my eyes for him to stay but I didn't know him enough to voice it.

# CHAPTER FOUR

## Saint

*I* guess I scared the nurses because they called security when
I left to move my truck to the garage. The overweight security guard trudged his way to the nurse's station but didn't say shit to
me though. A part of me felt like I should get my ass up and slide to
avoid any conflict, but the other part of me recognized that Ava clearly
didn't have anybody in her corner. The look she gave me as the nurse
escorted her to the back signaled that she wanted me to stay.

Sitting back in my chair, I sighed deeply and ran my hands down
my face. My mind replayed my actions in the emergency room waiting
area which had the nurse and security guards whispering and glancing
my way. Stepping in when a man was threatening to harm a woman
wasn't out of my character. I'd be remiss if I sat idle while some shit
like that went down in front of me. However, I didn't even know
where that protective nature came from when we arrived at the hospital. I had never been in the midst of a situation like this, yet I jumped
into action and did what I had to do to get Ava care.

I shot Carl a text so he would have my phone number.

**Me: This Saint. Lock me in and let me know what time you
need me there tomorrow.**

**Carl: I just looked at the schedule. Our first job is at noon so meet me at the shop no later than 11:15am.**

**Me: I'll be there. Would it be cool if I was paid daily just for this week? You know I'm fresh out and I have a few things to handle.**

**Carl: Sayless, I got you! Setup a Cash App or something and I can send you the money now.**

**Me: Alright, I'll try to see what I can do. If not, I can wait for the cash you bring tomorrow and then the daily pay from there.**

**Carl: Bet.**

I slid the phone back in my pocket and thought about leaving again until I felt Ava's purse in my lap. The black oversized tote bag contained her essential items and that made me decide to stay. At least until I could give it back to her. It wasn't like I had anywhere to go anyways, from the line building, I already knew the shelter was full by now, and I didn't even have enough money to shower at one of the truck stops.

Then my mind went to Ava, she clearly needed somewhere to stay as well so leaving her there could mean she'd have to fend for herself on the streets tonight. At least I had a car to sleep in, Ava didn't even have that. Deciding to stay put, I leaned back in the chair, drafting and deleting a message to Natalie at least ten times. I just needed to shower so I could be presentable for work tomorrow then I would be out of her way.

A few minutes later the same nurse that wheeled Ava to the back returned through the same doors, scanning the waiting room until her eyes landed on me.

"Sir, you can come back now," she stated.

I hopped up, praying that Ava and the baby were good with each step I took. They led me to a hospital room where the door was ajar. Ava sat on the edge of the bed, vomiting again while another nurse stood in front of her with a bunch of shit to hook her up to an IV.

"Okay, sorry. I'm ready now," Ava still looked weak as hell but was more coherent now. "You're the same nurse they had to get to do it last time after the new nurse played around with that needle in my arm. They weren't about to stick me multiple times today."

"I remember you from last time so I'll be quick and gentle," she chirped.

The nurse used her gloved hand to lift Ava's arm, examining it for a vein. Ava squeezed a small red ball in her free hand and the nurse asked her to change hands, examining that arm as well. I silently sat in a chair as Ava looked up at me, offering a faint smile. Returning the gesture, I was surprised that she was able to offer a smile in her condition. "You're so dehydrated, I don't see any veins," the nurse explained, trailing her hands down to Ava's knuckle. She suddenly stopped rubbing along Ava's hand and offered a confident grin. "I can definitely get this one," she nodded, pulling her supplies closer. Ava closed her eyes and remained still as the nurse started her IV. She flinched when the needle went in and I observed everything in silence. The nurse took a few vials of blood then got her started on fluids.

"We already notified your OB and he is going to admit you this time since you're a frequent flier. He's currently prepping for a c-section then he'll be around to check on you. I'm going to get your blood and urine sample to the lab and we'll keep you updated when we are going to transport you to a room. In the meantime, try to relax."

"Thank you," Ava replied, leaning back on the bed.

"You're welcome."

She exited the room and Ava glanced over at me. "This is so weird, what's your name?"

"Saint," I chuckled. "Nice to formally meet you Ava."

"Nice to meet you as well. Thank you so much for stepping in and protecting me at the shelter and transporting me to the hospital," she teared up.

"Chill," I responded, unsure of how to reply to her tears. "It's not a big deal. I'm happy that I was there. What are the doctors saying? It must be serious if they are going to keep you overnight."

"Nothing that I didn't already know. I have a rare pregnancy condition called HG. In layman's terms, I am going to throw up all day everyday, no matter what I do to prevent it. Last time I was admitted to the hospital for a week, so ain't no telling how long I'll be here this time," she explained then paused for a moment. "Since they are at least going to keep me overnight, would you like to stay with me?"

"Yeah, I'm cool with that," I accepted her offer, happy as fuck too because I wasn't planning to ask that. The car was going to provide me with shelter for a second night. The room fell silent and was slightly awkward until one of the nurses returned.

"Ms. Jamerson, we are going to take you down for an ultrasound to check on the baby and other organs," she bubbled, entering the room with a wheelchair. The nurse pulled the bag of fluids from the metal pole behind Ava and placed it on the pole connected to the wheelchair.

"Would you like to come back with her?"

I almost wanted to spin around to see if the nurse was addressing someone behind me but reality quickly made me realize she was speaking with me. "Uhhhh, nah, I'mma stay here."

"Understood, I will bring her back in one piece," she assured me before exiting the hospital room.

They were gone for less than thirty minutes and as soon as Ava was back in bed, we were informed that she would be transferred to another room. I carried Ava's things and listened in on everything the nurse said when they got her settled in the bed. However, I didn't understand shit they were discussing. The nurse administered a few medications that the doctor ordered via IV and told Ava that she would be back when her test results came back.

"Do you guys have any covers for the pull out couch for him?" Ava requested.

"I'll send the tech in with some."

"Appreciate you," I chimed in.

The fact that Ava even thought about me weighed heavy on my heart. After everything I'd been through in the last twenty-four hours, that small gesture meant a lot, it reminded me that everybody wasn't out here for themselves. When the nurses left, I did remember them saying that visiting hours were over at eight o'clock and it was nearing that time.

I don't know what they gave Ava but she was knocked out in bed, beautiful and peaceful as ever. Exiting the hospital room, I went to my car to retrieve my Walmart bag filled with my clothes, toiletries, rag, and towel. When I returned, Ava was still asleep and I took the opportunity to take a quick shower and rid myself of the dirt, stress, and uncertainty for the day. There were covers on the couch and I wasted no time laying down and catching some z's. This would probably be my most comfortable sleep for a while.

The next morning, I woke up to the sound of Ava speaking with someone else. I sat up on the pullout couch and allowed my eyes a moment to adjust to the light. Before I could gather myself, the doctor exited the hospital room.

"What were they saying?" I pried, then paused for a moment, realizing that I had no business questioning her health. "My bad, that's not my business but I just wanna make sure you're straight."

"No, you're okay to ask. If it wasn't for you, ain't no telling what would've happened to me," she clarified. "My doctor said that I am to the point now where the HG has led to metabolic acidosis, which basically means that there is too much acid in my blood. I'm also almost completely depleted of potassium and magnesium."

"Well what they gotta do?" I inquired, listening intently to all of this medical shit because I was learning a lot.

"I got Zofran and Phenergan through IV when they got my IV started last night. I haven't even been able to keep down the pills so I'm sure that's why I've been weak and dizzy. They are also going to start me on another medicine called Reglan through IV too today. Then after I finish this banana bag, they will start me on potassium through the IV drip. That shit burns bad so I told them to do that first, then they will give me magnesium the same way. It's a lot, I know. Enough about me though, I'm not trying to bore you with my issues," she rambled on.

Her voice was therapeutic. Always calm and soothing, with a gentle tone that made me want to relax. Just listening to her speak felt like a great way to reduce stress or decompress after a long day of work. Clearing my throat, I suppressed the urge to tell Ava that I could listen to her talk all damn day.

"You good, Ava, I'm happy they are getting the shit together for you. I was terrified yesterday, knowing your condition, you gotta take it easy."

"That's easier said than done when you are doing everything by yourself," she lamented.

"Understood. What are they saying about the baby?"

"Although this pregnancy is about to take me out, the baby is just fine. Since I'm not keeping anything down at all for days at a time, the baby is taking what it needs from other sources in my body."

I silently nodded my head, accepting all of this information because I wasn't sure how I should respond.

"Now that you got in my business, can I get in yours a little?" Ava interrupted the silence in the room.

"I guess," I shrugged.

"What made you decide to be so nice to me? You didn't have to step in and you didn't have to give me a ride, I'm a complete stranger."

I thought we already addressed this topic last night but Ava was bringing it up again so I would have to answer. "What type of man would I be if I stood by and watched that shit play out? Or see that you need medical attention and not help you get it?"

"I don't know, I guess I'm just not used to people being nice to me," she confessed.

"I was just doing what's right. Wouldn't change shit about it. Now can I ask you something?"

"Umm hmm."

"Where your people at? You look just as young as me if not younger. Why did you move your stuff in storage and go stay in a shelter?"

"It's just a temporary thing. My mom is a mentally and verbally abusive woman, I couldn't go to her for a place to stay if I wanted to. I was raised by my dad and he was murdered when I was in high school. I don't have any family beside her and my boyfriend of ten years decided that this was too much for him and disappeared," she detailed, not missing a beat. I'm not sure what pushed me to ask that, but I was curious as hell and appreciated her honesty. "Now it's your turn, where are your people at? Why were you at the shelter?"

Now I really regretted asking Ava that question because I didn't feel like rehashing all of the bullshit that I'd been through. For a brief moment, I was afraid of judgment but as I scratched my neck out of angst, I realized that I didn't have anything to be ashamed of. My past *doesn't* define me and I was going to make the best out of my life now that I was free. This setback wouldn't keep me down.

"I just got out of prison two days ago. I did eight years for a crime I didn't commit and the arrangements I had upon my release fell through but I'm in the process of fixing that shit."

Although I wasn't embarrassed by my story, I was still anxious as I waited for Ava's response. Visions of her kicking me out of her room and asking me to stay away from her were playing out in my head. Her expression didn't waiver though so I couldn't read her.

"Do you mind me asking what you did?"

"Nothing, I did time for a crime that I didn't commit."

"Oh yeah, sorry, you did say that. What were you accused of?"

"Possession of a firearm, robbery, and assault with a deadly weapon," I listed the charges and braced myself for her response.

"Saint Carmichael?" Ava's eyes damn near bulged out of her head when she made the connection. "This is how I know I was sick, I didn't recognize you and you still look the same."

"You know me?" I asked, sounding stupid as fuck.

"Well, not really. We did go to the same high school but I was a freshman when you were a senior. I love basketball, it's my favorite sport, so I was at every game. Then when you got arrested, a bunch of kids from school followed your case. Even back then I didn't think you did it. I remember you having the flyest whip at our school, you were always dressed, and I heard you had a rich brother so it didn't make sense to me that you would be breaking into people's houses. You were preparing for the biggest game of your career when that break in occurred," Ava perked up.

"Yeah, shit crazy man," I rubbed my hand across my waves.

"I always thought you took the charge for someone else. Can the nosy chick in me ask do you know who did it? I'm not asking for a name, but the gun was found in your car."

"To this day, I really don't know who's gun it was," I clarified. "I was on track to hit the NBA, ain't no way I would sit down and take them years for anybody."

"Well if it's any consolation, everybody from the lower grades at our high school didn't believe you did it. I'm happy you're out now and I'm so sorry you had to endure that."

"You don't have to be sorry, the only people responsible for ruining my life are the prosecutors, detectives, and the system. Ion call that shit a *justice system*, ain't shit *just* about it. These motha fuckas pick a target and go for it, they don't really give a fuck about making the streets safe because whatever nigga really did that shit is still walking free."

"Don't I know it," Ava shook her head and smiled big again. "This is such a small world."

My alarm went off, notifying me that I had thirty minutes to make it to work. "I ugh, gotta get out of here to make it to work on time," I informed her, folding the covers on the pull out couch.

"Do you ummmm... wanna come back when you get off work?"

"Sure, I'll come back." Returning to the hospital wasn't a part of my plans because I didn't want to make Ava feel weird but she offered and it didn't seem like a terrible idea while I worked my shit out. "Lock my number in so you can text me if you need anything. I can bring you whatever you want to eat back."

"I'm NPO," Ava expressed, accepting my phone and clicking around.

"What's NPO?"

"I'm not allowed to have anything by mouth, just this good old IV. I promise the fluids are heavenly." She smiled for the first time since I met her yesterday and I noticed how perfect her teeth were. I didn't need any further explanation, that smile let me know she was telling the truth. Her phone vibrated in her lap and she lifted it while passing my phone back to me. "I'll text you if I need anything. Thanks again."

"You're welcome."

I pulled my toothbrush and toothpaste from the Walmart bag and went to the bathroom to prepare myself for the day. "I'm not sure what time I'll get off today but I'll text you when I know."

"Okay, ummm... have a good day at work."

"Thanks, you try to relax and feel better."

"Oh, Saint, there is one minor favor that I'd like to ask," Ava called out to me, digging around in her purse. "Can you see if maybe my

34

books fell out in your car? I need it to keep me occupied while I'm here. I had to cancel my Kindle Unlimited subscription for the time being."

"I'll check, if it's not in my truck, what type of book should I grab for you?"

"No, you don't have to do all of that," she refuted.

"I got you on the book, Ava. What's your favorite genre?"

"I'm not picky, as long as the characters are black, I'll be happy."

"Alright, see you when I get back."

She smiled and I returned the gesture before exiting the room. Life as a free man was interesting as fuck so far. I went to work, did my shit, and Carl paid me as promised. With the money in hand, the first thing I did was put some money on my phone then I bought paper and envelopes to send Bishop a letter to give him my phone number so he could call me. I asked Ava if she needed anything before I returned to the hospital and she declined. My mood changed drastically now because I would be able to get on my feet real quick.

# CHAPTER FIVE

## Ava

"Don't be nervous, shit is going to be straight," Saint attempted to ease my mind after the doctor left the room.

My doctor informed me that they wanted to place a PICC line before discharging me from the hospital to administer my medication intravenously at home. He explained that when I was in the hospital, receiving the medication directly into my bloodstream, I got better, but when I'm discharged and had to take the pills at home, I regressed. This was my sixth hospital admission for complications due to HG and probably the fifteenth time I'd been to the hospital for dehydration. After the havoc HG wreaked on my life, I was willing to try it, but I was scared as hell.

Day four hooked up to all of these machines, being poked, and prodded for the sake of my baby was a lot for some but I was willing to push through for my nugget. Seeing the pictures of the long catheter inserted through the vein in the arm all the way to an area just above the heart made my skin crawl but I was bracing myself for it.

"I'm scared," I admitted, staring at my phone.

"Stop looking at all of that stuff online. It'll only drive you crazy," Saint grasped my phone and placed it on the nightstand. Every time he touched me I wanted to shudder, but I fought the urge. "Think about what your doctors said and base your decision off of how you feel."

"What do you think?" I pondered.

"I think it's your decision because you're the one that will go through it. All I know is Ion ever wanna see you as weak as you were when I brought you here. It can't be good for you or the baby."

"I'm going to go through with it," I confirmed, staring up at Saint when I noticed the time on the clock behind his head. It was a quarter past ten and he had to be at work by 10:30. "Go ahead and get to work. I don't want you to be late. Can you ask Nurse Jessica to come in on your way out?"

"Alright, everything is going to be straight," Saint gripped my hand for a brief moment before exiting the room.

When Nurse Jessica entered the room in her bright blue scrubs, she instantly made me smile. I had her as my nurse a handful of times since I'd been admitted to the hospital so much and we built a rapport. "Dr. Mitchell told me you weren't sold on the PICC line," she noted, sashaying over to her bed. Nurse Jessica was always upbeat and vibrant and I enjoyed watching her in my weakened condition.

"I'm going to do it. Dr. Mitchell said he could get me in today, if so, I'd appreciate it. I just want to get it over with because my nerves are bad."

"I'll let him know," she chirped, rushing out of the room.

In order to clear my mind, I got on TikTok and scrolled through cooking videos. Since my physical relationship with food changed drastically during this pregnancy, watching cooking videos was my new hobby. I couldn't wait to have this baby and get back to myself, I was going to cook all of these new dishes I'd learned. Nurse Jessica informed me that they would take me down for the procedure in a few minutes.

As if he could read my mind, my phone rang and it was a call from Saint. I couldn't help the smile that spread across my face, I answered and my anxiety instantly subsided. This was his first time calling my phone, we didn't communicate when he was away from the hospital. I believe we were both trying to avoid invading each other's space too much.

"Hello," I answered.

"I hope you're not in there stressing."

"I'm trying not to stress, they are about to take me down for the procedure in a few minutes. I have been watching cooking videos on TikTok to keep my mind off of it."

"So that must mean you don't know how to cook?"

"Quite the opposite, I've learned some of my best cooking tips from the internet," I snickered.

Nurse Jessica entered the room with a male transporter. "Thank you for checking on me. I have to go because they are here to take me down."

"Okay, let me know when you're all done."

"I will, bye."

I ended the call and relaxed for the ride. I'd regained a lot of my strength and the doctor cleared me for a liquid diet on day two. I promise vegetable broth never tasted so damn delicious and I was able to keep it down thanks to the intravenous medication. That thought helped put my mind at ease, I was doing the right thing.

After the procedure, I took a nap thanks to the medication they gave me after the PICC line was in place. When I woke up, I thought about my current situation. Saint was here around the clock unless he was at work and I happily accepted his company. These last four months of my life were lonely as hell. In high school, I was that socially awkward girl and didn't make friends outside of Jermaine. We were both in the band, he played the drums and I played the clarinet, allowing us the opportunity to bond over our love for music, reading, and anime shows. Although I'd been lonely, I really learned to stand on my own two feet and fell in love with myself again.

Sore and bored, I cracked open my book to read it. Just when it was getting messy, the incessant ringing of my phone on the night-stand ruined the experience for me. When Saint left the hospital the other day, he found one of my books in the car but one was still missing in action. I was thankful for the book that he did recover because reading became my greatest escape from my harsh reality. Since I knew I'd be staying in a shelter for a few days I only kept two books from my collection and it was my all-time favorite urban fiction series, *Crushing On The Plug Next Door* by Lakia and my favorite autobiography, *Assata*. Luckily, Saint found *Crushing On The Plug Next Door*, Dro and Yola were so funny to me and I needed the comedic relief.

Viewing the name flashing across my screen, I wished I could disappear into my books for real now. I hadn't heard from Jermaine since the day he left the house. His trifling ass knew I lost my job and couldn't secure another one in my condition, yet he didn't give a fuck to check on me, leave me with a penny, or pay up the rent. I didn't want him to disturb my peace. This was my first time feeling well in a week and Jermaine wasn't about to ruin that for me. Silencing the phone, I returned to my book and got lost in the pages.

Two hours later, Nurse Jessica came in to hook me up to the potassium drip and I had to brace myself for this shit. The last time it caught me off guard because the nurse I had didn't warn me about the burning. "You already look better than you did when you came in here a few days ago."

"I feel so much better too," I beamed, happy that I had the energy to smile today.

The burning sensation started and I closed my eyes and braced myself for the next few hours. "Do you need anything before I leave?"

"No, I'm fine. Thanks."

"You're welcome, I'll be back in to check on you."

I relaxed in my bed and looked up at the ceiling until the door swung open again. My heart started beating rapidly when my eyes landed on Jermaine. I didn't know what the hell was about to happen next but I could tell he was furious.

"So you moved out the crib, took everything, and got another nigga chilling up under you?!" Jermaine roared, storming through the hospital room door.

"I don't see how *anything* I do is any of your concern. This family shit was **too much** for you right? Then you blocked my number and disappeared."

"So you go fuck another nigga? Or you been fucking him?"

"I'm not fucking nobody, Jermaine!" I argued, tears streaming down my face. It was *the audacity* for me. This nigga didn't care how me and this baby were fairing until he heard about another man in the equation.

"Probably ain't my fuckin' baby anyways!" Jermaine scanned the hospital room and noticed Saint's backpack on the pull out couch.

"You sound stupid as hell but the DNA test will confirm that she is ninety-nine point ninety-nine percent your daughter when she arrives!" I exclaimed. "Now get the fuck out and don't come back until you got some sense," I tried to distract Jermaine but he wasn't phased by my yelling. He marched over to the bag and snatched it off the bed as Nurse Jessica re-entered the room.

"Sir! Security is on their way up so I suggest you leave peacefully."

"Fuck you *and* this bitch!" He scolded Nurse Jessica before tossing Saint's bag to the floor and addressing me. "Just like I disappeared before, I'll do it again. Fuck you and that baby, whatever nigga you fucking can take care of it." I waved his ass off and stared out of the window as he approached the door. It would've been too much like right for Jermaine to leave quietly though. "Just tell me where my shit at?" He asked, referring to his clothes and other items he left at the house. When Jermaine got up and left, he only took a duffle bag of clothes and a few pairs of shoes.

"Jermaine, it's been four months, a hundred and twenty days, your shit is **gone**. I had to do what I had to do to survive. You know the insurance only pays for a week's worth of Zofran and I had to pay for the other medicine some way so I sold your stuff," I shrugged. "Didn't think you were coming back for anything. You were on Instagram living it up in Atlanta before you blocked me so I thought you were starting over there."

"Fuck you, Ava."

I honestly didn't understand why Jermaine was upset, *he* left me and ruined the bond we shared. Not me.

"Okay, get out, now!" Nurse Jessica waved her hands towards the door as the tech walked in with her blood pressure machine. Jermaine knocked it over and kicked the trash can into the hallway before storming off.

"Stupid ass bitch!" Jermaine exclaimed as a security guard rushed him and shoved him up against the wall.

"That's destruction of property and the police are already on their way up here," the security guard informed him.

Jermaine struggled against his grasp but the bulky security guard had him by at least a hundred pounds, his scrawny ass wasn't going anywhere. I sat in bed, watching everything unfold in the middle of the hallway. An officer appeared out of nowhere and took Jermaine down, he squirmed on the floor as the officers handcuffed him, yelling obscenities while glaring at me. I wanted to feel sympathy for him, but there wasn't an ounce of fuck to give. This man left me in my darkest hour and I hope he used his time in jail to reflect on his life and get it together for this baby. We were *done*, there was no reconciling for us.

The officers asked the nurse and tech to step out and speak with them. Once I was alone, I allowed the tears to flow, Jermaine was no longer the man I fell in love with. The revelation hit me thirty days into his disappearance but seeing him today reopened a wound that I fought to heal. My lover and best friend was gone and it was just me and my baby now. Holding my stomach, the sobs grew louder as I allowed myself to feel my emotions, it was better to let them out than hold them in.

"Are you okay, honey?" Nurse Jessica questioned, returning to the room.

"Yeah, I'm fine," I sniffled, using my hospital gown to dry my tears.

"You're under enough stress dealing with HG as it is and you don't need him adding drama when you're this close to the finish line. Security has been put on notice and he will not be allowed back up here if and when he is released from jail."

"Thank God," I sighed.

"I got you, boo, don't let him get into your head. Unfortunately, I overheard everything and you don't need his negativity rubbing off on you and the baby. Focus on the people that you have in your corner and forget the judgment from the naysayers."

Offering her a slight smile, she returned a huge grin before exiting the hospital room. I sat in the bed, pondering over the mess of my life for a few minutes before the door opened again. When Saint came in from work, I was actually ecstatic to see him today. It was a pleasure to be in his presence everyday but I needed human interaction after Jermaine's antics.

"You okay? You seem tense today?"

"They had to give me more potassium through IV and it burns, I hate it," I offered Saint a partial truth.

"This shit is crazy, I wish I could do something to make you feel better."

"Just you being here so I'm not alone is enough for me. I really appreciate it." While I was speaking, Saint walked over and placed a gift bag in my lap. "What's this?" I eyed him, unable to hide my jovial expression.

"A little gift for you."

I used my free hand to dig in the bag and pulled out a paperback copy of *Assata: An Autobiography, Lil Mama: Tales From The Hood 1-2* by Ms. Street Cred, *Sweet Licks 1-3* by Lakia, and *Yayo* by Lisa Austin.

"Awww, Saint," I teared up at his kind gesture. "You didn't have to do this."

"I know you're probably tired of reading that same book over and over again."

"I could never get enough of this book," I chuckled. "Dro and Yola make me wanna live in the pages."

"I remembered you mentioning that you enjoyed those first three books but I read *Yayo* while I was locked up and it was straight."

"Do you enjoy reading?"

"Shit, that was the only thing keeping me sane over the last eight years," Saint clarified.

"What's your favorite book?" I bubbled.

"It's a toss-up between *Yayo* and *Animal* by Kwan," he detailed. I nodded, taking notice of his selections.

I tried to fight it but I knew I was blushing hard as hell while looking a mess in this hospital bed. The burning sensation from my IV knocked the smile off my face and I was wincing in pain.

"You straight?" Saint questioned, rushing over to my bedside.

There was that concern again, it sent butterflies through my stomach. Dating back to high school, I thought Saint was fine as hell. He had cinnamon brown skin, identical to mine, with a sexy wide nose, full juicy lips, and waves that could've been crafted by the king of the sea. All of the freshman girls at our high school crushed on him and Asim from afar. After previously gawking at his looks, it was refreshing to know that Saint was beautiful all around. When he held that emesis bag up to my mouth and cleaned my face, I could've melted if I wasn't on the brink of passing out. Our eyes were locked for longer than they should have been and I quickly turned away because that shit left me nervous in my vulnerable state. I didn't want to read anything that wasn't there. Plus neither of us were in a position for a love connection. We were homeless, clearly broke as fuck, and I was pregnant with a fuck nigga's baby.

"I'm okay, I uhhh... the shit just burns," I clarified. "Let me read some of my faves to you so you can tell me what you think about it. We can start with *Sweet Licks*."

"Your voice is so therapeutic, I'd actually love that," he pulled a chair up to the bed and I cracked open the paperback book.

We spent the next hour flipping the pages as I read the book aloud, talking shit about the characters in the book. Saint was *different*, this intimate action of me reading him a book did it for me and I could admit that I *thoroughly* enjoyed his company now.

# CHAPTER SIX

## Saint

*I* was winded carrying the heavy ass dresser across the grass. Beads of sweat poured down my face because this was probably the hottest day since I was released from prison. Working in this heat wasn't no joke, it had a nigga ready to pass out. We sat the dresser down in the last bit of space on the truck and I rushed off to grab my bottle of water from the passenger seat. My phone vibrated on the seat and Ava's name flashed across the screen. Concern immediately took over me because she never called me. I snatched the phone up to answer the call before she hung up.

"Hello, you good?"

"Yeah, I'm fine and the doctors decided that I could go home today since I kept some of my food down," she beamed. I could hear the smile in her voice. Watching her eat yesterday was weird as hell because the first four days, she wasn't allowed anything at all then the last two days she was only allowed to drink room temperature water and eat broth. She seemed to enjoy it either way, I'm sure I probably would have too if I was in her shoes. Even when I was sent to prison, the food looked nasty as hell but I only held out on not eating for a full twenty-four hours before I caved.

"That's what's up," I celebrated.

"And if I can get to my new apartment before the office closes at six o'clock, I can move in today."

"That's what's up. Did they say what time they are going to discharge you?"

"He said he was writing the orders up now," Ava informed me.

"Give me a minute, I'm going to see if I can get off early today so I can be there to pick you up and take you to handle your business."

"Thank you so much, I really appreciate it. If not, it's no rush, just let me know."

"Alright, I'mma text you."

I ended the call with Ava, thankful that Carl hired three new dudes today and we were done moving the items out of the house ahead of schedule. Carl was speaking with the homeowner near the front door and the three new dudes hopped on the truck to grab their bottles of water and engage in light banter about the sun. When Carl finished speaking with the homeowner, I jogged over to him before he could make it down the driveway.

"Wassup Saint?" He questioned.

"I know it's short notice but I was hoping I could get off early today. My friend is getting out of the hospital and needs a ride, you got more hands than we've had all week..."

"You don't have to explain," Carl stopped and pulled three crisp hundred dollar bills out of his pocket and extended them in my direction. "I wouldn't care if you had eight bad bitches waiting for you back at the crib, it's your first Friday as a free man and you trying to lay up with some chick you just met because I know you ain't asking to leave early to grab some nigga from the hospital. I feel you, if I was locked down for the last eight years, the last thing I would be doing is working at somebody's job. Pussy, money, liquor, and weed would be my only concern," he laughed.

"Nah, it ain't like that. I'm really going to help a friend." Carl waved me off and continued down the driveway.

"I'll shoot you a text on Sunday to let you know what time to come in. Take the weekend off and enjoy yourself."

"Thanks Carl, you have been a Godsend for real."

"You're welcome, Saint, I wanna see you win. Stay out of trouble."

"Always," I nodded and jogged over to my whip.

Since there wasn't enough room for all of us in the box truck I drove over to the location and I was happy as fuck that I did that now. I didn't have to wait for a ride back to my whip and I could go straight to the hospital. We were over in Seminole Heights so I had a short trek to the hospital. As soon as I hopped on the interstate, I received a call from an unknown number. I immediately answered it, praying that it was Bishop finally calling. The automatic message confirmed my assumption and I pressed **one** to accept the call.

"My nigga fresh out, how the fuck it feel, lil bro?" Bishop shouted into the phone.

"Come on Carmichael, you just got out of the hole," I heard someone addressing Bishop in the background.

"My bad bro, my baby brother fresh out," he addressed who I assumed was a guard, then refocused on our conversation. "How you feeling, lil bro? Shit straight? Are you getting everything you need to restart your life?" He quizzed.

I froze up for a moment, unsure if I wanted to offer the truth or a lie. When I sent my phone number to Bishop via mail and Jpay, I didn't plan this far ahead. Thinking back, I remembered how the other men on the units behaved when they learned that their women were fucking another nigga, getting married, or knocked up by another man. It was like they lost all hope and didn't give a fuck about crashing out behind a bitch. Natalie's betrayal crushed my soul so I knew that it would do a number on Bishop. Not only did she marry another nigga and have his baby, it was also clear that Bishop's money was long gone.

"Shit straight," I blurted out. "Carl put me on with a job paying good. I'm leaving there now. I've been chilling with this chick named Ava I met the day after I got out so I'm about to go pick her up. She's been a good friend so far."

"What happened with Shalana? I fucked with shorty."

"Man fuck her," I laughed.

"Oh she really fucked up if you speaking on a woman like that, Mr. Respectful," he cackled.

"Did you at least get the pussy before you kicked her to the curb?"

"Man, chill Bishop," I shook my head.

46

"Well what happened? Y'all seemed all in love and shit."

"Let's just say she was after my money, only wanted me because of what she thought *you* could do for *us*."

"I'm glad she showed her hand early. You ain't need to be tied down fresh out the pen any fucking ways. Have your fun, fuck all the bitches but make sure you strappin' up. Keep condoms on deck, never let a bitch bring condoms to the party... they play dirty and poke holes. Don't fuck bitches who don't got shit going for themselves. Ya feel me?"

"Yeah," I nodded, hopping off the interstate.

"Good, you can't have any jits before they let me loose. Hell, first thing I'mma do is put a baby in Natalie, give her the daughter she always wanted," he vented.

I cringed at his inner thoughts and quickly changed the subject. "How are you doing though? Do you need anything?"

"You know I'm straight, met with my lawyer today, and he said he might be able to get me out on early release but I ain't gone speak on that until it's in motion."

"Shit, I hope so. I miss you, bro. I gotta get my shit together to see if they'll approve me to visit you. We went from seeing each other twice a month to barely communicating at all."

"I know man, I'm coming home soon though," he assured me.

"I hope so."

*"You have one minute remaining."*

"Did Natalie tell you about the account I had her set up for you?"

"I'mma ask her about it," I informed him.

"Alright, get on that so you can use it for whatever you need."

"I will and thanks for the Tahoe," I acknowledged the gift that I received eight years later.

"You're welcome. When I get out of here I'm upgrading that bitch to wha..."

*"Thank you for using Global Tel Link."*

The call ended and my music resumed.

# AVA

The nurse removed my IV and passed me the discharge papers, leaving me free to go. While waiting for Saint to pick me up, I scrolled on my phone looking for work from home jobs. If I kept feeling as well as I did now I could at least do something over the phone. My doctor already gave me light bed rest orders and I wanted to stay out of the hospital so my little ass was definitely going to comply.

My phone rang and it was an unknown number. Hesitantly, I answered the call and immediately sucked my teeth when the monotonous voice informed me that it was a collect call from the Hillsborough County jail. I didn't let the message fully play before clicking the red button. Jermaine had some nerve calling me from jail after everything he put me through over the last four months. His ass could rot in that cell for all I cared. He better lean on his mother or whoever else he had been hanging around to get him out of jail. All of my money was tied up in deposits and fees on my new place, even if I had a million dollars, I wouldn't bail him out. Saint entered the hospital room a few minutes later and I was surprised that he made it there so fast. I'd showered, changed, and was dressed in my own clothes instead of the hospital gown for the first time in days.

"You ready?" Saint eventually broke the silence.

"Yeah, I'm ready," I confirmed, standing from the bed.

"Aht aht. Sit down, Ms. Frequent Flyer, you have been admitted to the hospital at least four times that I can recall so you know the drill, we will wheel you out," Nurse Jessica chirped, rolling the wheel chair up to the bed.

"Saint, take good care of her."

He nodded. "I'm going to pull the truck around and call you."

"Okay." Saint gathered our belongings and exited the room.

"Whew, you got one fine ass man and a dusty nigga pulling up about you," she chuckled and I immediately blushed.

"Oh no, it's not like that. Saint is just a friend," I refuted.

"Girl, even a blind man can see the attraction between y'all. I know you're probably on some, *I'm pregnant, I can't be dating*, shit but I met my husband when I was pregnant with someone else's child. Love doesn't have rhyme, reason, or time. It's not ideal but we are ten years strong," she flashed a beautiful rock on her ring finger.

"Now you're really tripping, I barely know the man," I let slip.

"Could've fooled me, he's so gentle and attentive. I heard y'all in here reading your books together. I wanted to melt into the floor, it was so cute."

"Oh my gosh, when?"

"Yesterday, when I came in to administer your afternoon dose of Zofran. Y'all were so into each other, you didn't even hear the door open," she clarified as my phone vibrated with a text from Saint letting me know that we could come down.

"Thank you for being so nice and non-judgmental," I smiled up at her. "Saint's ready, we can go down now."

"Let's go!"

On our way to the elevator I waved at a few of the staff members and thanked them for taking care of me before we left. I was weak and delusional when we arrived at the hospital, leaving me with no idea what type of car Saint drove. Suddenly, I was nervous because I didn't know what car to direct her to. I didn't want Nurse Jessica to learn that I just ran into this man at a homeless shelter then invited him to stay in my hospital room. Exiting the hospital, I frantically scanned the area for Saint and noticed him hopping out of a Chevy Tahoe. I was relieved that he was such a gentleman and saved me the embarrassment of my bleak circumstances.

He opened the passenger door and helped me out of the wheelchair and into the car. I wanted to tell him that I had enough energy to do it on my own but silently accepted his help instead. Jessica stood to the side grinning big as hell and giving me a knowing look. I smiled and waved goodbye before Saint closed my door. Jessica and Saint exchanged words and shook hands before he joined me in the truck.

"Where am I taking you?" He questioned.

"Ummmm, the apartment is in Nuccio," I informed him. "Do you remember how to get over there?"

"I actually do," he confirmed, easing away from the curb.

We drove in silence and I nervously fidgeted with my hands, wondering if I should speak my mind. I'd been debating on my next move all day. Glancing in Saint's direction, he even drove his truck sexy as hell, it was only natural that I swooned over him a little. Nurse Jessica was right, he was gentle and attentive, and I'd forever kick myself in the ass if I didn't extend Saint a helping hand after the way he was there for me over the last few days.

"If you haven't made other arrangements, you can stay with me until you get things situated. When I get my things out of storage you can sleep on the couch," I offered.

"You sure?"

"Yeah, I appreciate you being there for me. Plus we can help each other. I don't have a car and I will need rides to the doctor's and stuff, if you don't mind."

"Alright, bet. I'll take the couch but I'm going to pay my own way until I can secure my own spot. I had to spend the money I made from working this week on getting my license reinstated so I could keep my job. When I get my next check, you can have it all, I just need money for gas and food through the week."

"No, keep the money you have for you and we can work out some type of payment when I have a clear mind," I advised him.

"I appreciate you, Ava. You didn't have to extend your home to me, but I appreciate it. I was planning to get a weekly room with the little money I have left."

"After the way you helped me, I'm more than happy to return the favor."

# CHAPTER SEVEN

## Bishop Carmichael

### *Two Months Later*

oday was shaping up to be exceptional for ya boy. My meeting with my lawyer went better than expected, I received some of the best news, and I was scheduled for my first video visit with Saint since he was released from prison eight weeks ago. We chopped it up once, sometimes twice, a week and my boy was out there working and doing his thing with this chick he met named Ava. Saint claimed they were roommates for the time being and every time I spoke with him, I could hear her in the background but I knew better than that. There was no way he left his bedroom with Natalie to slum it in the hood with some bitch unless the pussy was immaculate. I ain't mad at him. Saint's life was snatched away from him before he could get started, he could wife her tomorrow, and I'd stand ten toes down behind him.

Sitting in the chair, I spent the first five minutes of the visit dealing with technical issues, like always. First, the system robbed you of your freedom then they robbed you of your paper. Everything in this bitch had a price and you and your family were responsible for the cost.

Phone calls, video visits, and commissary. Hell, they charged a hefty fee just for sending money to your loved ones. Just when I was about to kick the fuck out of the bullshit ass system they had in here, that bitch connected and Saint's face popped up on the screen.

"Yooooooooooooo! My youngin' looking good," I shouted, cheeks spread, displaying all thirty-two pearly white teeth.

"Yeah man," he smiled, rubbing his hands across his waves. Lil nigga even looked studious with a pair of rimless glasses. "Above all else, I'm feeling good. How are you holding up?"

"I'm straight, you know me," I shrugged. "How is Natalie? Her crazy ass has been tripping since I got locked up and we ain't been getting along for real these last six months. I snapped on her a little bit about barely answering and rushing me off the phone and she ain't took my calls since. Hollin' that you don't know how hard it is being out here alone while you're in there."

"Ion know, Ion really see Natalie. I live and work in Tampa, don't leave the city much," Saint clarified and my focus was already on some other shit, noticing his corded headphones he was using to hear me. "Tell Natalie I said to buy you some Airpods ASAP. It's 2023, we don't use them corded shits no more."

"Nah, I like what I like. Ava got a pair of Airpods, I had to wear them once because she needed me to listen to something on her phone but I ain't fucking with them," Saint laughed. The system didn't break my brother and that was enough to make a nigga's cold heart smile.

"You called me?" I heard a female's voice in the background then saw a visibly pregnant woman wearing a sports bra and leggings enter the frame and my heart dropped. The voice matched Ava's and that fucked my head up, Saint ain't need no kids right now. The closer she got, the more I realized that her stomach was too prominent for the child to belong to Saint. He'd only been out for two months and she was at least four or five months pregnant.

"Oh nah, I'm on a video visit with my brother, he is trying to play my headphones and I was telling him I tried your Airpods once and I ain't like it," he explained to her, all googly eyed and shit.

"I told you to upgrade to Airpods," Ava chortled, walking away from Saint. "I'm going to make chicken and rice for dinner, do you want some?"

"Nah, relax, you haven't been having a good day today. I'll grab Pollo Tropical or something once I finish up, go lay down and chill," he coerced her.

"You sure?"

"I'm positive and as soon as I get off here, it's gone be time for me to give you another dose of Zofran, on time," Saint nodded his head.

"Thank you, Saint," she bubbled, walking past the camera frame again.

I leaned back in the chair, watching their entire interaction, trying to choose my words carefully. Ain't no way I was letting my brother go out like a sucka ass nigga. He was too young for this shit, had too much room to grow and thrive, and taking care of the next man's kids wasn't a part of his future.

"What the fuck is up? Why you ain't tell me the chick you been up under was pregnant?"

"I mean, it kind of wasn't your business, besides, we are just friends. She ain't some chick I'm laying under."

"I'm letting you know right now Ion like the shit. You need to dead that and take yo ass home and..."

"No disrespect Bishop, but I ain't that same eighteen year old boy I was when I went to prison. I'm my own man and you better get used to that shit," Saint interrupted me.

"I know and I get that but you ain't never really dealt with grown women. These hoes be after that bread, on they *city girl* shit, ready to run a nigga's pockets! I ain't saying all you got to offer is money, and you my brother so of course you're a handsome ass nigga, but lil mama mismanaged her pussy and let the wrong nigga nut in her, that ain't on you. She on your dick before she could drop that load."

Saint stood from his chair and I noticed the background moving, he was stepping outside looking mad as hell but I was just looking out for my brother. "We ain't even like that, I told you we are roommates."

"Did you reach out to my nigga Rambo about running skills sessions with his kids? I told you the nigga got eight jits now, all boys, and he is looking for someone to train them up."

"Nah, I ain't have time to do that yet."

"See what I'm talking about? You haven't had time to handle business but sounds like you over there administering her pills like a fuckin' nurse. What, she don't have hands?"

"Man, stop speaking on shit you don't know about. When I said I was going to give her medicine, I was talking about giving her meds through IV. Ava got some shit in her arm that allows her to receive intravenous drugs and I do it for her."

I shook my head at this nigga, playing nurse, stepdaddy, and *roommate* after meeting the girl two months ago. The pregnant pussy had my brother drowning in her shit.

"I'm going to reach out to Rambo and get shit setup." He assured me.

"You better, you busy worrying about a bitch that probably ain't no good for you."

"Make this ***the last time*** you call her a bitch, Bishop!" Saint scolded me. If the nigga could've swung on me, he probably would have. He was really feeling this girl and that shit made my head hurt.

"**Bitch, bitch, bitch,** you think I give a motha fucka about you getting mad. Ava trying to get chosen by a young nigga with money just like Shalana!" I spat.

"***What money***, Bishop?" Saint retorted. "That money you left Natalie is gone and the bitch..." Saint's rant was cut off but I could still see his lips moving.

I gently tapped the raggedy ass system and the screen went completely black. Throwing the chair down, I exited the room and went to my cell to calm down for a minute before joining the line for the phones. There ain't no way that shit Saint said was true, Natalie couldn't have run through my fucking money already. She had been down for me since the beginning and that girl was my heart. "Ain't no fucking way!" I mumbled to myself, feet tapping against the dingy floors. It was taking everything in me not to spaz out in here.

I stepped up to the phone and dialed Saint's number but he didn't answer. Repeatedly slamming the phone down on the receiver, I was about to lose my shit until I remembered the news from my lawyer.

That was the only thing that was able to soothe me. Sauntering back into my cell, I laid down on my bunk and thought about my problems. My bitch fucked up, the niggas that owed me money fucked up, and I was about to shake some shit up real soon.

# CHAPTER EIGHT

## Saint

"*W*hat money, Bishop?" I retorted. "That money you left Natalie is gone and the bitch..."

The screen went black before I could finish my statement and I took that as a sign from the universe to keep my fucking mouth shut because I was about to let him have it. Ever since I could remember, Bishop never had to get on me too much, that nigga was my older brother and wild ass best friend wrapped up in one, but I'd definitely witnessed him talk to other people like he ain't have no fucking sense. About *Ava* though, I'd get into it with his ass.

Sighing, I was happy the connection was lost, I ended the chat, not even sticking around to see if the connection would fix itself. Speaking right now would be detrimental because we were both on edge. Bishop would probably wreck out if he learned that Natalie was married to another nigga, with a child, and raising a *whole* family in the crib he paid for. With six months remaining on his sentence, the nigga needed to lay low. As soon as Bishop was released I'd inform him of Natalie's misdeeds so he wouldn't have egg on his face like I did.

I understood how things could look to Bishop because he didn't have the entire truth. Plus that shit with Shalana was still fresh. Bishop could have lectured me until he was blue in the face and I would've listened to the shit without a complaint but disrespecting Ava, calling her *a bitch*, would never fly. Ava played a pivotal role in my current position.

Two months out of prison and I was able to stack most of my bread, had a stable roof over my head, and was able to enjoy life as a free man. The bond me and Ava shared was one of best friends for real. She wasn't up for leaving the house much. With the PICC line in her arm, people tended to stare instead of minding their business. Plus, Ava had to be admitted to the hospital twice this month but when Ava was having a good day, we ventured to the grocery store so she could pick out her own produce or to the library to grab a few books. After that it was back in the house because she didn't have energy for much else.

The bond we built was some shit that no man could break, not even Bishop. If it wasn't for Ava, I probably would've spent most of my money on a weekly hotel and that would've made it almost impossible for me to save for my own spot. I had enough money to secure my own spot but that was proven to be more difficult than I expected because felon friendly apartments were practically non-existent. Luckily, Ava wasn't pressing me to get out, she assured me that it was okay and I could take as much time as I needed.

Since living here, I kept the kitchen stocked with anything her pregnancy cravings desired, paid for the medications that her insurance didn't cover, and paid the utilities. Although Ava was approved for six months of rent payments from the county due to the end of the pandemic, I still slipped her half the rent money. We argued about that shit on the first for the last two months and I eventually left the money in her dresser, whatever she chose to do with it was up to her, but allowing a woman to take care of you was never a part of our repertoire.

Carl gave me Rambo's phone number a while back but I never reached out because Ava ended up back in the hospital the day I received it and I needed to be there for her before anything. Rambo's phone rang once and he answered the phone sounding like he was out of breath. Sounded like he had an entire daycare running wild in his house.

"Tyrone! Get yo motha fuckin' ass down before I drop kick you!" He shouted before lowering his tone. "Who dis?"

"This Saint, Bishop's brother. He told me that you were interested in skills training for your kids."

"Man fuck yeah! First, welcome home jit. He been told me you were out and I was waiting for the call. Now fuck the pleasantries, when can you start? They gotta get in something because they are out of school for summer now. Eating up all my goddamn cereal! Why you eating cereal at six o'clock in the afternoon when you know yo mama in there cooking Jamel? This the shit I be talkin' about, it's like you want a nigga to go in yo chest. How many times I gotta tell y'all? Cereal is for breakfast, in the morning. Do it look like it's morning to you?"

"No sir," a juvenile's voice answered.

"Then make this my last time asking Jamel and you better eat all of yo dinner!"

I wanted to laugh because the man was clearly going through it.

"Can you pull up today? My jits ain't bad, it's just a lot of them and they need to get out my motha fuckin' house. My hard headed ass baby mama didn't meet the deadline to enroll them in camp for spring break and the shit full now so they home all day and..."

"Boy, keep talking that shit and you and these kids will be put out. Keep on!" I heard a female talking shit in the background. It was taking everything in me not to laugh because they were both enter-taining.

"Nah, I'mma leave yo ass in here with them by yo fuckin' self then I'mma be all type of fuck niggas. Pipe down, Gigi," he stated before I heard a door slam shut and the background grew quiet. "Like I was saying, they ain't never played ball before so Ion wanna throw my jits into a league and have them embarrassing a nigga. Other jits talkin' shit and I'll be done smoked they daddy in the parking lot, ya feel me?"

I didn't feel this nigga at all, because my mind never went to shooting someone over trash talking but this was Bishop's homie and he must've trusted the nigga to let me go around him so I would roll with it. "Yeah, I can get them started with a quick drill today if you aren't too far away. Bishop told me you got eight boys, right?"

"Yeah, eight hard headed ass boys with one baby mama. I should've spread these motha fuckas out between women, ya feel me? Then I wouldn't have everybody under one roof at the same time. A nigga would have some peace then."

"Shit, Ion know about that," I blurted out before thinking.

"Nah, you right, child support, messy bitches fucking with my lady, and I can't wack they hoe asses. Then Gigi, yeah, that motha fucka tough as a nigga in the skreets, I would've had to cheat to have any kids outside of her and she would shoot a nigga and make sure her lace straight for her mugshot," he vented some wild shit, all I could do was shake my head. "So wassup, how much you charging per jit? Don't try to break a nigga's pockets because I got money either."

"Ummmm, I can do one or two sessions a week and it's seventy dollars per session," I answered confidently.

Ava helped me research other sports camps and how much they charged so I was earning what I deserved and remaining competitive in the market. She was intelligent and extremely business savvy and I loved learning from her. I decided to name my company *Saint's Hoop Dreams,* and last week Ava randomly inquired about the direction I wanted to take my logo in, then she surprised me with a logo that matched my vision perfectly. Thinking about that day made me smile for more reasons than one.

*"Look what I did," Ava spun her phone around and allowed me to view the screen.*

*I eased up to the edge of the sofa and eyed her phone. When the image registered with my vision, a huge grin spread across my face. The black and gold basketball disappeared into a trail of black and gold stars. It gave the illusion that the basketball was a shooting star that disappeared on the cusp of my business name* **Saint's Hoop Dreams**. *It was relaxed, laid back, and fit my personality perfectly.*

*Looking up, my eyes caught Ava's growing belly before I could take in her face. Since getting that PICC line she was able to gain a little weight and her belly seemed to double in size. She still had days where she couldn't keep anything down but the baby was still growing. Staring in her face, I promise I was lost in her beauty. Ava was always gorgeous but the added weight looked even better on her. Not only did Ava look out for me in a major way, she supported my dreams. Standing to my feet, I wrapped Ava up in a hug and I swear I felt her melt into my chest. Glancing down at her, she stared back at me. I literally felt our hearts beating in sync. Leaning down, I was going in for the kill, prepared to grace her perfect lips then I caught myself and changed courses. Connecting my lips with Ava's forehead, I closed my eyes, fighting to put my feelings back in check while simultaneously praying that I didn't make her feel uncomfortable in her own home.*

*"Thank you, for everything Ava. I don't know how I could ever repay you,"* *I smiled, trying not to seem too happy.*

*"You're welcome, I just want to see you win," she commented and I could feel the sincerity in her voice.*

That was the only time I'd almost wiggled my way into territory I had no business in. When I did finally move out, I had to do some big shit to show my appreciation. Shaking those thoughts off, I gave Rambo my full attention again. I already did the calculations and eight kids, twice a week at seventy dollars an hour would bring in an extra $1,120 a week. That on top of my salary from Carl Hauls was going to have a nigga living lovely.

"Alright, I got you. Do you accept cash app?"

"Yeah, I just got it setup. I am not sure where you're located but since you have so many kids, I don't mind making it easier and coming closer to you."

"Yeah man, we have a basketball court in our community. I'll pay you gas to come over here and get shit poppin'," Rambo offered.

"Yeah, that'll work. Can you text me the address and I'll be on the way?"

"Already sent it. Just let me know when you 'bout ten minutes out so I can gather my herd and drive them over there."

"I got you."

We ended the call and I checked to see how far he was. Homie lived wayyyyyy out in Land O Lakes so I needed to get on the road. Re-entering the apartment, I sauntered over to the storage closet on the patio and grabbed the sack of balls. Ava was seated on the balcony, with her face buried in a book. Lil mama had a vast collection of books and I quickly learned that she didn't enjoy ebooks, she only had a Kindle Unlimited subscription to read new releases while she waited for the paperbacks to come in the mail. I had to buy Ava a second bookshelf to house all of them, she was keeping a portion of the books in storage containers, we had to stop that.

Since moving into the apartment I completely transformed the balcony into a reader's paradise because that's where Ava spent most of her waking hours when I was away. I installed a fan that was pointed directly at her wicker hanging loveseat. It was big enough to fit two people so her petite frame fit in the chair perfectly. It was black and turquoise, her favorite colors and that was probably her favorite piece of furniture.

I also added waterproof blackout curtains to provide privacy or shade when Ava wanted it. There were two other patio chairs and a glass table for times when I sat outside with her. She placed her turquoise tassel bookmark in the book to save her position and peered up at me, clearly comfortable in her position. I smiled, enjoying the sight before me and happy to share the news with her.

"My brother's guy Rambo wants me to start training his kids today so I'm about to head over there. It's way out in Land O Lakes so I'm heading out. He has eight kids so I'll make some good extra cash off of just him alone."

"Congratulations, Saint!" She bubbled. "Why don't you seem more excited?"

"I am kind of nervous, still in shock, and trying to process everything," I lied. The truth was, Bishop still had me hot with that shit he said but I didn't plan on explaining the situation.

"Don't be nervous, you got this," Ava beamed, standing to wrap her arms around me. I felt my previous angst decreasing the longer I remained in Ava's grasp. We stood there stuck for a moment, staring like a pair of lost puppies until Ava finally broke the silence. "You better get going, I don't need my basketball skills trainer late for his first gig. This is what you've been preparing for and I feel like a proud mama bear," she excitedly jogged in place.

When Ava had energy her ass was extra as hell. "Calm down before you get sick again," I shook my head. "I'll see you when I get back."

"Okay, what do you want to eat for dinner? We need to celebrate!"

"I'll grab dinner on my way home, read your book and relax. Come on here so I can give you your medicine," I waved towards the interior of the apartment and Ava strutted inside.

After washing my hands in the kitchen, I found her in the room prepping all of the items. Ava hated doing it herself so the home health nurse taught me how to complete the task during her first visit. I was squeamish about the shit at first but I got over it and turned into nurse Saint for Ava. She laid back on the bed and I was happy to see that she at least gained a little weight. When we initially brought Ava's things home from storage I took notice of the picture of her pre-pregnancy and this baby was doing a number on her. She was always a naturally petite girl but she lost twenty pounds and looked super thin now.

I put on my gloves and administered the Zofran like I was a certified medical professional then trashed the empty Luer lock syringe. "Thank you so much." She smiled.

Leaning down to kiss Ava's forehead for a second time felt right at that moment. Her pleased facial expression confirmed that I made the right decision. Grabbing my sack of basketballs, I exited the apartment and locked the door behind me. When I arrived at the address, I noticed a Sprinter Van ease into the parking spot next to me. Laughing to myself, I sat in my car and observed the man that I could only assume was Rambo, step out of the van and open the side door. All eight of his boys rushed out of the truck and over to the basketball court where he made them run a lap. At least he wasn't lying about the boys being well behaved. I could tell this would be the easiest bread I made in my life.

# CHAPTER NINE

## Bishop

***Two Weeks Later***

*J* spent the last two weeks in my cell thinking about all the shit that could be popping off on the outside. We were on lockdown because of some dumb shit so it was hard to get to the phones and I couldn't call Saint. They turned the internet off so I couldn't send him an email either. It was probably for the best, Saint's words, *"What money?"*, consistently replayed in my head while I was idle in my cell. I didn't need him to elaborate more, everything made complete sense now. He was living with Ava because he needed shelter and that bitch Natalie didn't hold up her end of the bargain.

"Carmichael!" The sweet sounds of my name echoing through the prison cell sent chills up my spine. A nigga had goosebumps and all that shit. I eased up to the edge of my bed and stretched my neck to the left then the right to prepare for the day. It was my turn to play in a few motha fuckas' faces. The cell opened and I followed the guard to Receiving and Release. I hadn't visited this area since I was processed into the prison two years ago. I dreaded the sight of these walls on my first day, but today, I was grateful to see the area, inhale the stale odor and see the raggedy bitches that worked in here.

I signed some forms and received my property and returned the prison shit. It was motivating as fuck to dress in something other than the prison issued uniform. Ion give a fuck that the Gucci sweatsuit was dirty as fuck. When I made it to the other side of that gate, Rambo was waiting on a nigga, as promised.

"My nigga, Bishop, free!" He celebrated once I opened the door to his Suburban.

Rambo's dreads dangled in every direction and surprisingly, he looked well rested. After having eight kids I just knew he'd be beat the fuck down. A lavender scent hit me and I inhaled deeply, that sweet scent really brought it home for me. A nigga was *free*. My eyes landed on a fresh set of clothes and I wouldn't have expected less from Rambo. We went back to middle school, similar backgrounds, single mothers who got the job done with no help. He was the first to jump off the porch between us and I was right behind him prepared to learn the game.

Pulling the clothes from the seat, I stripped out of my current attire and redressed in the simple Nike basketball shorts and white t-shirt that Rambo brought me right on the side of the road. I didn't give a fuck. I had to get out of this sweatsuit underneath the scorching May sun. Looking back at the prison one final time, I flung both of my middle fingers in the air and waved them around before hopping in the truck.

"Let's fucking go! I got a few motha fuckas to handle." I exclaimed.

"Where are we going first? Them niggas that owe you money or to Natalie's crib?"

"You taking me to the city and I'm handling this shit. I can't have you getting into no shit with me when you got all of them kids to get home to," I shook my head.

"Fuck that, I been cooped up in that house with Gigi and them motha fuckin' boys all summer, retirement sucks bro! No action or nothin', I need some excitement in my life. Plus them niggas ain't no threat, it's light work."

"Exactly, them niggas light work and I can handle it dolo."

"Nah, I grabbed two AR 556 Rugers and I'm trying them out on a nigga today," he confirmed. The nigga clearly wouldn't take no for an answer so it was whatever. I'd be able to mow them niggas down faster and handle the shit with Natalie and Saint all in one day.

"I'm hitting them niggas that owe me money first. If what Saint said is true and Natalie ran through that money then the bitch ain't gone have shit to give up, I'll handle her last. My priority is collecting that cheese from the niggas that owe me," I detailed.

"Say less," he grinned and mashed on the gas.

Six hours later, we were sitting outside of Marco's trap. I shook my head thinking about how generous I was to these niggas. I had love for the jits because they were around Saint's age and I gave them a few bricks on consignment. That was truly out of my character, I ain't fuck around. I used to ask for my money upfront but I let a handful of up and coming niggas slide. A nigga did me that solid when I first got on and I wanted to return the favor. However, these niggas were supposed to drop the remaining balance to Natalie when I got locked up and she hadn't received a dime yet.

Rambo pulled the guns from the backseat and sat one in my lap. I admired the deadly device and smiled, this bitch was sexy, now I understood why Rambo couldn't wait to use them.

"So how we gonna do this?" Rambo queried.

"Spin the block and I'mma turn this spot into Swiss cheese. If he survives, he can pay up, if he dead, the nigga just dead," I shrugged.

Rambo put the car in drive and was about to pull off but the door swung open and I grinned at the sight. "It's a two for one special tonight, there go that nigga Kelvin," I pointed out. Kelvin was the other nigga that failed to pay up and now he was ruining my plans for Marco too. Knowing I couldn't hit the nigga drive-by style now, I jumped out of the bucket we switched to when we made it in the city. Rambo was up the driveway before me, the nigga was so eager.

"Bishop! Rambo! What the fuck?" Marco questioned with his hands in the air. Kelvin was right beside him, fear undetected, staring at both of us with a grimace on his face.

"I already know what this 'bout. Yo girl said we ain't drop that bread to her," Kelvin suggested. His demeanor didn't surprise me, the lil nigga reminded me of myself in my early twenties. He was the only reason I agreed to front their trio with a few bricks. I thought Kelvin would steer them niggas in the right direction and make sure I got my paper. Clearly, I wasn't the best judge of character because now he was about to make me put a bullet in his head. I placed my gun to his temple and glared at him in disgust.

"Precisely... so either cough up my motha fuckin' money or you'll be gator food by morning," I gritted.

"We paid yo girl, I *personally* delivered all of our bread and I got proof. I felt like the hoe was on some snake shit as soon as we met up because she was with this nigga named Vince that's around our age and he been thirsty as fuck to get on. I didn't take you as the type to have a young nigga like him watching over your girl but it wasn't my place to interject. And, I didn't have no way to get in touch with you so I went along with what you set up, but I had my phone recording the whole thing for my own protection," he detailed.

Staring at the nigga, I didn't sense deception and I always fucked with him so I wasn't trigger happy anymore. At this point, I didn't put shit past Natalie or these niggas but video footage would determine their fate.

"If you got video let me see. Which pocket is your phone in?" I eased up off him, my gun still aimed at his head.

"The right," he answered.

I stuck my hands in and pulled out the phone and passed it to him. "Pull up the video."

My breathing became erratic as I waited for Kelvin to produce his evidence. Either he was dying for stealing and lying or I was really about to kill Natalie. Ain't no way she ran through the money I left her and the money these niggas owed me. On top of that, she left my brother to struggle when he was fresh out the pen, after everything I'd done for her. I wasn't the perfect nigga, I cheated in the beginning of our relationship but I corrected myself without her knowing. Natalie never had to deal with bitches coming to her as a woman or none of that shit. My love and appreciation for Natalie ran so deep that I would've allowed her to keep the money and move on if that's what she wanted to do as long as she made sure Saint was straight when he came home. The thoughts swarming around in my head were diabolical. This shit cut deep as a motha fucka. Growing impatient, my right eye started twitching.

"This nigga don't got shit, let's smoke they young asses," Rambo broke the silence and a few moments later, Natalie's voice came from Kelvin's phone. He spun it around and I backed up off him to watch the video while keeping aim. Even if the nigga decided to be froggy, he would catch a bullet in the process.

Rage flowed through me as I observed the exchange on the video. Kelvin was holding his phone upside down to keep his shit discreet but I could see everything as clear as day. Natalie and some young, light skinned nigga approached Kelvin in the middle of the abandoned warehouse parking lot. Her face was crystal clear throughout the entire exchange. Kelvin's entire story checked out, from his apprehension to the amount given.

*Natalie approached Kelvin and accepted the duffle bag from his grasp with a big ass smile on her face. She unzipped it to verify its content, then zipped it back up and passed it to that nigga.*

*"No disrespect but since Ion know y'all like that, can you count it in front of me real quick? It's all banded up so it won't take long," Kelvin requested. "I just don't want any discrepancies later on down the line. I know Bishop don't play and I am handing you mine and two of my niggas' money so it's a hundred grand in there."*

*"Yeah, that's fine," Natalie shrugged. The nigga she was with unzipped the bag and held it open for her. Natalie shuffled the money around in the duffle bag and looked back at Kelvin. "All hundred grand is accounted for."*

*"Alright, be easy," Kelvin stated and got back in his car.*

The video ended and I lowered my gun and tossed the phone back to him. Waving my hand at Rambo, he begrudgingly followed suit. "You said the nigga she was with name Vince?"

"Yeah," Kelvin nodded. "He some rapping ass nigga out of West Tampa. When you got locked up, the broke ass nigga was suddenly riding around in a new whip, rocking high end shit... niggas in the hood thought he had a lil motion in the streets but I knew better. I figured it was your money because Natalie was front and center in a few of his videos, that shit wasn't making no noise like that so he was back begging to be put on."

"Good looking out. I'm man enough to apologize," I admitted. "I had a few of them thangs sitting when I got locked up, y'all boys can come grab 'em when I get my shit together. Ion even want no cheese for 'em, just take 'em."

Kelvin and Marco nodded, and I headed back to the truck. Rage consumed me and I needed to ease my nerves before I lost my shit. Pulling the blunt I started smoking but didn't finish, I took two hard pulls and allowed the weed to fill my lungs as Rambo drove off.

"Why the fuck you ain't tell me Rambo?"

"You heard that nigga Kelvin, she's fuckin' with some young nigga. Do you think I be around them jits? Fuck no! Ion speak with none of them, Ion fuck with West Tampa niggas either so how would I know? Natalie ain't never liked me and I ain't never like her either so how was I supposed to know? Only motha fucka you need to be mad at is *that bitch*. Shit got me tight for you, let's go smoke that nigga Vince since she wanna play in ya face and steal ya bread."

I sat back, finishing the blunt while Rambo maneuvered through traffic. This hoe almost had me smoke my favorite young nigga on top of everything else she did. The pussy hoe had to be dealt with.

"Take me back to your spot and let me borrow one of your whips until tomorrow. I wanna deal with that hoe alone. If all this shit people saying about Natalie is true, that mean she probably got rid of my cars for this nigga and I need to be able to move around."

"This shit fucked up, Bishop," Rambo shook his head. "I ain't like Natalie but I definitely didn't see her doing you dirty like this man. Make me wanna go home and move some shit around for me just to be on the safe side."

"You better, these hoes ain't loyal," I grumbled.

The rest of the ride was silent. When we got to Rambo's house, he passed me a set of keys and pointed at an Audi Q8. I didn't give a fuck if it was a Honda Civic, I was sliding. "I'll get up with you tomorrow," I expressed.

"Bet," he dapped me up and I noticed the Sprinter Van in front of the Audi.

"Nigga, you bought a Sprinter Van?" I chuckled.

"Fuck yeah, all these jits gotta ride somewhere. Don't worry about what's in my driveway, just make sure you don't do anything to land you back in prison on your first day out. Street shit is one thing but *domestic shit* is what be fuckin' niggas up for real."

I waved Rambo off even though I knew the nigga was speaking facts. Honestly, there was no talking to me at this point. Rambo lived thirty-five minutes away from my crib and I did the dash, cutting that shit down to twenty. When I eased into the driveway it was about ten o'clock at night. Natalie's Benz truck was parked in its usual spot and an unfamiliar candy red 1989 BMW 325i Cabrio. The black rims and matching black interior with *Money Making Vince* etched in the seats let me know that this shit was custom. Laughing to myself, this hoe showed out with my money. I approached the door and stuck my key in, to my surprise, the shit worked. When I entered the living room Natalie was asleep in this nigga's lap with a baby on her chest. Vince was leaned back on the couch, mouth wide open, snoring like the king of this castle. Pulling the door all the way open, I slammed the door with so much force, the living room shook.

Natalie's eyes widened when she saw me standing at the door. Placing her hand on the baby's back, she sat up and tapped the nigga's chest. His eyes slowly opened and by the time they looked back at me, they were met with the barrel of my AR.

"Congratulations money making Vince, you came up off a dumb ass hoe and that shit gone cost you your life!"

I would've let off a shot but Natalie and the baby were shielding him. "Move Natalie! Bitch ass nigga supposed to protect you, not the other way around. You left my brother to the streets so you could lay up with this weak ass nigga?"

"Bishop, please," Natalie pleaded, stepping closer to me. I was numb after the shit this bitch did. If she would've kept it real, I wouldn't even be this enraged. I could've been in there fucking them CO bitches if I knew she was out here fucking broke niggas, making babies with them, and living in the house I paid for. The weak ass nigga made the ultimate fuck boy move and pushed his way towards me, using Natalie and the baby as a shield. As soon as he was within reach, I knocked his ass with my free hand. Vince tumbled to the ground and I rushed him, beating the shit out of him with my gun. Natalie rushed off while yelling for me to stop. I couldn't see myself beating her ass but I was definitely going to town on this nigga's face.

"Bishop, please!" Natalie returned, pulling on my bloodied shirt. "You're going to kill him! Bishop, please stop, he's my child's father and you don't want to go back to jail for murder this time!"

This nigga was done for. I turned my anger toward Natalie and gripped her chin with my bloody hand and pushed her up against the wall behind her. I never got like this with Natalie before, she never gave me a reason to spazz out. Her normally light skin now resembled a cherry tomato and a sliver of sympathy rose within me. I released the firm grip I had on her chin, prepared to calm myself down when my eyes landed on the atrocity behind her. A picture with me, Natalie, and Saint at his eighth grade graduation previously hung there, now it was a picture of Natalie and her new family. Regripping Natalie's face, I cocked back and punched the oversized picture frame right next to her head. It tumbled to the floor, shattering upon impact. I stomped that bitch and tossed another punch at the wall, leaving a gaping hole.

"What? You gone snitch on me, Natalie? After stealing my money, lying on my niggas saying they didn't drop my bread off with you, and leaving Saint to the wolves, you'd turn around and snitch on me too?" Shoving her face out of mine, I scrutinized her with disgust and picked my gun back up.

"Where is my money? And don't lie to me because you know motha fuckas talk plus you could never get away with lying to me, no matter how big or small! I fucking know you better than anybody else around this motha fucka!"

"I spent it," Natalie choked out, sliding down the wall until she was in a squatting position with her hands over her face. The baby upstairs started crying and that was the only thing saving these dirty motha fuckas from an early grave. Me and my brother grew up with a single mom who passed away when Saint was ten. I saw how the absence of both parents plagued Saint so I didn't want to put an innocent child through that.

"What you spent my money on, Natalie?"

"Cars, jewelry, studio time, music videos," she confirmed Kelvin's assumptions.

"For this non-rapping ass nigga? How fuckin' dumb could you be?"

"I'm sorry Bishop, please! I was honest, I told you the truth now, please don't hurt us. We can pay you back."

"Bitch how? He ain't about to get no money in this city and his rap career ain't taking off, so how the fuck y'all gone come up with that type of money?" I paused and took a deep breath. "Get that crying ass baby and this bloody nigga out of my shit."

"Bishop!" Natalie sobbed, eyes widened at my request.

"Don't say my name, don't **ever** speak on me again after tonight. Forget I exist, pussy hoe!"

"But where are we going to go?"

"Do it look like I give a fuck? Figure that shit out like you made Saint. You always said he was like your son, right? You left your son to the streets over this nigga. Now go before I change my mind," I barked.

Natalie hopped up and rushed up the stairs, hiccupping and snotting like I gave a fuck. I stepped over that nigga and sat on the couch. Natalie rushed out of the door with the baby and her nigga started waking up on the floor. Letting a shot off that swirled past Vince's head and went into the floor, he hopped up, disfigured jaw leaning to the left. He gently tapped at his jaw, wincing in pain as he slowly peeled himself off the floor. I lifted the gun and aimed it at his head. "Your jaw doing the gangsta lean gone be the least of your worries if you don't get the fuck on. Make that shit quick before I change my mind about letting you live."

"Come on Vince! Let's go!" Natalie rushed back in, grabbing Vince and pulling him out the door.

I watched their lights disappear out of the driveway and relaxed on the couch. If the bitch ass nigga decided to spin the block tonight I'd be here waiting for him. Wasn't shit pussy about me. With my idle time, I shot an email off to the same chick who sold the house to us to put it back on the market. I ain't want shit to do with the house anymore but I'd be damn if them motha fuckas was gone build a life here. Plus I had some young niggas pull up and grab Vince's car, whatever money they could get for it in a chop shop was theirs to keep, I just wanted the shit out of sight.

After that was done, I looked to see where Saint and Ava were staying. It was a lil minute away and I would make that drive tomorrow after I got my shit together.

# CHAPTER TEN

## Ava

Saint's business picked up rapidly and that left me at home alone for most of the day. This was nothing new, I'd been lonely as hell throughout the duration of my difficult pregnancy. He worked with Rambo's boys Tuesday and Thursday. On Monday and Wednesday, he picked up another set of boys whose parents noticed what he was doing with Rambo's boys at the basketball court. He was almost making more with his side hustle than his nine to five. I felt like a proud mama seeing him off everyday but I was jealous that I had to share him now.

It was back to eating dinner alone for me because when Saint finally made it home after his full schedule, he was exhausted. After showering and eating, Saint barely kept his eyes open long enough to read with me before he was falling asleep so he could do it all over again. I was still getting in where I fit in though, ensuring that I woke up before he went to work so I could enjoy a quick breakfast with him. The mornings were still pretty rough for me so I mostly watched him eat bacon, eggs, and toast, he never switched his breakfast up either. I guess I shouldn't talk much because I ate a dragon fruit smoothie every morning for breakfast and if I wasn't throwing up after that, I'd do something small like a bagel.

I found myself drowning in my thoughts while seated on the edge of my bed. Rubbing my small belly through my purple maxi dress, I eased out of my bed and walked into the kitchen. I prepared a glass of lemonade and dropped in a handful of frozen dragon fruit chunks before making my way to the patio. Today, I planned to dive into these new paranormal books I ordered. The moment I was comfortable in my seat, there was a knock at the door.

Taking a deep breath, I couldn't believe that someone popped up on my doorstep before I could sift through the stack of books. One of my favorite things to do outside of reading was having a mini debate about which book to read first out of a stack of new books. Due to my financial situation it had been a long time since I was able to order a bunch of new books. Since Saint insisted on leaving money in my dresser, I decided to finally spend some of it. The rest I spent on baby stuff because my daughter had nothing. Just thinking about that infuriated me, Jermaine really wasn't shit.

The knocking started again and I jolted from my seat with an attitude. That feeling grew exponentially when I caught a glimpse of Bishop on my doorstep. Although I could only hear Saint's end of their video visit, it was clear that Bishop saw my belly and expressed his disapproval for whatever we had going on. It felt amazing to hear Saint defending me but Bishop's disapproval brought me back down to reality. I was a pregnant single mom and Saint was fresh out of prison with enough on his plate already. The feelings I had for Saint would need to remain at bay, no matter how strong they'd become. Everything about that fine ass man was perfect.

Louder knocks assaulted the door and the feeling of confusion and apprehension heightened. When did he get out of prison and why was he popping up here when he clearly didn't like me? Taking a deep breath, I finally said something.

"Who is it?" I decided to play stupid in an effort to buy myself additional time.

"Bishop, Saint's brother," his deep voice answered.

Unlocking the door, I swung it open and came face to face with the man I'd only seen across the gym at my high school basketball games many years ago. I know it might be weird that I could remember him from all of those years ago but I'm positive that almost anybody who attended those games would remember Bishop's face and possibly his voice too. He was the loudest in the building while cheering his brother on and talking shit simultaneously. For some reason I could even remember his favorite line, *them fuck niggas can't see you, Saint.* Me and the other girls from school always snickered at his antics because he had the other parents flustered. I even remember a time or two when the coaches asked him to tone it down.

"Hello, ummm, Saint isn't home," I faltered, nervous as hell now that we were face to face. Attempting to quell my nerves, I focused on the lines on his black and gold Versace shirt.

With Bishop out of prison, my mind went into overdrive. Would Saint leave me alone to go live with Bishop? Would he listen to Bishop and end our friendship? Why was I asking myself these questions when Saint didn't belong to me? I helped him out in his time of need and he did the same for me.

**Bwuahhhhh!**

All of the questions and the fear of the unknown took over and the next thing I knew, vomit was spewing out of me. I was able to grab a bag from the counter behind me to catch it and then...

**Splash!**

Bishop jumped back, disgust evident, and I noticed that the black Louboutin sneakers he wore had fluids on the tips. "What the fuck?! Did you just piss on my new shoes?"

"No, my water just broke! Oh my God, please take me to the hospital," I groaned as it felt like my stomach was hardening and pain shot through me at every angle.

"Fuck no!" he exclaimed, rubbing his hands across his waves in frustration. Bishop now wore a look of panic while staring down at me. I glared back at him, realizing that he was tall as shit now that we were close up. "I just bought this whip and I'm not putting you in my shit like that to fuck up in the first twenty-four hours. Let's call you an ambulance."

"Fine, I'll call Saint," I rolled my eyes, not surprised by Bishop's response, the nigga clearly didn't like me. He grabbed my hand and ushered me to the couch as that thought crossed my mind and I was thankful for that. When I heard Saint's voicemail, I hung up and dialed his number again only to receive the same results. Bursting into a fit of tears from frustration and pain, I couldn't believe that my birth story would transpire in this manner. At my home with a man who clearly didn't see it for me.

"Okay, lil mama, relax with all that crying and shit. I'mma take you to the hospital," Bishop finally offered.

"Okay, can you go in my room and grab my keys off of the night-stand? There is a black duffle bag next to it, can you grab that too?" I choked out my request while attempting to cease my crocodile tears.

Bishop returned with the requested items plus the comforter from my bed and my fresh towels I needed to fold and put in the linen closet.

"What? I said my whip is new. You gone have to sit yo wet ass on this," he declared.

I wanted to laugh at him but another pain hit me and I froze up. Closing my eyes, I breathed through it, just like the nurses taught me. Bishop ran downstairs and left me alone while my eyes were closed. With the door wide open I saw Bishop placing the comforter over the backseat of his Range Rover. When Bishop re-entered the apartment he grabbed my hand and led me to his truck. When I was safely inside he sprinted back to my door to lock it with his ear glued to his phone.

"This nigga Saint and Carl both ain't answering," Bishop shook his head and pulled out of the parking spot.

The urge to push hit me and I panicked. I didn't know what to do. My only instructions were to breathe through the contractions but them motha fuckas were hitting me left and right and the urge to push grew stronger. Bishop was driving and looking between me and the road every few minutes. "You okay back there?"

"No!" I screamed, reaching between my legs, I could feel my daugh-ter's head.

"Oh my God! I gotta call 911. I can feel her head!" I screamed.

Upon reflex, Bishop glanced into the backseat and his calm facial expression flipped to mortified as he swerved into the other lane. "Oh shit!" The driver next to him laid on the horn and Bishop turned back around to focus on the road. I don't know if his outburst was for the view of my baby's head hanging out of my vagina or the fact that he almost killed us. Either way, I didn't care, my heart was beating so fast as the call to 911 finally connected.

"911, what's your emergency?"

"I'm nine months pregnant and my water broke. We are on the way to the hospital but I can feel the baby's head, he can see the baby's head and I... I... aghhhhhhhhhh!" I screamed, dropping the phone because the contractions and urge to push hit me simultaneously.

Following my body's command that time I pushed, long and hard, holding my hand low enough to catch my baby. I remember reading that women's bodies were made for pregnancy and that would always offend me because the trauma I went through during this pregnancy wasn't normal. There were days that I was afraid I would die. My first OBGYN came to my bedside when I was ten weeks pregnant and dropped me as a patient because *I was too sick*. This entire process was hell. However, as my baby slid out of me in the backseat of Bishop's truck and I caught her tiny body in my hands, I could finally relate, my body was made for this. Using one of my hands, I placed the phone on speaker.

"I'm finna throw up!" Bishop gagged in the driver's seat as he pulled over. I ignored his ass and focused on my baby and the phone.

"She's out! Oh my God! What do I do now?" I panicked into the phone.

"Ma'am, do you have something to clean out the baby's mouth and nose?"

"Uhhhh, yes," I explained, as Bishop passed me the towels before rejoining traffic. While using the towels Bishop commandeered from my apartment to get the job done, I was happy that his behavior actually paid off in the long run. My baby's tiny cries filled the car and I joined her, sobbing like a big ass baby. I was a proud ass first time mama who beat HG just to experience this moment.

"Okay mom, how far are you away from the hospital?"

"Fo' minutes! Please have somebody at the entrance to get them up out my shit! Got me sick to my stomach. I ain't never seen no shit like this, and in my new whip. Ion know how the fuck Gigi and Rambo did this with all them jits over there," Bishop complained and I couldn't help but to laugh at him.

"We will have people at the entrance," the operator assured me. "Mom, I need you to place the baby on your chest and focus on keeping you guys warm while dad drives."

"That crazy man in the background is not her father," I noted.

"Why you gotta say it like that? I'm a good nigga," Bishop questioned, glancing in the backseat again. He looked like he saw a ghost when he caught a glimpse of the umbilical cord sticking out of me and attached to the baby. I couldn't help but to laugh at his cringey expression before he quickly whipped his head back around to focus on the road.

I covered me and the baby up with the comforter as I continued staring at the top of my baby's amniotic fluid covered head. As long as she was healthy, that's all that mattered. Now that my adrenaline subsided slightly I realized that Saint hadn't called me back, that wasn't like him and I was growing concerned. Since the 911 operator was still on my line I couldn't call him myself.

"Bishop, can you call Saint again? He never ignores my calls and I'm getting worried," I confessed.

"I just called him again and he ain't answer. I'm about to call Carl now," he informed me.

"I hope he's okay," I sighed, holding onto my baby in the backseat.

Today was definitely an eventful day.

# CHAPTER ELEVEN

## Bishop

*A*s much as I wanted to go home and wash my eyes out with bleach to erase the memories of seeing that baby slip out of Ava's pussy, I couldn't, Saint would probably kill my ass if I left her there alone. Of course I wasn't scared of Saint, but I already pissed jit off enough by suggesting he get the fuck away from Ava. Now that we were both home, my main goal was to ensure that his business was successful and our bond remained unbreakable. It was *us* against the world.

Ava and the baby were getting cleaned up so I excused myself from the room to give them privacy. Baby girl looked just like her mama, they were both beautiful as fuck. They captured my heart in the short time I knew them so I knew Saint was about to be head over fucking heels in love with them. After last night, one would assume I'd grown an immense hatred for women after what Natalie did, but nah, that bitch did some fucked up shit and she was the only one responsible for that. Taking my anger out on other women was some pussy shit. Plus, Ava pushing that baby out in my backseat gave me a whole new respect for women. She possessed some next level strength that I didn't even want to think about.

Even after delivering her own crying baby in the backseat of my truck, Ava was still worried about Saint. I assured her that Saint was straight, his phone was probably dead so she could relax and focus on the baby. Since I didn't have a signal in the hospital, I took the elevator to the first floor and the urge to smoke hit me as soon as I inhaled the fresh air underneath the sun. After sixteen years in the drug game and two years in prison, I have witnessed some real wild shit. Ava pushing her daughter out took the cake though.

I went to my truck to smoke a blunt and continued calling Carl and Saint. Once I was relaxed and high, I gathered myself to go back inside when Carl called me as I approached the hospital's automatic doors.

"Man, what the fuck is y'all niggas doing? I been calling you and Saint, back to back for the past two hours. I just had to deliver a baby in the backseat of my Range Rover! Tell Saint we at Tampa General," I barked on Carl and his goofy ass laughed into the phone.

"Well damn, welcome home. Let me go find Saint," he stated. "We right down the street at The Mirasol Apartments. The signal in this motha fucka is weak as hell," he paused for a moment and I heard an elevator ding in the background.

"Saint, Bishop is on the phone, he said Ava just had the baby."

"Fuck! What hospital?" He hollered in the background.

"Tampa General, you right down the street, I can run you down there real quick," Carl informed Saint.

"See y'all in a minute," Carl stated then disconnected the phone.

I decided to wait for Saint to turn up because they were only a four or five minute drive away from the hospital. Ava and Saint shared some shit I'd never seen before. She pushed out a baby and was worried about Saint while my brother disregarded the entire fact that *I* was delivering the news about Ava going into labor. Saint was so wrapped up in Ava that he didn't question how the fuck would I know if I was still in prison?

Shaking my head, I noticed a little boy rush past me and towards the moving cars in the drop off lanes. Lunging into action, I snatched him up by his arm and pulled jit back to safety. He cowered under my glare, but I wasn't mad at lil homie, I was pissed at his parents. Observing his appearance I was prepared to break my foot off in somebody's ass when I noticed his light up shoes were smoked the fuck up.

Jit was one scuff away from exposing his toes in these sneakers. I had to save Ava's ass, now this lil jit, what was the universe coming to?

"Chill out jit, you can't run out in the street," I scolded the boy who looked to be six or seven as he fought to free himself from my grasp.

"Off! Me!" He shouted, struggling against my grasp, but I wasn't letting up.

"Yo parents ain't teach you to look both ways before crossing the street?" I questioned, looking towards the door for his parents because any stranger pulling up might mistake this encounter for the wrong thing.

"Off! Me! Off! Me! Off! Get off meeeeeeeee!" He screamed.

"Jibri!" A frantic woman sprinted out of the hospital and over to us.

"Mom! Mom!" He confirmed, pointing his finger at her.

I released my grip on jit and he rushed over to his mom. Noticing that his mom was dressed nicely in a matching Nike leggings and tank set with a pair of fresh Air Max's on her feet, I shook my head. She was fucking gorgeous, dark chocolate skin glistening underneath the sunlight, her long jet black tresses swaying with each movement so I knew it was the expensive shit. If I caught her on the streets jogging with her curvaceous body in those skin tight leggings, I definitely would've swerved off the road to grab her number. But nah, we had to meet while she was displaying piss poor parenting skills. Unable to hold my tongue, I exposed my disapproval for this entire situation. "Your boy is running wild, could've gotten hit if I wasn't out here, and lil man is wearing shoes that's damn near talking. Do better."

"Fuck you bitch ass nigga," she covered her son's ears and yell-whispered, while hugging her son.

"Nah, I never fuck with bitches who don't keep they kids up. That's setting myself up for failure," I scoffed and refocused on the big ass box truck pulling into the drop off area.

Saint hopped out of the truck and rushed towards the automatic doors. My boy was really a hardworking man now, a yellow Carl Hauls t-shirt and his sweaty forehead were a testament to that. His ass was laser focused, barely noticing me until I called his name. "Saint!"

"Bishop?" He puzzled, reality hitting him as I embraced him in a hug.

"In the motha fuckin' flesh," I grinned at him when we broke the hug.

"Why didn't you tell me you were getting out?"

"The same reason you ain't tell me the bitch spent my money and left you to the streets," I mugged him.

"Man, Bishop, I didn't want you wrecking out behind that bullshit. You were six months away from your release and we had plans. I needed to see you home," Saint explained.

"I'm your big brother, Saint! I look after you, not the other way around."

"Where you stayed at when you first got out?" I stared a hole in Saint and he looked beyond me like he always did when he knew I wouldn't like his answer.

"I stayed in my car the first night, then I met Ava the next day at a homeless shelter. One thing led to another and I wound up sleeping on the pull out couch in the hospital with her until she was discharged."

Breathing deeply, I was enraged to hear that shit. I set shit up so my brother could come home to the best conditions and that shit fell through because I wasn't here to orchestrate it. "You out here struggling for no fucking reason, Saint. I ain't stupid enough to leave all my money to a bitch. No matter how much I loved Natalie, the only two souls I truly trust to not fuck me over are you and ma. Natalie only had an eighth of my shit and there was an account setup for you in your name for when you were released as soon as I got sent up the road. We'll handle all this shit later, just go see about your girls for now, they need you." I lectured him.

"I told you Ava's just my friend."

"Yeah yeah yeah," I waved him off. "Y'all both just saying this type of shit because of the situation but the feelings are mutual, all she kept worrying about was whether or not you were okay because *it's not like Saint to ignore my calls.*" I repeated that last line with my best impersonation of Ava's voice. "I was there for her but she wanted *you.* Treated a nigga like I wasn't shit. They in room 560."

Saint pulled me in for another long hug. "Welcome home Bishop!"

I nodded my head and he rushed off towards the entrance.

"Welcome home Bishop! Hit me when you get yourself situated, I gotta get back to the job," Carl's sweaty ass shouted from the truck.

"Bet, you know we gone throw some shit together. We'll let you know, thanks for looking out for my bro while I was locked up."

"Always!" The cars in front of him moved and he followed the flow of traffic. Now that Saint was here, I had to smoke another blunt and ease my mind for real.

# CHAPTER TWELVE

## Saint

*R*apidly tapping the button for the fifth floor, I felt all types of emotions running through me. I couldn't believe that I missed the shit but I was happy that Bishop was here for her. Bishop didn't have to tell me, I already knew he was off that dumb shit he was spitting before about Ava. After the way Ava looked out for me I could never turn my back on her and baby girl, no matter what.

The door closed and I took a few deep breaths while we ascended to the fifth floor. Stepping off, I immediately saw Nurse Jessica leaned up against her computer on wheels, chatting with her co-workers. She caught a glimpse of me over their shoulders and excused herself from their conversation.

"Good genes run in the family," she bubbled. "They were all over here asking who that tall dark handsome man was leaving out of here about twenty minutes ago. Ava told me he's your brother Bishop and he was quite the gentleman. Y'all mama raised y'all right."

I almost laughed in her face, *gentleman* and *Bishop* weren't often utilized in the same sentence. If the ladies were impressed by him, I wouldn't block his shine, maybe one of them could tame Bishop's wild ass. "Yeah, that's bro," I confirmed.

"Well I'm glad you're here, me and Ava were both worried about you. Her room is the last door on the left," she bubbled, leading the way.

I trailed behind her and the squeaky crocs she always wore. They were a welcomed distraction because something in me felt like my life was about to change. Whether it was a positive or negative change, I had no idea, but I was bracing for it. We entered Ava's room, door creaking in the silent room. Ava sat on the hospital bed, legs dangling off to the side while she breastfed the baby. I froze up at the beautiful sight before me. The love between the two was evident.

"Oh, I can ummmmm... wait outside. Just call me when you're done," I announced once Ava looked up at us.

"No, you can come in, it's natural, Saint. I'll be breastfeeding for an entire year if my body allows it and I don't plan to cover my baby up in my own home," Ava detailed.

"Are you sure?"

"Boy, come on, she said it's cool," Nurse Jessica waved me in.

I hesitantly entered the room, in awe at the sight before me. The baby looked just like Ava and I could already see the overflowing emotions threatening to spill out. Without a word, I knew why she was emotional, it took so much for Ava to get the baby here. I washed my hands and joined them near the bed. A lone tear slid down her brown cheek and I fought with myself not to kiss it away. *We are just friends. We are just friends.* I chanted to myself. Noticing a box of tissues on the table next to Ava, I snatched two out and used it to dab her tears away.

"I'll excuse myself," Jessica grinned before exiting the room and closing the door behind her.

"I'm so sorry I wasn't here but you did it, Ava. Congratulations," I apologized. "What did you name her?"

"I haven't thought about it yet. Fear of losing her wouldn't even allow me to pick a name," Ava confessed. The baby popped her head off the nipple and Ava quickly fixed her top. Baby girl smiled up at us with the most beautiful dark brown eyes. Her eyes fluttered a few times then she was knocked out with her mouth agape like she worked a ten hour shift. Smiling at her actions, this girl already had me smitten and I'd just met her less than five minutes ago.

Gripping Ava's free hand, I pulled it up to my lips and planted a gentle kiss on her knuckle. "She's here, beautiful and healthy, you did it and now it's time for you to start thinking about those names."

"I know," she breathed deeply, standing to place the baby in the bassinet. "Although I haven't thought about a name, I was keeping a list of pretty ones I heard while pregnant. I'll consider one that starts with a B since she was born in his truck."

"What?" I spluttered.

"Yep," Ava chortled.

She plopped back down on the bed next to me as she brought me up to speed on the events from today. The shit was wild and Bishop's antics didn't surprise me at all. I might've fainted if I saw that shit myself. After an hour there was a knock on the door and Bishop entered the room.

"I thought you left after the traumatic shit you saw today," I laughed.

"Nah, how was you gone get home if I left? Carl dropped you off and I drove Ava here."

"Well, in that case, let me go grab my truck, take a shower and change, then I'll be back. Do you need anything from the house?"

"No, just hurry back," she responded. "I already told my doctor I spent enough time in the hospital to last a lifetime and I wanna go home asap. If everything is looking good we out this bitch tomorrow."

"I got you."

"Thank you again Bishop. It was nice to formally meet you, sorry it was such a hectic introduction."

"Hopefully, next time, shit will be chill," he shook his head, cringing with each word.

I laughed, pushing him out of the hospital room. The elevator ride and walk to the truck was silent. When Bishop hit the button to unlock the doors to a new Range Rover, I turned to him.

"This you?" I inquired, raising my fist to my mouth.

"Paid for, dropped cash on it as soon as they opened up this morning."

"So you weren't playing when you said Natalie didn't have access to all of your money?" I questioned.

"When have you known for me to play 'bout my money?"

"Never, toss me the keys, let me whip it." I held my hands open for the keys. Bishop tossed them over my head and I jumped to grasp them.

"That lil nigga still got it," he snapped, rushing around the truck to the passenger seat.

"Fa sho," I commented. "You got plans tonight? I need help putting the baby stuff together so Ava doesn't come home stressed and can focus on the baby."

"Fuck no, nigga. I'm not putting shit together in that shoe box y'all been living in. By the time Ava is discharged from the hospital, y'all gone be in a house. Since y'all roommates and shit, you need a room right? Not a couch and the baby needs a nursery and room to grow. Plus I can't have you staying in the hood, the fuck I look like? My realtor chick is already on it with a list of places for you to look over just tell me which one. She can get you the lease and keys tomorrow and I'll handle the rest."

"Damn you got it like that?"

"She owns a few properties and she knows I'm good for it," Bishop commented.

I eased into traffic and got choked up at my reality. Bishop raised his left fist and I glided my right fist to meet his. They collided like we used to do every time before I left the house. "I love you, baby boy."

"I love you too, big bro," I expressed.

"Don't get all soft on me in this bitch. I ain't even done yet." Bishop pulled an envelope from underneath his seat and passed it to me.

"What's this?" I queried, focused on traffic.

"You were going to college whether on a basketball scholarship or not. I had this set aside for when you graduated from high school to cover your tuition or start a business, it was up to you. Now, it's time for you to do what the fuck ever you wanna do with it. I wanna see you shine on these fuck niggas, Saint!" He rubbed the top of my head and sat the envelope in my lap. "We are about to get you a website, some social media promo, and get shit poppin'."

"Bishop, I appreciate you bro. I'm happy you're home, please do whatever you have to do to keep it that way," I expressed.

"I'm thirty-five years old and officially retired from the dope game. All legit shit from here on out. Shit got too hot for me."

My phone rang and it was Ava calling, I snatched the phone up and answered it. "Hello."

"Hey Saint, can you grab me a pair of flip flops from my closet so I can wear them as shower shoes?"

"Yeah, I got you. Do you need anything else?"

"No, that's all. Thank you so much," she bubbled and ended the call.

"*Do you need anything else?*" Bishop mocked me from the passenger seat. "Nigga, you damn near released the steering wheel to answer that call. I thought we was gone wreck out. Miss me with all that, *we friends* shit," he cracked. "Got me delivering babies and shit, I ain't even been out a full forty-eight."

"We are friends, Bishop."

"Alright, keep fucking around and you gone get pushed out of the way," he shrugged.

"Ava is like my best friend, she would never let that happen."

"Where is her baby daddy?"

"Ion know, I just know that he abandoned Ava while she was pregnant and they don't speak," I provided the minimal details I had.

"You know niggas love coming back for their families," he threw out there.

I couldn't lie, that comment ignited some shit in my chest but I kept it under wraps. Everything was changing and I had to take a moment to process my current reality.

# CHAPTER THIRTEEN

## Bishop

"*I* swear to God you buying me the whole bar when we link tonight after this shit," Rambo exclaimed, knocking his dreads out of his face so he could have a better view of the nail he needed to drill into the blush pink crib. "This shit right here is exactly why I'm not having any more kids. My boys' ain't the hard part. Putting all they shit together is what be about to take a young nigga out."

"Cap! Every time I get on the phone with you, you yelling at them bad ass jits," I retorted, pulling newborn sized diapers out of the packs and placing them onto the shelf of the changing table I just finished building. Usually, I paid motha fuckas to do this type of shit but we were crunched for time. Carl sent some of his dudes over as soon as we got the keys this morning and they got the living room and bedroom furniture moved in and that left us to handle the nursery.

"That's only natural," he laughed.

"You think this shit is traumatic? This is light work. Man, after I beat on that nigga Vince's ass and put them out of the house, I stayed there for the night to see if he would come back so I could smoke him. Of course the pussy never showed. The next morning I copped the whip..."

"And left my shit at the dealership and didn't say shit. Don't ask to borrow shit else, nigga!" He waved his fingers near his throat to signal no.

"Man, I said my bad, shit got crazy and I'm about to tell you why. When I pulled up at Saint and Ava's crib, her water broke and I had to take her to the hospital in my new whip. Man she had fluids, blood, and shit everywhere and I saw the baby's head hanging out of her. I'm still traumatized, that's why I couldn't call you," I explained, my face frowned up.

"You a weak ass nigga. I watched three sets of multiples come up out of Gigi. I'm damn near an OBGYN my damn self," he affirmed proudly.

"Shit you might as well be. Save you money on hospital bills," I suggested.

"Nah, I got a vasectomy, we are six years free of pregnancy."

"Shit, don't jinx yourself."

I placed the wipe warmer in the small groove on the changing table and looked back at all of our hard work. "We pulled this shit together real nice with a twenty-four hour notice," Rambo pointed out now that he was finished with the crib. "I gotta slide, my kids get out of school in an hour and I gotta get back to Land O Lakes."

"Bet, thanks for coming through man," I dapped him up before he departed.

Gathering the trash from the floor, I stuffed it into a small black trash bag positioned near the nursery door. The house Saint chose was located in Westchase. It was a three bedroom two bathroom house with a two car garage and massive backyard. My brother was really moving like a family man and I was along to support him in every decision he made.

Ava's daughter was so fucking adorable that I was even smitten by her. Saint texted me a few hours ago and let me know that Ava finally decided to name her Jordyn. I held Jordyn yesterday and rocked her to sleep while Ava took a shower. In that short amount of time she definitely stole my heart, I completely understood why Saint was enthralled with them.

Moving to the living room, I organized the gifts that Ava and

Jordyn received from Saint, Carl, Saint's co-workers, Rambo, and myself in the middle of the living room floor. When I heard that Ava lacked friends and didn't have a baby shower, I decided to accept the gifts and set them up for when she came home from the hospital. Jordyn didn't lack in any area, the newborn had everything she needed and then some.

Saint informed me that her favorite color was turquoise so I grabbed a table cloth, balloons, and cupcakes in that shade of blue. Clearly, I wasn't one to throw parties, women loved extravagant shit, but I could only do so much. The cupcakes, a fruit and veggie spread, and sandwich platter were placed on the table for them. Once everything was in place, I exited the house. It was nearing three o'clock and I wanted to make it back to the hospital to pick up Ava, Saint, and Jordyn before the traffic got outrageous. My dumb ass decided to retire from the game and move downtown so I knew how ugly that shit could get. When I decided to move into the luxury unit, I didn't factor in the traffic and that shit could get ugly. Exiting the house, I set the alarm and locked up.

My Range was parked against the curb because Carl's moving truck took up the entire driveway when I arrived this morning. Strolling along the driveway, I admired the massive yard sign that read *Welcome Home Ava and Jordyn*. When I spun around to face the truck some fat shit caught my attention out of the corner of my eye. Licking my lips, I admired her melons bouncing along the sidewalk as she pushed a stroller in my direction. Ava gave me a new appreciation for single moms so I wouldn't count her out just because she had a stroller aged baby.

"Excuse me," I gripped her arm and she ceased her jogging to smile at me, exposing her perfect smile. Barking came from the stroller and my eyes immediately flew in the direction of the growing sound. The stroller was absent of a child but carried five baby Yorkies and they were all dressed the fuck up with lil side bangs, resembling a Karen, ready to ask an employee to speak with the manager at any moment. Hair bows, sweater vests, dresses, and shit were covering all of the dogs.

"Oh no, you that rude ass nigga from yesterday," she sassed, hands now planted on both of her hips. Between her titties, these dressed up dogs, and her mouth, I was overstimulated for a second, this shit caught me off guard. "I couldn't dig in your ass like I really wanted to because my son was standing right there and..."

Initially, I was confused but her last few words helped me figure this shit out. This was the chick whose son almost got hit by a car. "Man move around," I laughed, cutting her off. "You got these baby Karens out here dressed better than your son and they are safely in a stroller. Some of you bitches are..."

**WAP!**

The slap didn't hurt but that shit left me stunned, I couldn't remember the last time anybody put their hands on me. Before I could respond the baby Karens started attacking my ankles. It was like the slap signaled for them to hop out the stroller and attack me. She stood there, calling their names, but the lil mutts weren't giving up.

"Look, I was out of line for calling you a bitch and I apologize for that but get these fucking dogs fo' I start stomping they asses!" I ordered. The only reason I was being lenient was because a few other neighbors were outside and I ain't need to catch no animal cruelty charges today.

She did some type of whistle and snapped her fingers then all five dogs ceased their attack. Her fine ass bent over to lift the dogs up into the stroller then zipped it shut and strutted off. I started towards my truck again but stopped at the sound of her voice.

"Although it ain't none of your fucking business, I'm going to tell you so maybe you'll think before you say anything stupid to a mother that's doing her fucking best. My son has *autism* and refused to wear any other pair of shoes that morning. Those are his favorite shoes and I ordered him another pair last week but Amazon sent out the wrong size so I had to send them back and we are waiting for another pair. Sometimes, my son looks a mess because that's what he wanted to wear and if I refuse, it could start an unnecessary meltdown. He likes what he likes and I allow him to dress how he wants to. His clothes are always clean, whether he is matching or not. I watch my son like a fucking hawk because of his special needs, but we were in the hospital to grab something from my old office when a ***code blue*** sounded off over the hospital PA system and he took off but I was right behind him. Next time, think before you judge someone, you never know what a person is going through."

She twisted off and I felt like shit after hearing her story. I watched her twist off, enjoying the view of her ass in the leggings even more now that I knew she wasn't a deadbeat mother. She turned into a driveway about three houses down and I climbed into my truck, setting up my GPS to figure out the fastest way home when the mystery lady re-emerged from the house and slid into the driver's seat of a Toyota Camry. I slowly rolled past her car and noted the make, model, and license plate before hitting the gas. She would see me again, I had to make things right after the way we met.

I beat the heavy traffic and called Saint's phone when I pulled up to the entrance. Saint came up with this dumb ass idea for me to pick them up from the hospital and say I had to make a quick stop to orchestrate the surprise. Sitting idle near the entrance, I let Saint know I was there then shot off a text message with the lil vibe's information to the same lil nigga that got me the addresses on Marco and Kelvin to see what he could find out for me. Images of the shorty running in them joggers had me ready for a night at the strip club. I had to get rid of these niggas asap.

While waiting, I peered into the backseat and shook my head at the sight of the car seat base installed in the backseat of my truck. This shit was too much for me, got me riding around like I'm somebody's baby daddy.

# CHAPTER FOURTEEN

## Ava

*J*ordyn's greedy butt was latched onto my breast again while we waited for Bishop to let us know that he was downstairs. I'm not sure what she did more, slept or nursed, all I knew was it was her world and I was on her time. They couldn't wheel me out of this hospital fast enough. My eager ass urged my doctor to discharge me yesterday after the twenty-four hour mark but he declined, stating he wanted to keep us for observation one additional night due to the complications I dealt with during my pregnancy and Ava being delivered in the backseat of a car. Bishop and Saint told me to relax and follow the doctor's orders so I did, but I couldn't wait to get back to the comfort of my own home.

"Bishop just texted me, he's outside, you ready?" Saint questioned.

"Now you already know," I bubbled and Saint laughed at me.

"Let me go grab the nurse," he informed me before exiting the room.

A few minutes later one of the nurses wheeled me and Jordyn out of the hospital while Saint trailed behind us, holding our bags.

Saint opened the rear passenger door and placed Jordyn's carseat in the base. He looked sexy as hell handling the baby with ease, I swear it was taking everything for me not to drool at the sight before me. Saint spun around and I prayed he didn't catch me damn near drooling over him. If he did catch it, the man was an expert at hiding his emotions. Gripping my hand, I stood from the wheelchair and hugged Jessica before Saint helped me into the truck. I waved at her one final time before Saint closed my door. He hugged her too and I caught myself feeling slightly jealous of the display of affection and wanting to ensure that it was just friendly. When Saint joined us in the truck, Bishop pulled off and we were on our way.

"Thanks for picking us up," I cut through the silence.

"You're welcome. How lil mama doing today?" Bishop inquired. It was clear he was falling in love with Jordyn just like me and Saint.

"She's good, full and sleepy," I advised him.

When I looked out of the window I realized we were headed in the opposite direction of my apartment. They didn't mention any pit stops so I was apprehensive about this. Saint didn't have to tell me, I knew that Bishop was in the streets before he went to prison. While in the hospital I did my due diligence and discovered that Bishop was in prison for assault with a deadly weapon. I wasn't trying to be in his business but I needed to make sure he didn't get locked up for anything that I'd need to worry about before I positioned myself or my child around a whole other man.

"Where are we going?" I questioned, curiosity getting the best of me.

"I gotta make a stop before I take y'all home," Bishop announced.

My level of angst grew with Bishop's answer. Being around men like Bishop wasn't foreign to me. My father was a dope boy before he was murdered while *making a stop* so I knew how they operated, making a stop usually meant some other shit.

"What kind of stop?" I drilled him, my disapproving eyes staring a hole in the side of his face.

"Damn Saint, what the fuck you been telling this girl about me?" Bishop laughed.

"Nothing, Ava went to my high school so yeah, she used to see you showing yo ass in the stands and ya know, she from the city sooo," Saint shrugged.

Bishop refocused on the road, and my fingers vigorously jabbed at my iPhone screen, literally moving a mile a minute. Seconds after I hit send, Saint's phone chimed loudly and I'm positive that Bishop knew it was me texting. At that point I didn't care if the nigga knew I was talking cash shit.

**Me: I'm not in the business of riding in the car when people have to make a stop. ESPECIALLY WITH MY NEWBORN!**

"I would never make a street-related stop with my brother in the car and since you and Jordyn are an extension of him, the same applies, chill out," Bishop eyed me in the rearview mirror. "I can't be mad at you for seeking clarity. We just met two days ago and you're protective of your freedom and I love that, it shows me that you'd look out for Saint in that same manner as well."

"Of course," I relaxed a little in the seat but I was still on edge.

The car fell silent, rubber colliding with the pavement serenaded the atmosphere until Bishop decreased the speed and turned off of Linebaugh and into a subdivision in West Chase. He stopped in front of a house in the middle of the block on the left hand side. Initially, I was on my phone sliding through my camera roll to choose the best picture to post of Jordyn. I narrowed it down to five pictures that were moved to favorites but I couldn't decide. Social media would only receive one picture of my baby for distant relatives on my dad's side of the family who didn't live in the state. When I finally did look up, a loud gasp escaped me as I read the sign, *Welcome home Ava and Jordyn!*

"Welcome home? What is this?" I puzzled. Unsure if this was really our new place or if it was an Airbnb he rented for a moment, either way I was excited. My apartment was small for all three of us to be cramped up in.

"This is for *us*, I signed a year lease and we moved all the baby stuff here. Everything is put together so we could both have our own rooms and the baby will have a nursery," Saint detailed.

"Really? You secured your own place and still thought about including us?"

"Yeah man, Ion need all of this space for myself and I'll pay the fee for you to break your lease or you can keep it for yourself and go home. It's up to you." Bishop's eyes darted at Saint and he mouthed for him to *man the fuck up and stop playing*. Saint mouthed back for him to *mind his business.* "I don't want you to feel like I'm rushing to make decisions for you and Jordyn. I'm just here to support you."

The car grew quiet and Saint exited the truck and opened my door. I slid out of the truck and my orange sundress was flowing in the wind like we were in the middle of a chick flick. Wrapping my arms around Saint's neck, I planted a gentle kiss on his cheek. There was a great height disparity between us so I was standing on my tippy toes to perform the task. Saint wrapped his hands around my upper back and I fought the urge to jump into his arms and smother him with kisses to demonstrate the intense feelings growing inside of me for him.

"Of course we are staying here, my baby needs room to grow. I'll start paying my portion of things as soon as I find a job when my six weeks are up. I'm going to pull my own weight."

"Don't worry about that right now, let me show you around," Saint replied.

"I'll grab the baby," Bishop announced from his side of the car.

I didn't object since he was the closest to her. Saint led me to the front door and passed me a set of keys. The moment he swung the door open and I viewed the balloons, gifts, and spacious fully furnished living room, I almost didn't recognize the deafening squeal that escaped me.

**Wa! Wa! Waaaaaaaaaaah! Waaaaaaaaaaah!**

"Come on strong lungs, yo loud ass woke Jordyn up," Bishop scolded me. Sitting Jordyn's car seat down on the brand new sectional, my baby was bawling.

"Shut up, I can't help how special y'all make me feel," I sobbed, brushing past him to pull Jordyn out of the car seat. "I really don't know what I did to deserve you guys but I appreciate you guys for everything."

I was ugly crying and there was no shame in my game either. The immense amount of joy I was experiencing had to be displayed.

"Let me get the baby before yo dramatic ass drops her," Bishop offered, pulling Jordyn from my arms and rocking her gently.

"No, it's okay, I got her," I reached for Jordyn but Bishop faked like he was dodging a tackle and swerved around me. They bopped into the kitchen and Saint led me into the nursery.

My mouth damn near touched the floor. The blush colored crib, changing table, and rocking chair were beautiful. Add in the sage colored three dimensional flowers that were popping off of the walls above the crib and the room was breathtaking. Sage fluffy plush rugs were positioned in front of the crib and changing table. It was simple yet beautiful, especially for a pair of men to pull together in a little under forty-eight hours. There were a few boxes of diapers and wipes stacked in the back corner disrupting the decor but I'd remove them later. I sat in the rocking chair, appreciating every item in this room.

Saint spun me around and I noticed the closet contained a slew of tiny baby girl clothes and I was unable to contain my emotions. "Saint! Bishop!" I squealed, pitch high enough to shatter an eardrum. I hugged Saint then rushed into the kitchen to find Bishop.

"Yo mama gone be annoying as fuck, I'mma make sure you have a room at my crib for when she pissing you off," Bishop cooed.

"Bishop! Don't be in here cursing in conversation with my baby," I chastised Bishop before gently hugging him.

"I really appreciate you too. Saint hasn't left the hospital so I know you played a pivotal role in pulling all of this together for us."

I rested my head on Bishop's shoulder for a moment before Saint pulled me to finish the tour. My bedroom had a King size bedroom set and the massive room was clearly the biggest in the house. "Saint, you don't have to give me the master bedroom, it's your house."

"This room is yours because it has a spa style bathtub and you'll be the one putting it to use. You looked out for me and I'm just returning the favor."

"I love it and I appreciate you so much but I have one request," I eyed him.

"Whatever you need," Saint offered. I closed my eyes for a moment, trying to refocus on the topic at hand because **babyyyyyy**... at *that* moment, I understood why so many women weren't able to wait the full six weeks before having sex and wound up pregnant afterwards. Although Saint was being his usual self, those words sent a scorching heat through my body. Swallowing hard, I had to do something to hide my body's involuntary response. Jordyn's cries filled the house and I finally found my voice again.

"Can you rebuild my reading oasis here?"

"That's the first order of business tomorrow," Saint kissed my forehead. "Come on and get Jordyn from Bishop, she clearly ain't feeling him anymore."

"Clearly," I chuckled and exited the bedroom.

# CHAPTER FIFTEEN

## Bishop

### *Two Months Later*

"Stop all that fucking running," I ordered, grasping Kimmy's waist with my right hand to assist me in guiding the pace because her immobile ass wasn't moving shit.

"I'm not running," Kimmy refuted while moving out of the position.

My left hand forced her back down into position because her arch was fucking horrible, it was damn near nonexistent, but she wanted a nigga to hit it from the back. Instead of enjoying the pussy I found myself wondering why I decided to fuck Kimmy again when she laid flat like a corpse when she finally gave up the pussy for the first time last night. Kimmy simply couldn't take dick and we both had to accept that. She waltzed her ass up in the party in this tight ass purple dress, rubbing her ass all on my dick, telling me that she wanted to fuck just to come in the room and run from the dick. Ion care how beautiful her ass was, I wasn't wasting another second on Kimmy.

She was one of the nurses who was fawning over a nigga at the hospital. I slipped her my number and we went out on a few dates over the last two months. Kimmy was cool as shit, we vibed, but the bitch couldn't take dick and she was too soft for me. I needed a chick like *mean ass* who slapped the shit out of me for talking sideways. Thinking about her had me fucking Kimmy harder and growing more annoyed because her ass was tensing up worse now. I already knew if I got a hold of her fine ass, she would match my energy, that slap told me all I needed to know. Unfortunately, she wasn't as easy to find because the car didn't belong to her.

"It's too much," Kimmy whined, reaching back to push me out of her. This was exactly why I loved women who fucked on the first night, at least I knew what I was getting myself into after that. Clearly, I wasn't going to nut in this position, even playing with her clit didn't help Kimmy's stiff ass relax. I pulled my dick out of her and slid the condom off.

"Come on Kimmy, bless a nigga with some head, it's my birthday," I persuaded her and she complied.

Sliding to the edge of the bed, she sucked all nine inches down her throat and played with my balls. I reached down to fondle her supple breast and this was what she should've been advertising. Kimmy couldn't take dick but she could deep throat one. She sucked my dick like a pro, real sloppy with the spit dripping from the sides of her mouth, a nigga was in heaven as my nut spit down her throat.

Peering down at Kimmy after she released my dick from her lips, I noticed she swallowed all of that shit. Smiling at her, I might not have to cancel this bitch after all.

"Where the fuck is Bishop!" I heard Rambo's loud ass yelling through the house.

**KNOCK! KNOCK! KNOCK!**

"Aye, is Bishop in there?"

"Say no, that nigga drunk as hell," I whispered to her.

"No, he's not in here," Kimmy hesitantly replied and Rambo moved on.

"I'm about to shower," I stated. Kimmy looked around for her clothes while I grabbed the rubber from the floor and flushed it down the toilet.

"Can I join you?" Kimmy batted those pretty lashes at me but I wasn't going for it.

"Nah, I'm trying to be quick," I declined her offer. Now that the nut wore off, keeping her around wasn't in the equation. I couldn't live off head alone, I needed a woman that had top tier pussy too and no, I can't be out here teaching her how to fuck, we are too old for that shit. As of twelve o'clock this morning I was thirty-six years old, I was ready to stop living wild and settle down with Natalie. Now I was out here back to my younger days, fucking with random hoes. After showering, Kimmy went in and I changed into a fresh outfit.

My phone chimed and it was a text from Saint.

**Saint: Where the fuck you at? Gigi only agreed to watch the baby for two hours and Ava only agreed to show her face for a quick minute. This is her first time leaving the baby with anyone else and you're not even at your own party!**

Shaking my head, I laughed at the message. Saint was probably the one who was ready to go, not Ava. Over the last two months Ava would bring Jordyn to the basketball courts when Saint trained Rambo and Gigi's boys, they built a rapport, and it was no surprise that they also fell in love with Jordyn. Gigi even insisted on being Jordyn's godmother since she didn't have any daughters. The community we were building was solid and I was proud to be a part of it. I had eight nephews and one niece that kept me on my toes and I loved this shit.

Descending the stairs, Rambo's drunk ass immediately noticed me. He was clearly searching for me while two strippers carried a two tier cake on a long tray that resembled an ancient litter without the covering. "Aye!" Rambo yelled over the crowded first level of the home. The nigga was so loud that even the people in the kitchen and outside by the pool heard him. The DJ turned the music down and all eyes were on me at the bottom of the stairs.

"They fucked up and freed my nigga from the feds two months ago and now he off parole just in time for his birthday! **Issa motha fuckin' real nigga holidaaaaaaaaaaaaaay!**" Rambo shouted, climbing onto the kitchen island in the middle of the house he rented for the night.

I ain't want no extravagant shit but Rambo refused since I missed out on celebrating the last two years. He raised his hand in the air like a conductor and the room followed along singing *happy birthday*. The strippers lit a few candles and I walked over to blow them out before thanking everyone for coming. I hated drawing so much attention so I swiftly made my way out of the area while they crowded around for cake. It was nearing eleven o'clock and that party had been going on since eight. These niggas had endless liquor and plenty of food so they were about to go all night. I grabbed a bottle of D'Usse to join the vibe and escape my inner thoughts.

I didn't miss Natalie, how could I after the shit she did? However, I did miss that family unit shit. Fucking one woman who knew what I liked and I didn't have to play around in these streets with bitches I could barely trust. I turned up the bottle of D'Usse and spotted Saint off to the side slowly sipping out of his cup. The mug he wore made me follow his gaze and it led me to Ava. She was sandwiched between my young niggas Marco and Kelvin as they discussed something that was clearly funny because Ava was cracking up. I hit them with those free bricks and we let the division Natalie attempted to drive between us go.

Wading through the sea of people in the room, I posted up next to Saint. The nigga was so mad he didn't notice my presence. "You need to shit or get off the pot," Saint finally tore his eyes away from them and glared at me.

Ion know why he was mad at me, it was Kelvin about to swindle Ava right from under him. The day that Ava was discharged from the hospital, I thought he was going to speak on his feelings but instead he kept denying them. Saint even said he wasn't going to tell Ava they were moving, he was going to give her the option because he didn't want her to feel like he was controlling her. I told him to step down then but he was still hollin' that they were just friends. The obvious attraction between them every time I went to see Jordyn damn near suffocated me. They needed to kiss, fuck, or something and stop playing.

"What?" Saint questioned me, then returned his gaze.

"Look, Ava dropped that load, threw on some tight shit, and got mother fuckas salivating in this bitch." His head swiveled in my direction and his face was frowned up. "Nigga, you *secretly* in love with her so you know she's fuckin' beautiful. Another nigga gone step in and play step daddy, have yo chest hurting, making it hard to breathe."

"Shut the fuck up nigga," Saint grumbled, taking a swig from his cup. "I don't like Ava mingling with them niggas but I don't want to interfere and seem like a crazy ass nigga."

"Go make up an excuse to steal her and keep her under you until y'all leave. It's a lot of dog ass niggas up in here and I fuck with Ava so Ion want her to fall victim to their bullshit. That nigga Marco to her left got four kids with four baby mamas and he been married since eighteen and none of his kids came from his wife so clearly they ain't leaving each other. He fuck on other bitches then go right back home to his wife. Kelvin just a young nigga with long money who don't even date, he fuck 'em and duck 'em. A younger version of me so I know he hell. Better get yo ass over there and save her."

Saint stalked off without a word and I was dying laughing at how fast he moved. Somebody bumped me hard as hell from behind as I turned up my bottle of D'Usse and it spilled down my shirt. I turned, prepared to choke a nigga, and realized it was shorty with all them fuckin' dogs.

"Damn Christmas came early," I mumbled to myself.

"I'm so sorry, the floor was wet and I slipped. Let me grab you..." her voice trailed off before she could finish her statement. "Nigga fuck you, I hope that shirt is brand new and the D'Usse leaves a permanent stain that even the dry cleaners can't get out."

"Even if it does, I'll just buy a new one," I explained, licking my lips. She rolled her eyes and spun around to leave but I gripped her wrist before her mean ass could take off. This was exactly what I was talking about, verbally abuse me bae, I love all that crazy shit.

"Kalesha, we gotta go, my husband just called me. The lil hoe babysitting Gideon thinks she is slick... she doesn't know we have cameras in the house and Herc always checks them when he's out of town and she snuck some dread headed lil boy in my house!" I immediately recognized Gabby's voice. She was Gigi's little sister and I could definitely see her and Kalesha being friends the way their mouths were set up.

"Wassup Gabby," I greeted her and she finally looked up from her phone to observe the scene before her. I side-hugged Gabby with my free hand and she pecked my cheek like she always did when I ran into her.

"Bishop, how do you know Kalesha?" Gabby pried, refocusing on her phone.

"She slapped me and let her dogs attack me like two months ago," I detailed.

"Dogs?" Gabby puzzled, looking between us.

"Nigga, you called me a bitch and tried to play on my top like I'm a dead beat mother."

"What?" Gabby looked at me with her hands on her hips.

"Come on, don't jump me. I made an honest mistake and I apologized. Tryin' to see what else I can learn from you to help me be a better man."

"Nothing, bye," she waved me off. "Come on Gabby before them teenagers be fucking on yo new couches. I told you to leave Gideon with my parents too."

"Yes bitch come on, ain't no way she gone break in my couches before me," Gabby fumed, initiating a call on her phone.

"Let me go, I know you heard my ride saying she is about to leave," Kalesha ordered.

"Stick around for a little longer," I encouraged Kalesha's mean ass but her frowned up face still hadn't relaxed since she recognized me.

"Yeah friend, Bishop is good peoples, you're in good hands with him. This is his welcome home party. He's the one you decorated the place for," Gabby informed her.

"Fresh out of prison, not surprising at all," Kalesha remarked. I grasped my chest, fake offended by her comment.

"Oh she answered the phone!" Gabby shouted and rushed out of the door talking shit with the phone glued to her ear.

I couldn't help but to eye fuck Kalesha, she was gorgeous as fuck with her hair in a high messy bun and a skin tight two piece crop top set hugging her curves.

"Relax, I'm going to take you home," I assured her.

"No and I have to go because I don't trust myself with you," Kalesha blurted out and a grin spread across my face as she became flustered and closed her mouth. The revelation was music to my ears, I would definitely work my way into her heart. "I mean, I don't know you... I... I don't trust you." Kalesha tried to correct herself but the damage was already done.

"Let me get your number."

"Absolutely not."

"You might as well give it to me, I'll give you a hundred dollars," I offered and her eyes squinted in confusion.

"You wanna pay me for my phone number? What kind of desperate shit is that? Do you always offer bitches money in exchange for their numbers? I know that shit works every time but I think it's creepy."

"Nah, Ion never have to do too much but you are *different* and I figured you would want the money because if you don't give me your number today, I'm going to hit Gabby's brother in-law and have him offer her a hundred for your number and she will give it up. I was just trying to cut out the middle man," I explained.

"Boy bye." I released my grip and salivated over her walking away from me yet again.

This time was different though, shit was going to go just how I explained it to her and we would be in each other's presence again soon. I had her panties wet and her mind flustered, she would definitely be *mine* soon. Taking another swig from the bottle of D'Usse I shut the door once I watched them drive off safely.

Saint appeared through the crowd with Ava by his side. "Happy birthday! Thanks for inviting us, Bishop!" Ava hugged me all bubbly and shit. That liquor clearly had her feeling lovely.

"You're welcome. What you thought about Kelvin? I know that nigga was trying to finesse his way into some pussy."

Saint's jaw clenched, that nigga wanted to jab me but instead refused to show his hand. "Shut up, Bishop. He was just being nice while Saint was busy with some of his old friends."

Ava moved through the door and Saint turned around and mouthed *fuck you nigga* before trailing her. "We out," Saint bumped me on his way out of the door and man, for the first time in years, I felt complete with my lil brother back home. Getting under his skin would never get old to me, I was on that until they put one of us in the grave.

# CHAPTER SIXTEEN

## Ava

*L*ife was better than good, it was marvelous. We were settled into our home, I secured a part-time work from home position at night. Jordyn didn't have to go to daycare because Saint would take care of her while I worked my four hour shift as a customer service representative. The village I had surrounding me was top tier, they really had my best interests at heart. I welcomed the love and support from my village with open arms. Rambo was definitely rough around the edges but I loved his wife Gigi.

We met at the basketball courts while I watched Saint train the boys one day. He now had a group of ten kids that he trained at that same time, Gigi and Rambo's eight kids, their nephew Gideon, and a boy whose parents heard about Saint through Gigi. Rambo must've been sick or something that day because she drove the Sprinter Van to the courts and let the kids out. After introducing herself, she immediately gushed over Jordyn and it was over from there. I didn't have a mother figure and Jermaine's mother never liked me so I didn't bother to reach out to her. Gigi stepped in and offered the support that I needed as a new mom. I don't think she knew it, but Gigi was filling a very painful void.

Saint sat next to me in the pediatrician's office and I reveled in the fact that Jordyn just received a clean bill of health. I was nervous as hell because she was about to receive her two months vaccination shots. The nurse re-entered the room and sat a silver tray with a few needles and vials on it on the counter.

"Okay mom, can you bring Jordyn over for me and lay her down?" she requested. I hesitantly stood up and carried Jordyn over to the table. The nurse picked up on my apprehension and offered me a smile.

"Relax, it'll be over quickly. She might have some swelling, redness, and pain at the site of the injection but I promise she will be fine."

The nurse placed gloves over her hands and filled the syringes with the vaccines from the vials and placed three bandaids on the silver tray. Like a pro, she grabbed Jordyn's chunky thigh and administered the vaccines. My baby's loud sobs filled the room and Saint was up out of his seat to grab her as soon as it was over. Although I wanted to be the one to comfort her I was glad Saint stepped in. Jordyn loved him and anytime she was having a rough time and I couldn't get her to quiet down, she would happily go to Saint. I think that Jordyn was at a point where she could sense him when he got off of work because that was the only time she pulled those long crying fits. Any other time she was my perfect angel.

Saint held Jordyn on his chest and gently patted her back. "It's okay Jordyn, it's all over. You're okay, Saint got you."

I watched them in awe, wanting to rub Jordyn's back but she was quiet for him. "The receptionist will have Jordyn's immunization record printed out for you by the time you get her dressed and come out. If she is a little fussy, you guys can do Tylenol or Motrin."

"Thank you," I nodded.

Saint laid Jordyn on the table and I gathered her clothes from the car seat and passed them to him. Within minutes Saint had her dressed and we were exiting the exam room to grab her shot record. "I'm going to take her to the car since she's falling asleep and it's so loud in here."

"Okay," I voiced, standing behind the woman checking in at the receptionist desk.

It took a minute to secure the forms then I rejoined them in the car. Jordyn was awake as soon as we pulled into traffic and she was cranky as ever. On the average day Jordyn hated her car seat and today was no different. I tried to entertain her with some toys but she wasn't going for it.

"Let's stop and grab Jordyn some Tylenol just to be on the safe side. She always hates the car seat but she hasn't calmed down yet," Saint suggested, pulling into a CVS along the route home.

"Cool," I agreed with him.

"Let's take her inside to see if she'll calm down," Saint suggested.

I unbuckled the straps of the seat belt and eased Jordyn out of the car seat. Jordyn immediately calmed down once we stepped out of the truck. We trailed Saint through the automatic doors and into the children's medicine aisle. I scanned the shelves for infant Tylenol and Saint gripped my shoulders, capturing my attention.

"I'm going to grab a bag of chips from the snack aisle. Do you want anything?"

"Grab me some Whoppers if they have those," I requested.

"Ion see how you eat that nasty ass candy," Saint commented.

He knew I loved Whoppers and talked shit about them every time. I settled on the small bottle of medicine and scanned the shelves for women's vitamins. With my vitamins in hand, I left the medicine aisle and followed the sound of Saint's voice. Jordyn was asleep in my arms and I held her tight, picking up the pace when I realized that Saint's voice was engaging in conversation with a woman.

"Well it's a pleasure seeing you again. I'm glad you're doing fine and still handsome as ever," she flirted as I stepped onto the aisle.

The girl was fucking breath-takingly beautiful. Super tall and thick with a long ass 613 straight weave and perfect acrylic nails. A tight ass spaghetti strap bodysuit clung to her curves and her titties were practically spilling out of the top and she was too fucking close for my comfort. She was eye fucking him so hard the bitch was probably already pregnant. Strutting over to them, I purposely made our presence known.

"Did you find the Whoppers, Saint?" I pried.

"Yeah I got them, let me have the medicine, since Jordyn is asleep you can take her to the car." Saint passed me the keys after raising my candy in the air.

I felt my fucking heart beating out of my chest after Saint's request. He was sending me off for this bitch. Shoving the medicine and vitamins into his chest, I stomped off with Saint right on my heels.

"Ava!" he called after me but I ignored him, my feelings were hurt.

The last thing I wanted to do was argue with a man who didn't belong to me in public while holding my daughter. Saint turned back to pay for the medicine and I marched to the truck and strapped my baby into her car seat. Jordyn was still asleep and I prayed she stayed asleep while I felt my emotions because the tears wouldn't stop falling. I played around and hid my feelings for too long and now Saint was chopping it up with other bitches. It just never seemed to be the right time to divulge my secrets. He was my only friend, my small slice of a support system, and I didn't want to ruin that.

Plus, I just had a baby, he didn't have kids and Bishop wasn't feeling the idea of us before so I'm not sure what he would say now. Supporting a platonic relationship between us wouldn't look much different from how we behave now but still, it was something to consider. Thoughts of rejection ate at me constantly. With all of that said, I was falling for Saint and the decline was steep, I don't think there was any coming back from this. My moment to sulk and debate about my next move was short lived because a private phone number started calling. Tucking my feelings, I took a deep breath and answered the phone.

"Hello."

"Wassup Ava," Jermaine's voice greeted me. "I heard you had the baby and you didn't even bother to let me know."

"How the fuck was I supposed to do that when you changed your phone number, Jermaine? You blocked me on everything and you're calling me private right now. Plus the last time I heard, you were in jail."

"You could've called my mama," Jermaine argued, sucking his teeth like the bitch he was. Taking a deep breath, I had to close my eyes and pinch the bridge of my nose to keep from spazzing on this sassy ass nigga. I didn't know when Jermaine turned into a bitch ass nigga or how I missed the red flags but I was stuck with the nigga now.

"Look Jermaine, your daughter's name is Jordyn and I am trying to leave the past in the past for the sake of our daughter, but you're making that really difficult. I was so mad at you to the point that I hated you for abandoning us but now I realize Jordyn deserves to know you, no matter how I feel about you," I vented.

"Good, I'm glad to hear that. I'll be in touch to set something up," Jermaine replied.

For some reason, I expected an apology but that clearly wasn't going to happen. "Cool, I'll watch for your call."

I disconnected the call to keep from cursing Jermaine out. Now I was seething for multiple reasons and I just wanted to go home and curl up in my bed. A few silent tears slid down my cheeks as I stared into space.

"Come on Ava, why are you doing all that crying?" Saint's voice shook me. I was so deep in my daunting thoughts that I didn't hear him open the door.

"Nothing, I'm just tired," I lied, wiping my tears while sitting in the backseat.

Saint's door was still open and the girl from inside walked by the truck and offered me a set of disappointing eyes. "I'm sorry girl, I didn't realize y'all were together."

Before I could respond Saint rudely closed the door in her face and pulled out of the parking lot.

# CHAPTER SEVENTEEN

## Saint

The car was silent as we drove home. I know that the shit looked terrible but it wasn't at all what it seemed.

Swaggering through the drug store, I grabbed a cart then ventured over to the snack aisle. Grabbing Ava five packs of Whoppers and a bag of sour cream and onion chips, I was about to find Ava and Jordyn when Shalana stepped into my path. She looked good, better than the last time I saw her, but she wasn't touching Ava, that girl was *perfect*. Plus Shalana's character made her a strong opp in my eyes.

Shalana didn't owe me shit when I got out of prison. However, Shalana's response when she realized I wasn't of use to her was a complete change from any of our previous interactions. I looked out for Shalana because I fucked with her, no ulterior motives, but it was clear her feelings for me were contingent upon what I could do for her. Or rather, what *Bishop* could do for her by way of me since he had the money.

"Oh my God, Saint!" Shalana bubbled, surprising the shit out of me when she embraced me in a hug. I hadn't run into Shalana since she dropped me off at my whip. Her greeting caught me off guard but I quickly broke the hug before Ava saw us.

"'Sup," I kept it simple.

"Nothing, how have you been?" She bubbled, probably noticing my fit and calculating the shit up.

"Good, just grabbing some stuff real quick. I gotta slide though."

"Well it's a pleasure seeing you again. I'm glad you're doing fine and still handsome as ever," she flirted as Ava entered the aisle with us.

As soon as our eyes connected I knew I fucked up. I promise I felt Ava's heart shattering as she approached us. "Did you find the Whoppers, Saint?" Ava pried and I immediately noticed that Jordyn was fast asleep after all of that screaming she did. Without thinking, I responded in the worst way possible.

"Yeah I got them, let me have the medicine, since Jordyn is asleep you can take her to the car." I passed Ava my keys after raising her candy in the air and at that moment, I realized I made shit worse.

Ava snatched the keys from me and I felt the pain residing in her. It was the same anger I felt at Bishop's birthday party last week when Ava was talking to other niggas.

"Ava!" I called after her, prepared to explain myself, but she was out of the door and I didn't need these weak ass employees trying to tackle me for stealing some shit I could afford. Rushing over to the line, I quickly placed my items on the counter and the cashier rang my shit up.

"I'm sorry, I didn't mean to make your lady mad. Well if that's your girl since you ain't been out long enough to have a whole baby," Shalana's voice irritated my soul at that moment. It was clear she was trying to be messy the way she made that comment and I wasn't going for it.

"That's my *whole fucking family* and my **entire** heart. Move around!"

"The total is $27.12," the cashier informed me. I pulled two twenties from my wallet and passed them to her. Snatching my bag from the counter I rushed outside. Ava was in the car, staring off into space with tears cascading down her cheeks.

If I'm being honest, I wasn't sure how to address the situation and the silent ride home bought me a few minutes to get my shit together. When we got home, Jordyn was still asleep and I carried her inside. After ensuring that Jordyn was down for real, I texted Carl to let him know that I wouldn't make it into work today before knocking on Ava's bedroom door.

"Go away Saint," Ava shouted.

"Ava, that was Shalana, the chick who picked me up from prison that I told you about. She was all up in my face saying hi and I told her to move around. Ion want shit to do with that girl. You and Jordyn are my family, my *entire fucking heart*. I don't be out in these streets because I got *what I want* at home already. Although I haven't expressed that, I know I've shown you."

The sound of the door knob turning caught my attention and I waited for Ava to meet me at the door but she didn't. I gently nudged the door open and my heart rate increased at the sight of Ava dressed in a black lingerie set, complete with thigh high stockings. Ava still wore a sports bra and leggings when she was doing her at home workouts so I knew the body was still perfect, it was even better covered in the thin fabric.

It was a little after three o'clock, the Florida sun was beating through her closed curtains, providing my eyes the best view of Ava's sparsely clothed body. My dick grew hard as a ton of bricks before I could think about controlling the urges that hit me. Grinding, ensuring that Ava was okay then the birth of Jordyn kept me occupied, I didn't have time to think about pussy. Ava's was on the forefront of my mind now.

"Ava, do you really want this?" I motioned between us then pulled Ava closer to me. "I *want* this, I've *been* wanting this... us... I've been wanting *you*. It never felt like the right time though."

"I want the same thing and there is no time like now," Ava confirmed.

There was nothing else to be said between us, the tension would finally be cleared. I covered Ava's lips with mine and savored every moment of the slow sensual kiss we shared. My tongue felt every ridge on her tongue as my hands slid down her body until they were positioned at her lower waist. I guided Ava back towards the bed and we collapsed on her pillow top mattress. My hands roamed every crevice on her body and I enjoyed the feeling of her soft hands roaming the length of my back. When they graced my scalp, I felt her body buck beneath mine.

Pulling my tongue away from Ava's lips, I trailed kisses down until her lower lips greeted me. Kissing them gently through the fabric she was wet and I pulled her thong to the side and licked at her nectar. It was addictive, just like her natural aura and I wanted to lick up every drop. Trailing my tongue between her slit, I found my way back up to her clit. Sucking it into my mouth, I slowly dipped my fingers inside. Ava was already creaming for me and I was about to drain her of everything she had. I tongue kissed her clit with the same passion I did her supple lips until I felt both of her hands rubbing in random directions across my scalp.

"Oh my... Saaaaaaaaaaaaaaint!" Ava shouted as she came on my fingers.

I pulled my fingers out and licked her juices off. She smiled down at me and pulled me up until I was kissing her lips. Ava's body convulsed underneath me but she still had enough strength to spread her legs and let me in. Pulling my joggers down, I couldn't slip my dick in fast enough.

"Oh fuck!" I reveled in the moment, slowly pushing my way through her walls. Ava was special and this pussy was made just for me. Her pussy took a moment to accept me in and her ass was scratching my back in the process.

"You feel so good," Ava moaned in my ear.

I lifted up and planted a kiss on her lips as I slowly dug her back out. Lifting her right leg with my left hand, she was at the perfect angle to guide all of my dick in her with ease. Ava fucked me back from below and our slow fucking quickly turned into me flipping her ass over and digging her back out. Her back was arched perfectly and she pulled a pillow to bite on as I hit her with back shots. The slapping sound in the room grew louder as Ava's moans increased a few decibels. Suddenly her pussy clenched me and her juices flowed down my shaft. I was in heaven, unable to control my nut with the influx of sensations, I came inside of Ava.

Frozen in place, I was terrified of what Ava would say as I pulled out of her. Ava collapsed on the bed, a fucking masterpiece in every way possible, I couldn't think about anything except how lucky I was to have her. Kicking my joggers and boxers fully off, I laid in the bed next to Ava, dick still damn near touching the ceiling.

She turned over, a smile on her face. "That was the best sex ever," she confessed, her small hands stroking my dick.

"Relax, I'm on the depo shot, it's okay," Ava assured me, reading my fucking mind. That's how in sync we were, it was scary as shit that I fell for this girl so hard.

"I love you," I leaned over and kissed her again.

"I love you too," Ava expressed once we broke the kiss. She pulled her bra off and eased over to where I was laying, slurping my dick in her mouth. My hands found their way between her tresses and I was about to enjoy every second of the view.

**Wa! Wa! Waaaaaaaaaaah! Waaaaaaaaaaah!**

Jordyn's loud cries came through the baby monitor, fucking up the vibe. I closed my eyes as Ava slowly eased up off of my dick. "Since you didn't pull out I have to take a shower so wash your hands and get Jordyn, I'll finish what I started tonight," Ava pecked my lips then rushed off to the bathroom.

I pulled my clothes on, washed my hands, and grabbed Jordyn's little cranky self. "Those shots got my baby upset," I bounced her up and down in my arms.

Jordyn laid on my chest and ceased her tears. After everything I'd been through, these simple moments made life worth living.

# CHAPTER EIGHTEEN

## Kalesha Warren

"All done, mom." Jibri monotoned, sitting up straight at his desk. He placed the mechanical pencil in his teal pencil holder and interlocked his fingers on his desk, so handsome and studious.

"Okay, can you read a book while mommy finishes these treat bags then we can go over your math problems?" I requested.

He raised both of his thumbs in the air and rushed over to the bookshelf. If Jibri wasn't building entire cities with his Lego sets, he was reading a chapter book. He was only six years old and in the first grade, but my son was already reading on a fifth grade level. Jibri excelled academically in all subjects which made this transition easy. We were in our second week of homeschooling and so far the experience was pleasant. The journey was unexpected, but I had to do what I had to do for my son. He was on the spectrum and his unique abilities made him an easy target for the disrespectful kids at school to bully him while the teachers and the school system barely met his needs. Kindergarten was rough, but Jibri was blessed with an amazing teacher who had superior communication skills, followed his IEP, and watched out for the other kids' shenanigans.

I wasn't naive, I knew Jibri would face additional challenges that other children didn't as soon as he was diagnosed in VPK at four years old. Plus, I joined a Facebook group with other local moms whose children had autism and read all types of hurdles that they encountered with the school system, after care programs, and therapy services. Even with all of that said, I thought that Jibri would at least have a few years before the heavy bullying started.

Jibri wasn't talkative unless he felt comfortable in the space he was in, he reverted to a toddler's vocabulary when he was uncomfortable, and by the end of the school year, he opened up with his teacher so I thought he was making progress and I was excited about starting first grade on a good note. Unfortunately, I quickly discovered that Jibri was more traumatized by the bullshit he went through last year than we realized because he ran away from his class during recess on the first day of school. His irresponsible teacher didn't notice until they were back in the classroom. Me and my parents rushed up to the school and my dad found Jibri in the back of the library reading a book. Meanwhile, I was in the office speaking with his uncompassionate teacher and when I didn't like her nonchalant responses about Jibri's disappearance, I turned that bitch every way but loose.

That led to me earning my first mugshot and the benefits no longer outweighed the bullshit. I pulled Jibri from school and he was doing so much better. Jibri was thriving and I was enjoying watching my son learn and grow on a daily basis. Plus it was a huge relief to know that my son was safe, I didn't have to brace myself for him to come home with disheartening stories of what kids said to him on the playground or constantly battle with the schools about ensuring that his accommodations were made. It was just me, Jibri, my parents, and his tutor involved in his education now.

While in school, Jibri required speech therapy and behavior therapy due to his frequent meltdowns. However, removing Jibri from school decreased his episodes drastically. Looking over at my son as his face was buried in *Stuart Little,* my heart felt full with all of Jibri's progress recently.

Turning back to the project on my desk, I stuck the Bluey stickers on top of the Pringles cans and moved them to the side. I had an order of fifty Pringles, water bottles, and chip bags to transform into the Bluey theme. My office space used to house my DIY crafts and the supplies I needed for my party planning business. Party planning used to be my side hustle but now it was my bread and butter with Jibri homeschooling. I used to be a fulltime dietician at Tampa General Hospital but I resigned to be there for my son.

My phone rang as I finished up with the cans of Pringles and it was a FaceTime call from my parents. Married for thirty years, Gail and Preston had the type of love that I knew I'd probably never receive. After going through what I went through with Jibri's dad, I'd probably never heal enough to allow that type of love into my heart. I was with Jibri's father for two years before we got married and I found myself pregnant shortly after that. Our lives were pure bliss until Jibri started to show signs that he might be on the spectrum and we started going through the process to have him evaluated. That was a point of contention that turned volatile because he didn't believe we should be *labeling* Jibri. Instead of obtaining the help our son desperately needed, he wanted to impose stricter punishments on our three year old son. He accused me of being a bad mom and that was my breaking point. We got into a major argument and the fuck nigga decided to leave in the middle of the afternoon while me and Jibri were at the hospital with my parents.

That Wednesday was a day that I would never forget, it was probably the worst day of my life. Up until that point, my twenty-six years on earth were very relaxed. I went to college, met my ex-husband and got married, secured a job, and began a family in our house with a white picket fence. However, that day wore my ass out. My father suffered a heart attack and my husband left without a word all within a twenty-four hour span.

My ex-husband filed for divorce and I didn't contest his demands. I acquired the house and he was ordered to pay child support but the slick ass nigga never complied with that shit. The child support office had been on his ass for the past three years without any response. I hadn't heard from his ass since the day he packed his shit. During the divorce proceedings, he didn't even show up to court and that's how I ended up with the house.

Last year, he was arrested for failure to pay and someone paid a thousand dollars towards his child support for him to be released from prison. I wasn't sweating his ass either. During our last conversation, he swore all Jibri needed was an ass whooping and I would earn a second mugshot if he did that to our son. Autism didn't make my son less than like his father seemed to think, it made Jibri unique, and I loved every part of my son regardless.

"Mom, your phone," Jibri stood in front of my desk, pulling me out of my thoughts. He nudged the phone towards me, annoyed with the incessant ringing.

Tapping the green button, I looked into the phone to see their jovial faces pop up on the screen. "Happy Friday!" They sang in unison and Jibri smirked, pushing his head into the camera. He didn't smile often unless it was in regards to a new book or his grandparents. If it wasn't for them, I probably would've lost my mind ten times over. When I needed a break, they gave it to me. I was short on rent this month and they covered the cost. There was nothing like having a supportive village to help you keep your head on straight.

"Happy Friday," I sang.

"Happy Friday, I'm weading *Stuart Little*. Mom is slow today," he huffed lowly. The "r" sounds were currently Jibri's focus in speech and I noticed that the corrections happened less frequently. I still listened for the mispronunciations and worked with Jibri on the corrections.

"Boy, I'm almost done with work for the day then we can go to the park," I chuckled. "Let's practice that word again. R... R... Reading."

Sighing deeply, Jibri repeated the word. "R... R... Reading. Reading."

"It's Friday and you only do review activities so I'm sure you aced it. Would you like to come over to build this New York City skyline Lego set we ordered you? Then when we are done we can read a few chapters from Stuart Little? If your mom doesn't have plans, you can spend the night and when we finish reading Stuart Little, we can watch the movie."

"There is a movie?" Jibri eyed them suspiciously and it was taking everything out of me to stifle my laughter.

"Yes, there is a movie," I assured Jibri with a gentle arm rub.

"Ohhhh, sounds promising. Can I stay at my gwandpawents?"

"Sure, I don't mind if you want to ditch me to hang with them but let's try that word again. Grandparents... grrr... grrr. Grandparents."

"Grrr... grrr... gwand..." Jibri paused for a moment and closed his eyes before restarting. "Grrr... grrr... grandpawents. Grandparents," Jibri practiced and I gave him two thumbs up.

"Good job, Jibri!" My parents celebrated, clapping too loudly for Jibri, and my eyes immediately darted in their direction.

"Grandparents, too loud," Jibri replied flatly, waving his index finger in the air.

"Sorry about that grandson, but you did an amazing job," my dad complimented him.

"Okay. I'm grabbing shoes now. See you soon."

"See you soon," my grandparents waved at him.

"We will talk to you when we get over there," my mom assured me before ending the call.

I refocused on my task at hand, placing the labels on the mini water bottles when Jibri re-entered the room with his shoes in his hands. "There is a man walking to the doow with flowews. I saw him out of my window, he has a lot of flowews."

Standing from my chair, I peeked out of the blinds covering the window that was positioned beside my work station. My breathing became erratic and Jibri looked up at me in confusion. "Do we need to call 911?"

"No, it's okay. Stay in here and read more of Stuart Little while I answer the door," I requested.

Sprinting out of the office, I opened the door before Bishop could knock. On the way home from the party I explicitly told Gabby not to give him my number but she clearly didn't listen and did the opposite. Swinging the door open, I caught a full view of the porch and Jibri was right, there were a lot of flowers on the porch. An assortment of pink roses were strategically placed to spell out *Date?*

"Why would you pop up here?" I badgered, folding my arms across my chest. Fighting to disguise my beating heart.

This was the sweetest thing any man ever did for me and I wasn't sure how to feel about it coming from Bishop. My arms folded across my chest only made my titties sit up higher in my sports bra, that in turn caused Bishop to glance at them before licking his perfect lips.

That simple gesture alone made me want to melt into a puddle in the middle of my porch just like he did last week at his birthday party. Although our first two interactions made me want to stomp his ass out, I couldn't pretend this man wasn't hand crafted by God. Smooth dark skin, low fade, and a full beard. During our previous encounters Bishop was iced out from his neck to his wrist draped in a whole bunch of designer shit but today he was dressed in a simple black Nike terry shorts, a black t-shirt, and matching sneakers with one chain gracing his neck.

"Gabby told me that you threatened to beat her ass if she gave me your number so she dropped your location instead," he smirked. His hands were holding a huge bouquet of pink roses on the left and two envelopes on the right. "Since I don't have your number I decided to pop up with a few gifts and a simple request." He stepped over the flowers, invading my space, and the scent from his cologne captivated me. Bishop was fine, smelled good, and apparently had a persistent romantic side. "This one is for you and this one is for your son." He stated.

My curiosity was piqued as Bishop slid the pink and blue envelopes into my hand. Pulling the flap open on the pink envelope, I observed the five hundred dollar Amazon gift card with my name on it and the blue envelope contained a two hundred dollar Roblox gift card. "Gabby told me that your son loves Roblox and you like to craft so I figured those would be the best options."

"Bishop, you didn't have to do this," I attempted to push the gift cards back into his hands but Bishop refused, backing up to give me a little space.

"Nah, those are for y'all to keep. Ion use either of them so please don't try to give them back. I don't have the receipt so you'll be throwing money away."

"Well thank you," I commented.

"So what's up with my question?" He motioned at the flowers on the porch. "Can I take you out on a date sometime?"

"No, it's giving stalker!" I belted louder than expected and I immediately heard Jibri's voice behind me moments later.

"Mom, too loud. Tell me when the gwandpawents get hewe, I'm

weady to go." He shook his hand, waving his index finger in the air before walking down the hallway back into the office where his nosey butt was supposed to be.

"Lil man just told on you, he got his bag packed and ready to go with his grandparents. Spend a little bit of your free time with me."

"I can't, I have treats and things to finish before the night is over," I informed Bishop.

"What if I help you with whatever you got going on?" Bishop offered.

"Ughhhh, that was just an excuse. I'll be done with my work stuff in a few hours then we can go to dinner," I caved.

The truth was, I could use a night out and doing it on someone else's dime was even better. Gabby got me the gig decorating for Bishop's welcome home party and that was supposed to be my night to let my hair down but her babysitter ruined that. I ended up back at my parents' house sleeping in bed next to Jibri for the rest of the evening. Gabby was really my only friend. All of the women I met in college got married and moved away with their spouses and the co-workers I had from the hospital were never real friends, more like acquaintances.

"Alright, I heard you love Rocco's Tacos so we can hit them up. What time should I come back to pick you up?"

"No, I'll meet you there," I declined while unlocking my phone and placing a FaceTime call to Gabby. "I don't know you like that. Matter of fact, let me call Gabby and make sure she gave you my address. I watch a lot of true crime tv and niggas be lying for real."

"Okay, cool," Bishop threw his hands up in surrender as I impatiently held the phone.

"I can't believe Gabby gave you my address," I talked shit.

"Gabby knows that I'm a trustworthy person," he replied right before Gabby's face appeared on the screen. "You were just telling this man all of my business, huh?"

"No, if I told Bishop all of your business, I would've told him how much you needed some dick in ya liiiiiife!" Gabby cackled and I was so embarrassed that I hung up on her ass. I swear that girl was no fucking good.

"I can help in that aspect too," Bishop professed, invading my space again. He was too close again and his presence ignited a desire inside of me. Afraid to move, speak, or even breathe, I stood there and allowed Bishop to embrace me in a hug that left me breathless. His voice and the scent of his cologne left me spellbound. Once Bishop released the grasp he had on me, he gently pecked my cheek and backed off of the porch. "You want me to help you carry these inside?"

I almost shouted hell no, I didn't trust myself with this man but I kept my shit together. "I got it, I'll grab them after I get my son packed up for the weekend."

"I'll see you later, my number is inside of your envelope."

I stepped back inside and closed the door, allowing myself to feel for a moment. A goofy ass grin spread across my face, "This is some fairytale shit happening in real life."

"Mom, language," Jibri chastised me.

"I'm sorry baby," I gulped, quickly getting my shit together before my parents got here.

The doorbell rang and I already knew it was too late. The flowers were still on the porch and my mother held a vase in her hands when I opened the door.

"What gentleman bought you these flowers?" My mom inquired with an enormous smile on her face. "I kept telling you not to close yourself off from the dating world. You're only twenty six, the right one will come along eventually."

"I barely know him like that yet," I commented.

"Well why does he know where you live if you don't know him like that?"

"Come on mom and dad, let me check Jibri's bag, he packed it himself, and y'all know he will throw his iPad in there and call it a day. No clothes, socks, or underwear," I quickly changed the subject before rushing into Jibri's bedroom. My mother's response didn't surprise me, my parents always encouraged me to get out of the house and date. They frequently caught an attitude because I would sit in the house when they picked Jibri up for the weekend. Truthfully, I just wasn't on that. I'd kissed enough frogs to last a lifetime and I didn't have high hopes for Bishop to be any different. However, I would go with the flow and enjoy the free food and drinks.

# CHAPTER NINETEEN

## Ava

*T*his entire house was amazing, a huge upgrade from our apartment, and the bathroom was immaculate. It was truly my oasis in the entire house. I had a walk in shower, garden bathtub with spa jets, and an oversized vanity mirror in the bathroom. Sharing it with Saint over the last week elevated the level of joy I received from the space. My hands were currently clasping the slippery walls for dear life as Saint fucked me from behind with my feet elevated off the shower floor. His hands gripped my hips as he slid me up and down on his dick, the fact that I had no leverage to hold myself up didn't matter as my body tensed up and the orgasm ripped through me.

Saint kept the grip on my right hip and pulled my hair back with his left hand. The pain was accompanied by intense pleasure and I was about to lose my battle with being silent. Jordyn was asleep on the bed and I was stifling my moans to keep from waking her but Saint always made that a difficult task.

"I love you, Ava," Saint whispered in my ear and licked behind the earlobe.

"Fuck, Saint! I love you too!" I couldn't hold that outburst in as another orgasm hit me. Saint pulled out of me and I dropped down to my knees, sucking him into my mouth. He always pulled out when he was about to nut and it was my mission to catch it. Although I was on birth control we went the extra mile to prevent pregnancy and I loved Saint even more for that.

After breaking the seal and elevating our relationship status, I couldn't get enough of Saint. This man was handcrafted by the universe for me. Mentally, physically, and emotionally, he kept my cup full. After sucking the nut out of Saint, I stood and washed off. He pecked my neck and I pushed him away because we had to leave the house in thirty minutes before we got in the shower so I'm sure we had about half the time left now. I exited the shower, leaving Saint to have his turn to rinse off.

Jordyn was still asleep on the bed, dressed in a purple romper with a pair of matching socks. We were preparing for Jordyn's first visit with Jermaine on this lovely Saturday and Saint just finished stuffing me with every inch of his dick so I knew my mind would be at ease for the trip. In an effort to keep the peace, Saint didn't know about Jermaine popping up at the hospital or his actions that led to him being arrested. It never came up, Saint never asked about Jermaine, and it honestly hadn't crossed my mind until this very moment.

Saint exited the bathroom with his towel around his waist. His perfectly toned body was better than a professional athlete and I was happy that I could openly gawk over it now. Out of sheer habit, I trailed my hands across his abs before entering the bathroom to brush my hair up into a ponytail. I noticed an old passion mark that I hadn't noticed before and pulled my makeup out to cover it up. After nearly a year of abstinence I almost forgot that my skin was easily bruised when sucked on. Plus, Saint's dick felt so good that I wasn't going to object to anything he did while in the moment.

Before brushing my hair, I took a moment to cover the bruises in an effort to avoid any confrontation. Ten minutes later I was dressed in a pair of jeans with a *Poetic Justice* graphic t-shirt and prepared to tackle the day. Sauntering into the living room, Saint held Jordyn in his arms and she reached for me. Shaking my head, I already knew what that meant, she was hungry. I hate to admit it, but Jordyn never tried to leave Saint for me unless she was hungry. When Saint was home, I was nothing more than the nutrients Jordyn needed to survive.

I took my baby and sat next to him on the sectional to nurse Jordyn. Once Jordyn was latched onto my breast, I shot a text to Jermaine's mother's phone. He still hadn't called me from his own phone, but I wasn't sweating it, I was trying to go with the flow of things for the sake of Jordyn. Saint leaned back on the couch watching highlights on Sports Center. I admired his handsome face and he noticed me staring at him. Saint smiled at me which in turn made me blush. He leaned over to kiss my lips then the top of Jordyn's head, I loved how much he adored me and Jordyn. Since the day I met Saint, he was protective of me and I couldn't have asked for a better person. He checked off every characteristic I wanted in a spouse. Gentle, protective, attentive, and caring. Jordyn finished nursing about ten minutes later and I quickly redressed before heading out.

When I prepared to tell Saint about meeting with Jermaine at his mother's house, I was apprehensive as hell. Thinking back on that day now I inadvertently smiled because my worries were unnecessary.

*It was storming outside, forcing Saint to cancel his Wednesday skills practice after work, and I was geeked because that meant I got to spend the evening with my man. Me and Jordyn often went to watch Saint at the basketball courts he practiced at but it was nothing like a movie night at home. Jordyn was knocked out cold, I pumped breast milk to last her through the night, and I sat on the couch with Saint curled up watching* **Coach Carter** *with a big ass glass of wine. The credits started rolling and Saint gently massaged my scalp as I used the control to find his movie pick of the evening. We decided to watch our favorite movies of all time, mine was* **Coach Carter** *while Saint's was* **Love And Basketball.** *As I located his choice, he started talking shit.*

*"I can't believe that's your favorite movie of all time. That shit ain't touching* **Love And Basketball,**" *he expressed.*

*"Liessss!" I argued. "I used to love that movie just like the next but now that we are grown, we gotta admit that it's the story of ultimate struggle love. The man was engaged to be married and here she come talking about some I'll play you for your heart," I mocked her. "Q wasn't shit from the day Monica met him being sexist talking about girls can't play ball. Then when she was balling out on his ass, he tried to take her head off."*

*"Aye man, chill out, they were kids," Saint laughed.*

*"What if it was Jordyn?" I posed.*

*"I'll stomp a lil nigga out," Saint blurted out and I burst out laughing.*

*"See, it ain't funny when it's Jordyn."*

*"You fuckin' right."*

*My phone chiming loud as hell interrupted our conversation and I quickly silenced it because Jordyn slept through a lot of things, but a phone ringing wasn't one of them. I silenced the phone and pressed play on the movie. When my eyes landed on the screen I saw that it was a text message from Ms. Mary, Jermaine's mother.*

**Ms. Mary: Wassup. I'mma be at my mom's crib on Sunday. Can you bring the baby through at 5?**

*"Why your body tense up like that?" Saint pried. I could tell from the verbiage that it wasn't Ms. Mary but indeed Jermaine.*

*"It's Jordyn's dad, he wants us to come to his mom's house on Sunday," I advised him.*

*"That's what's up, what time y'all need me to drop y'all off and pick you up?"*

*"Five."*

*It was the day after we made things official and Saint still supported me in this decision like every other one I made. I loved that he didn't attempt to inter-ject in the relationship between Jordyn and her father.*

*"I'm glad homie is stepping up to the plate because Jordyn needs that. I know how it feels growing up not knowing my father and I want to support the bond between Jordyn and her dad in any way that I can. That's **my** baby girl though and even if that nigga chooses to go back to doing dumb shit, I'll always be here for Jordyn," Saint leaned down and planted a kiss on my lips.*

*"Thank you, Saint," I smiled and pressed play on the movie before sending Jermaine a confirmation text.*

"Once I drop you guys off I'm going to gas up the truck for the week and then stop at this park to see if anybody is hooping out there," Saint informed me, easing into the driveway of the address I entered in the GPS.

"Yeah, that makes more sense than driving all the way back home then turning around to come pick us up again," I responded.

"You don't have to get out, I got the baby," I told Saint.

Truthfully, I didn't want him to exit the truck and risk Jermaine seeing him. Saint clearly wasn't pressed about Jermaine but I'm not too sure if I could say the same about him. Throwing me his questioning eyes, I swiftly moved past Saint because I knew questions swirled around his head. He was the type to carry Jordyn or anything heavy for me and I was the type to let him. Grabbing Jordyn out of the backseat at record speed, I waved at Saint on my trek towards the door.

Knocking once, Ms. Mary opened the door, peaking her nosey ass head out of the door before retreating to the interior of the home. She didn't offer a greeting, so I was instantly on edge, regretting my decision to come here. "Hello, Ms. Mary," I stated, placing Jordyn down on the couch. Her blinds were open so I could see Saint backing out of the driveway and I had to fight the urge to call him.

"Hey," she replied dryly before going into the kitchen to wash her hands. I leaned down to pull Jordyn from her car seat as she exited the kitchen. "Jermaine!" Ms. Mary shouted down the hallway, startling Jordyn.

"Let me see her chile," Ms. Mary extended her hands in my direction as she plopped down on the couch.

This lady had been miserable since I met her and I quickly learned that she condoned Jermaine's bullshit. Hence, why I never reached out to her. When he disappeared during my pregnancy I called her once to see if she heard from Jermaine, this old bitty told me, *"Stop calling my phone, Jermaine is a nigga, and he just doing what nigga's do."* Thinking about that shit made me want to roll my eyes.

Jermaine's light bright ass sauntered down the hallway looking hungover, pulling a shirt over his head while emitting a stank ass yawn that I smelled across the room. Jermaine desperately needed a haircut, shower, and to brush his funky ass mouth. I kept my mouth shut though and passed Ms. Mary the baby. Jermaine stood over us with his hands folded across his chest like he was waiting for something. I frowned my face up at him, not liking the feeling of him hovering over me after our last encounter in the hospital. My nerves were on the fritz and I was starting to think this was a terrible idea, especially because I hadn't told anyone about how Jermaine behaved in the hospital.

"Do you want to take a seat?" I offered, eyeing Jermaine.

His eyes were glossy and I realized he was high, off of what, I don't know. Peering over at Ms. Mary, I noticed that she was examining Jordyn's face and now I was completely uncomfortable. Standing to my feet, I was prepared to take my baby but she beat me to it.

"Hea, this ain't none of our kin. She don't look nothin' like our people," Ms. Mary groused, shocking the shit out of me. "Hea! Plus I told you I saw this gal in the hospital with some other dude when I was in the emergency room about my blood sugar back in February," She growled.

Jordyn screamed and I took my baby from Ms. Mary. I couldn't refute her claims about another dude being in the emergency room with me because Saint was there every step of the way. Now I had the answer to a question that plagued me, I always wondered how Jermaine knew I was in the hospital with Saint that day. "Well she looks just like me, so yeah, thanks for stating the obvious, she doesn't look like y'all."

"Jermaine, get this gal and that other nigga's baby up out of my house since she can't be respectful," Ms. Mary scolded him.

"Ava, let's just swab the baby and y'all can go," Jermaine piped in, pulling a Q-tip like item out of his pocket. It wasn't wrapped up in anything and had a piece of lint on the tip."

Shaking my head, I knew Jermaine was on something heavier than weed now. He stepped in my direction and I immediately placed Jordyn in her car seat and pulled my phone out and placed a call to Saint. "Move Jermaine! You are not putting that dirty shit in my baby's mouth. The child support office will be in touch to set up a DNA test."

"I'm already turning around Ava!" Saint barked into the phone.

"Okay," I teared up and dropped the phone into the car seat so I could carry Jordyn out of the house.

"Fuck you, Jermaine! If that's what you wanted, you could've just said that instead of asking me to bring the baby over like y'all wanted to meet Jordyn!" I grabbed my crying baby off the couch and rocked her gently on my way out of the door. "It's okay mama."

"Ava, the girl don't look like me, my mama ain't lyin'," Jermaine stated.

"Stop talking to me, Jermaine," I exploded on him.

"That's the same nigga that you was at the hospital with, ain't it?" He questioned as Saint was pulling into the driveway and I was relieved to see him. Saint always had a way of making things better and I was two seconds away from placing Ava on the ground and beating Jermaine's face in.

"Sure is, *he's* the one taking care of your daughter since you're too much of a deadbeat to do so," I barked and stomped off but Jermaine stepped in my path.

"Dead beat? How I'mma deadbeat when Ion even know if the lil girl is mine? You running off at the sound of a DNA test so shit definitely looking funny."

"You can have an official DNA test so we don't have to discuss anything further," I screamed at Jermaine, tears streaming down my face as Saint stepped out of the truck.

"Ava, chill with the baby in your hands," Saint's relaxed voice soothed me as he pulled me towards the truck.

"Nigga, that's my fuckin' daughter, mind yo business. You just footing the bill, pussy nigga. If me and Ava gone yell out this bitch, that's what the fuck we gone do. Get back in the truck, she'll be there in a minute. You'll be lucky if I don't take her back for the fuck of it. Ava still wants me, that's why she named the baby Jordyn to go along with Jermaine." He talked shit as Saint guided me to the truck.

"Cap, *I* named Jordyn," Saint shook his head and I immediately saw the dagger pierce Jermaine's heart.

"Saint, let's just go," I calmed myself to keep Saint relaxed. The same nigga who was just questioning the paternity of the baby was so stressed in his chest now that he saw Saint. It was actually comical but I knew how much Saint wanted to avoid trouble, he was on a mission to redeem himself after all of the bullshit he went through. I placed Jordyn's car seat in the car and was about to slide into the backseat with her because she was still crying.

"Bitch, you let another nigga name my daughter?" Jermaine raged, approaching the truck. Saint turned around and knocked Jermaine in the mouth. His shit was leaking and he stumbled back, holding his face. Opening the door, I rushed over to grab Saint and pull him back towards the car.

"I called the police as soon as y'all started that arguing and I got your license plate so you're going to jail!" Ms. Mary announced, rushing to Jermaine's aide. The nigga was dazed and confused and I regretted bringing my ass over here.

# CHAPTER TWENTY

## Bishop

*L*eaving Kalesha's house had me hype as a motha fucka. Gabby told me Kalesha was a hard ass, didn't take no bullshit from anybody, and rarely left the house if it wasn't concerning her son. I didn't know shit about autism until I met Kalesha that day at the hospital. Although Kalesha tried to fight it, the chemistry between us was *instant* at the party and she already admitted that she couldn't trust herself around me. My persistence was going to win Kalesha's heart, the only question was how long would it take?

I had my fun after being released from prison but Kalesha had all of my attention now. When I called Rambo and he told me that Gabby brought her son to his crib to play with the boys, I was on my way over there to have a discussion with her face to face. Gabby didn't put up a fight about giving up Kalesha's information, in fact, she sat with me in the living room and taught me about autism and how it affected Kalesha's son. I'd only seen Kalesha in action with her son on two brief occasions but it was clear that she loved her son. When his little ass came to the door to be nosey, I peeped that he had on a new pair of those same light up shoes.

Kalesha texted me an hour ago and told me to meet her at nine o'clock, providing a few hours to take care of some business. My prison stint was unexpected, it was some heat of the moment type shit and I had a lot of business to complete now that I was out. Prior to getting sent up the road, I was in the process of investing my money and watching it grow. Stepping out of the game and into a legitimate business used to be a daunting thought for me. After involuntarily being out of the game for two years, I felt it was best to stay out. That's why I passed them bricks off to Kelvin and Marco and bowed out of the game once I was out of prison.

Pulling up to Saint's gym I smirked at the sign that was finally hoisted above the building. *Saint's Fitness* was underway and I couldn't wait to showcase this building to my brother. I was pushing Saint towards skills training for this reason alone. Once we opened up, he could hold his classes here and run his own business. I wasn't shit like Saint, he wanted to work and become a productive member of society. I'd hustled to take care of us for long enough, I was looking forward to living off the money I made and finding passive sources of income to manage if I get bored. Hell, if push came to shove and I wanted to do something other than relax with Kalesha, I would have Saint give me a job at the front desk of this gym.

"What do you think?"

"Shit is straight," I nodded, admiring the brown LED backlit channel sign above the building. "What's the inside lookin' like?"

"I can show you better than I can tell you, let's take a tour," Charles, the manager of the construction company I hired, waved towards the door and I followed behind him. "The crew is doing touch up shit and working on lighting then the cleaning company can come out to do their thing and the final step is the inspection."

I admired the empty space and my vision was coming to life. The pool and sauna area looked amazing but I had to use my imagination for the rest of the amenities the gym would offer. Initially, I was going to purchase a franchise but Saint's name was one that deserved to be posted above the building. Saint might've lost his shot at following his dreams with college basketball and the NBA, but it's never too late to create new goals to achieve.

This project was two years in the making. When Saint was up for parole, I started the process of scouting the best area, then sitting down with an architect and coming up with the design. This wasn't an overnight project, I put in the work. Then Saint decided he wanted to finish his sentence instead of getting caught up in the grasps of probation and parole. I didn't agree with Saint's decision, I wanted him home, at the same time it wasn't my choice and I couldn't do shit about it. The land was paid for and contracts were signed before Saint informed me of his decision to finish his sentence. I wanted Saint to be a part of the process and since he wasn't, I decided to make it a surprise. Shortly afterwards, I got locked up but the project moved forward thanks to my bank account. I kept this a secret from everyone, even Natalie was in the dark when it came to this.

"This shit is looking real nice. I appreciate you and your crew for working on shit while I was away," I dapped him up, smiling big as hell. This was the first time that I could actually see my vision coming to life and it was exhilarating.

"Of course, your boy Rambo came up here a few times to make sure the job was coming along as we detailed."

"Had to make sure my money was put to use with all the delays and other things y'all had going on but I appreciate you for the tour," I commented as a text from Kalesha came through on my phone.

**813-823-5555: Hey, it's Kalesha. Can we do eight o'clock?**
**Me: Absolutely.**

"Alright Charles, call me when everything is 100% together so I can come down to view the final project," I advised him after sliding my phone back into my pocket.

"I got you, boss."

I hopped into my truck and headed in the direction of my condo downtown. The view was magnificent and the corner unit I secured allowed me to overlook the city from almost any location that wasn't in my bedroom. After retrieving a bottle of water from the refrigerator, I enjoyed the silence after spending most of my day at Rambo's crib. His jits were bad as hell.

~

Fifteen minutes before eight o'clock I pulled my car up to the valet and passed them my keys and a fifty dollar bill. I was feeling superb all day but I was elated now.

"Punctual, I like that," Kalesha's voice caught me from behind just as I was about to walk off.

I turned around and baby girl was fucking beautiful. Her hair was flat ironed bone straight, complimenting her oval shaped face. The messy bun I'd seen her rock during our past encounters were cute but this look on her was perfect. Kalesha wore a pair of wide leg denim jeans with a cream button up shirt that was tied into a crop top and a pair of nude heels. Her makeup was done, although she looked just as amazing natural, but it was clear that she came to take my heart home in her pocket.

"Of course, I had to finesse my way into this date, I'm about to soak up every minute of it," I explained, passing the valet attendant money for taking Kalesha's keys.

She caught up to me and I wanted to take her hand but instead, I followed her lead and headed for the restaurant. When we approached the door, I opened it and allowed her to walk in front of me. We were immediately seated in a booth and I scanned the menu because I hadn't been here in years. Kalesha's eyes were fixated on me when I looked up. She immediately looked away and that caused me to smile.

"What?" Kalesha questioned, placing her hands on the table.

"Why you trying to act shy? You already slapped the shit out of me, told me *fuck you,* and called me a stalker."

"I'm not being shy," she chuckled.

"Oh you ain't want to get caught staring a nigga down?" I licked my lips.

"Don't flatter yourself," she rolled her eyes. "I'm only here because you seemed so desperate."

"Never that," I shook my head and stood from my side of the booth and slid beside Kalesha. She wanted to play *uninterested* and I wasn't one for playing games. Goosebumps instantly rose on her skin and I had to stop myself from sinking my teeth into her flesh. Kalesha's breathing pattern was prominent with the tight ass top she was wearing, her chest heaving slowed, and I smirked at her.

138

"Good evening, what can I get you guys to drink?" The waitress returned to take our orders,

"I'll take a strawberry basil," Kalesha uttered, staring at the menu while my eyes were on her.

"I'll take whatever she ordered."

"I'll have it right out for you guys," she bubbled, walking away.

"Why did you come over here?" Kalesha finally looked over at me.

"I felt like maybe I needed to be closer to you since you were trying to play me. Maybe I gotta invade your space like I did earlier to get that same result. Plus, this the best seat in the house," I expressed, placing my arm on the back of the booth, making myself comfortable.

"What do you usually order from here?" I questioned, pulling my menu to our side of the table.

"Birria tacos."

"I'm following your lead tonight," I expressed as the waitress returned with our drinks.

We placed our orders and I requested another round of these girly ass drinks Kalesha was drinking. While drinking our first drink, we got over the prerequisite questions about children and current relationship status. Kalesha finished the first one just in time for the second round and I loved to see her loosen up.

"So Bishop, when you aren't stalking beautiful women and critiquing their parenting skills instead of minding your own business, what do you enjoy doing in your free time?"

"Come on man," I laughed at her smart ass mouth. "I'm going to apologize again. I should've been minding my business but I'm glad I didn't because if I did, we wouldn't be having this conversation right now and I would've never learned to mind my damn business. You never know what people are dealing with when it comes to their kids."

"I accept your apology for real this time," Kalesha smirked. "I just had to give you a hard time."

"Yeah, where was them lil mutts at when I pulled up to your house?"

"Those weren't my dogs," she chuckled. "My son is homeschooling from this point on because we had a few challenges with the school system. That resulted in me leaving my job and I had to get creative with my income to cover our bills. I do DoorDash, Shipt, UberEats, and Rover."

"What the fuck is Rover?" I pried, processing her story.

"It's an app for people who need help with their pets. I used to walk a bunch of women's small dogs from your neighborhood when they have to work late or if they are out of town. Multiple women needed my assistance that day."

"Damn, you really are out here hustling. I love that shit, it makes you even sexier," I leaned closer to Kalesha as she blushed. "Relax," I whispered in her ear and she fucking shivered.

"I'm relaxed," she straightened up in the booth and scooted in the opposite direction from me. I didn't want to come off as a pussy hound so I allowed her the space but if she was trying to give it up, I was definitely going to catch it. Those eyes Kalesha was giving me told me she wanted this dick though, I was an expert at reading women.

"Let me change the topic before yo ass be sitting in a puddle over there and that'll require me to lick ya clean." Kalesha bit her bottom lip and took a deep breath before gripping the oversized martini glass and sipping from it. "So what's up with yo baby daddy?"

"Why do you care about him?" Kalesha puzzled.

"I don't give a fuck about that nigga, but I'm trying to see if I'mma have beef for wifing you. That's all," I admitted.

Kalesha took a big ass sip from her glass then looked at me. "You won't have to worry about my ex-husband. He made it clear that he doesn't give a fuck about us when he abandoned us when Jibri was being evaluated for autism. It's been me and him ever since."

"Damn that's fucked up but he losing out, not the other way around," I hooked my finger underneath Kalesha's chin and pulled her closer.

The desire burning in her eyes told me what Kalesha needed at that moment. I leaned in and felt the craving burning deep inside of me. Gently gracing my lips on Kalesha's, I enjoyed the feel of her lip gloss covering mine. Kalesha placed her hand on my chest and it was over from there. Placing another soft kiss on her lips, I felt Kalesha slip her tongue into my mouth and I accepted it, enjoying the strawberry flavor from her drink. I sucked on her lips for a moment and these juicy motha fuckas tasted even better than they looked. A low moan escaped Kalesha and that shit shot my dick to the ceiling. I needed to feel her but I broke the kiss to keep it respectful.

"I told you I didn't trust myself around you," Kalesha breathed, taking a seductive sip from her glass.

"The feeling is mutual," I admitted aloud.

"How far away do you live from here?"

"About ten minutes," I confirmed.

"We should get our food to go," Kalesha challenged me, reaching underneath the table to caress my already hard dick.

"Aye miss!" I shouted to our waitress but she didn't hear me so I placed a hundred dollar bill onto the table and gripped her hand.

"Wait, I want the food first," Kalesha chuckled, backing up on me. Her soft ass crashing into my hard dick made shit worse. I wrapped my arm around Kalesha from behind and planted a kiss on her neck before leading her towards the exit.

"You can order the whole menu off UberEats on the ride to my house. It's your world," I whispered in Kalesha's ear.

We stood at the valet stand waiting for both of our cars to pull around. For a Friday night, they weren't too busy and it didn't take long. The entire time we waited Kalesha swayed to the beat she made up in her head underneath the beautifully lit area. I gave her my phone to order the food off UberEats. When our cars finally pulled around Kalesha slid into her Toyota Rav4 and I kissed her lips and instructed her to follow me before closing her door. The smile Kalesha displayed was contagious, shit made me want to ensure that it remained there. Ten minutes later I keyed my passcode into my door and we were granted entry.

"This is amazing," Kalesha gasped, staring out of the windows.

"Almost as amazing as you," I planted a kiss on her neck.

"You know what would make this view better?" Kalesha pried.

"What?" I played her game. The anticipation building between us was a new experience for me and I was enjoying the chase.

"If your pretty black dick was out," Kalesha bit down on her lip and approached me.

She stuck her hands down the front of my Valentino track shorts, feeling the dick without the fabric as a barrier. My shit shot straight up after all of the work I did to get it to go back down before maneu-vering through the hallways of my building. Shocking the shit out of me, Kalesha dropped down to her knees and I came through with the assist, pushing my shorts down to give her easy access.

Gripping the base of my dick with confidence, Kalesha spit on the head and used her hands to spread her saliva all seductive and shit. The sight of her pretty ass handling my dick like she knew what to do with it grew my anticipation exponentially. I closed my eyes for a moment to stifle my excitement and missed the introduction between Kalesha's lips and my dick because she swallowed me whole. Her head bobbed up and down with the perfect rhythm and she hadn't gagged once.

"I love it here," I admitted. "Suck this dick just like that, bae."

Kalesha smirked up at me, unbuttoning her shirt with both hands while sucking my dick simultaneously. Hands free head was some new shit for me and I made up in my mind that I was never giving Kalesha up. When her buttons were undone I reached down to pinch her nipples through her bra, happy that I was tall with long arms. I pulled the bra down as Kalesha placed her hands on my dick again and proceeded with the sloppy head. The sight of her perfect Hershey-kissed nipples combined with the slurping and sopping sounds filling the condo pushed me closer to the edge. Then Kalesha swiped the tip of her tongue across my balls in a windshield wiper motion while my dick was down her throat and I felt my toes curl. That shit felt marvelous and I couldn't warn Kalesha about the load of nut that spit down her throat.

"Fuuuuuuck!"

Was all I could get out. It took everything in me to hold onto the kitchen island and stop myself from moaning out like a bitch in here—that shit felt so fucking good. Kalesha wasn't about to show me up in here tonight. As she swallowed my nut with a smile on her face and her seductive eyes on me, I pulled my pants back up and lifted Kalesha off her feet.

"Take them fucking pants off," I commanded.

"You sound so demanding like I didn't just suck the soul out of you," she flirted, kicking off her heels. *Damn she did all of that with them heels on too.*

"Please," I replied.

"That's more like it," Kalesha smirked, following my request.

I slid one of my dining room chairs across the floor and over to the kitchen island that Kalesha stood in front of. Without uttering a word, I gripped Kalesha's slim waist and lifted her onto the kitchen island. I paused for a moment to admire her perfectly sculpted body, placing a kiss on the few stretch marks that motherhood blessed her with. Shaking my head as my kisses got lower, I tore her thong off and took my seat in the chair. If Kalesha wanted to keep that frilly shit she should've got rid of it.

Barrier removed, I dove face first into her pussy, lapping up her juices with each flick of my tongue. Her legs were already shaking and I hadn't even gotten into that pussy how I planned to.

"Fuck Bishop!" She emitted a dulcet moan that almost didn't match her harsh verbiage. That juxtaposition turned me on even more.

Peering up with my mouth latched onto her clit, I saw her head leaned back with her hands caressing her titties. Her essence satisfied my craving. I loved eating pussy but you had to be special to earn that privilege and Kalesha was already something special to me. Kalesha had that same infatuation with giving head, I could tell with the effort she put into satisfying me. That thought made me want to go harder. Kalesha thrust her pussy into my mouth and I dug two fingers inside of her, filling the area with a melodic sound.

"Shit, Bishop! I'm about to cum!" Kalesha squealed, holding my head in place. I allowed my tongue to rapidly swirl around her clit. Her hips thrust forward as her moans grew louder. Kalesha clearly needed this nut and I wasn't going to deprive her of it. Her body shot up, ***"Eat this pussy just like thaaaaaat!"*** I felt her walls tighten around my finger before pulsating rapidly. My tongue lapped up her juices until there was nothing left.

A knock at the door caught my attention as Kalesha attempted to catch her breath. It couldn't be anybody but the UberEats driver and that food could wait on the doorstep until we were done. I removed my fingers from her pussy and licked her juices off, not willing to waste a drop that seeped out of her. Leaning over, I gripped both of her titties and sucked them gently, my dick begging to enter her. Our lips connected and the passion between us was mind blowing. I kissed her long and hard like I had a point to prove her and the universe. Guiding myself onto the island with her, I heard my phone ringing but ignored it, pulling my dick out of my shorts. I was ready to risk it all but Kalesha broke the kiss and knocked some sense into us.

"Do you have a condom?" She panted.

"Yeah, let me grab one out of the room," I confirmed, easing off of her. My phone rang again and I pulled it out of my pocket to silence it on my way into the room. When I noticed it was Ava calling, I quickly answered, she had my number but never used it before so red flags were firing off in my mind.

"Wassup? Y'all straight?" I quizzed, praying she wanted some trivial shit, my dick had a new home to rest in.

"No, I ughhhh... Saint's in jail and I... I don't know what to do," Ava sobbed into the phone and I heard Jordyn crying with her ass in the background. This news made my dick soft and I ceased my stride and turned around to face Kalesha, playing with her pussy on the kitchen island. Taking a deep breath, I was going to fuck Saint up when I bonded him out. I met my freaky twin flame and he was ruining the fucking vibes.

"I'm going to get him out of jail. Just chill and relax, you got the baby crying and shit, Ava."

Kalesha's face frowned up and she laid flat on the island after hearing what I said. Our freaky ass nightcap was over and I was just as disappointed as her.

# CHAPTER TWENTY-ONE

## Saint

*A few hours earlier.*

"*Hello*," I answered my phone after pulling away from the unfamiliar home.

I didn't want Ava to feel any type of way about me not trusting this visit but a funny feeling hit me when we pulled up to the house. Following my intuition, I went to the corner store around the corner and backed into a parking spot to make it easy for me to pull out. I didn't even want to be stuck in the middle of the pumping gas if Ava called me to come pick her up early. Although I'd never stand in the way of Jermaine playing a role in Jordyn's life, I'd never let the nigga play with her either. I'd been here since before Jordyn was born and I loved that girl like she was mine biologically. Blood didn't mean shit to me.

My phone rang but it wasn't Ava, it was an unknown number. "Hello."

I quickly answered to be on the safe side and the unfamiliar voice left me worried. "Hello, is this Saint Carmichael?"

"Yes, this is Saint," I sat up in my seat, anticipating their response.

"Wassup man? This is Coach Chef. I saw flyers for your skills training classes at the rec center and had to reach out to you. I'm so proud of you man, Saint."

"Oh, what's up Coach Chef?" I greeted him, a huge smile spread across my face. "How have you been?"

"Wellllll, I'm living, aging and about to slip into retirement," he admitted.

"That's a beautiful milestone, nothing to frown about. Why do you sound like that? Don't most people celebrate leaving the workforce after putting that time in?"

"Oh, I'm happy about retirement but hate that I have to leave my boys. I have a great group of boys on my AAU team and I hate to let them down, but I promised my wife and she's been fussing about my retirement since I was coaching you," he chuckled.

"Trust me, I remember how she used to be, making them sly remarks," I confirmed.

"So you know what I mean," he got excited then his tone evened again. "The replacement coach I had decided to take another job, now I'm left scrambling for this upcoming season unless you're interested. Due to your background, I'd have to remain the coach as we work on expunging your record but you can still work as much as we can work around."

"Oh man, Coach Chef, I'm definitely interested."

"Well, let's set up a time to sit down and discuss the specifics," he suggested and my phone beeped in my ear. Pulling my phone away from my face I immediately knew something was up when I saw Ava's picture on the screen.

"Yeah, we can definitely set something up for next week. My girl is calling and I need to make sure she's straight. Can I hit you back at this number?"

"Of course, this is my cell number, call or text me anytime."

"Alright, I'll be in touch," I expressed before clicking over for Ava.

*"Move Jermaine! You are not putting that dirty shit in my baby's mouth. The child support office will be in touch to set up a DNA test." Ava's high pitched yelling had my adrenaline going.*

"I'm already turning around Ava!" I barked into the phone.

"Okay," Ava teared up and then the phone sounded muffled. I could make out the yelling voices but couldn't make out what was being said.

I pulled into the driveway and spotted Ava and a nigga that I could only assume was Jermaine standing on the porch. They continued arguing and I threw the truck in park and hopped out, prepared to intervene. I wanted to diffuse the situation before making shit worse. "Ava, chill with the baby in your arm," I requested, pulling her towards the truck. Next thing I know, the nigga was spitting bullshit and I knocked his shit loose.

It was like everything went in slow motion once that lady rushed out of the house yelling that she called the police. Nah, I didn't want to go back to prison but about Ava and Jordyn, I'd sit down for the rest of my life. Plus, this was an assault charge, nothing too crazy, and Bishop would get me out. We pulled off but didn't get far because the police pulled us over. With Ava and Jordyn crying in the truck I was arrested on the side of the road. I felt like a fucking failure being processed into jail for a second time. On the day I walked out of those prison gates, I promised myself that I would never step foot into another jail. Yet here I was. On the bright side, I was aware of my rights this time and exercised them to the fullest extent of the law.

After being questioned and sitting in a cell for a few hours I was released. The gate slid open and I spotted Bishop's truck in the parking lot. He drove over when I was in view and unlocked the doors when he was in front of me.

"Cheer up, young nigga, you gone beat the charges and move past this. You were protecting your family," Bishop stated as he drove off.

"It's not that," I huffed. "Coach Chef just hit me with an offer that would get me a step closer to my new dreams. He wants me to work with his AAU team while I work on getting my record expunged then take over the team. It will likely be a slight pay cut from my current job with Carl but..."

"Fuck that job with Carl. Take Coach Chef's offer and we can get a lawyer started on the process of expunging your record," Bishop sounded off, all excited and shit. "I can see it in your eyes, you *want* it, go get that shit, Saint. A lil money lost in salary won't hurt you."

"It's not just me now," I confessed. "Me and Ava are official now and I have an entire household to take care of."

"Don't get offended..."

"Then don't say shit offensive," I cut him off.

"Shut up, nigga," his eyes shot in my direction. "This is why I initially had concerns about you and Ava. Becoming a parent is a lot for any 26 year old but especially one who is fresh out of prison. You're here now though and let me just say there is more where that hunnid grand came from. When your lease is up, I already planned to buy you a house, that's just some temporary shit while I get a few things off the ground. If you're no longer working at Carl's, you'll have more time to do your skills training thing. Also, with the type of clientele you have, start charging them niggas more. They got it and they love you so they won't complain. Trust me. Plus, you travel to them, parents usually have to transport their kids to extracurricular activities. I remember lugging yo ass around to all the shit you were into when you were a jit, that's definitely worth the extra thirty. Shit is going to be straight," he lectured and I noticed he was going in the opposite direction of my house.

"Where you going?"

"I gotta show you something. Relax."

I got comfortable in the seat because I knew he wouldn't give a fuck about my protests and I was too tired to get out and walk home. After a twenty minute drive I was annoyed as fuck in the passenger seat. Sitting up to protest, my vision was snatched by the brown LED backlit channel sign that read, *Saint's Fitness.*

"Bishop, what the fuck?" I gawked over the sign above the stand-alone building.

"This yo shit and I wanted to surprise you with Ava and Jordyn in attendance but you needed to see this tonight. I'm gone always make sure you straight, you can quit all that shit you do to make money right now and still live comfortably. What the fuck you think I hustled for? As soon as the gym is complete, everything will be transferred over to your name."

I stepped out of Bishop's truck, speechless, as I allowed the tears to slide down my cheeks. After so much strife in my life this shit hit me in my chest. Bishop exited the truck and came to my side of the truck. "I would take you on a tour but they are still working on the light fixtures so it'll be dark in there and we don't need to fuck anything up. We already had a few setbacks and I'm ready to open this bitch up and turn a profit. You can hold your skills training courses here, have the AAU team practice here for free, and save on your gym membership fees. The options are limitless, you just gotta execute them."

Pulling me in for a hug, I allowed myself to feel my emotions. "I still can't formulate words of gratitude for you and everything you have done for me throughout my life. Not just this gym either. Taking care of me after mom died, never missing a visit, always looking out for me. We've been through some shit and you always made sure I was straight through it all."

"I'm your big brother, you don't have to say thank you," Bishop roughly grasped my head after breaking the hug. He hated when I got like this but he always looked out, there was never a time when he didn't come through.

"Thank you Bishop. I appreciate everything you have ever done for me and I pray that one day I'm able to return the favor."

"Shit, I got ten years on you so just don't put me in a nursing home. I wanna go out in my crib. Can you do that for me? Get me a nurse with some big ass titties to take care of me, oh and my wife Kalesha, can't forget her. She's around your age so make sure she's straight."

"When the fuck you get a wife?" I inquired, laughing at his silly ass while wiping my tears.

"Don't worry about that. You ruined our first date with your bull-shit," Bishop shook his head. "Now that you have a little motivation to keep your dreams alive, let's get you home to Ava. She was in that bitch crying with Jordyn last time I talked to her," he laughed. "Take care of your girls and continue to handle your business. I'll worry about getting your charges dropped."

# CHAPTER TWENTY-TWO

## Ava

*J*ordyn's ear-piercing wails had my head pounding. My emotions were all over the place and so were hers, we both wanted the same thing, *Saint*. When Jordyn got like this at night, she was overtired and wanted Saint. This wasn't the first time Jordyn pulled this stunt, when Bishop and Saint went out for drinks one night and she wanted him, she cried for an hour straight until finally falling asleep in my arms. All of the excitement from today probably made the situation worse because we got home three hours ago and Jordyn was still in an uproar. She was probably pissed off with me for subjecting her to that foolishness with Jermaine and Ms. Mary. Fuck the both of them. After what happened with Saint, Jermaine didn't have to worry about me or Jordyn. Jermaine and his mama wanted to play dumb when he knew Jordyn belonged to him. Having a paternity test done wasn't even the issue but he wasn't sticking that dirty Q-tip in my daughter's mouth and the fact that he didn't see an issue with his actions spoke volumes.

"It's okay Jordyn," I placed her on my chest and gently rubbed her back. "Saint will be home soon."

I was sick to my stomach because I knew how Saint felt about going back to jail and he was there again and I played a role in putting him there. Glancing at my phone, I checked to see if Bishop called or texted but he hadn't. My tears started again and me and Jordyn would have my shirt soaking wet in no time. The doorknob turned and Saint entered the house unscathed with Bishop on his heels.

"See I told you, they were both over here crying," Bishop nudged Saint like it was funny before going into the kitchen to wash his hands.

"Saint, baby. I'm so sorry," I hopped up and Jordyn sobs grew louder at the sight of Saint and Bishop.

"It's not your fault. Disrespect towards you or Jordyn will always get me out of character," Saint planted a kiss on my forehead then my lips. "Let me shower that jail off of me so I can get her."

Bishop returned and took Jordyn from my arms. "Ava, please calm down and stop crying, you're making baby girl fussier than she already is."

"No I'm not, she's crying because she wants Saint," I explained, using the back of my hands to dry my tears.

My slippers led the way into the kitchen and I poured myself a glass of wine while Bishop attempted to quell Jordyn's tears without any success. She usually loved when he came over to spend time with her but she wasn't feeling his ass either. He was bouncing her up and down on his lap. On the average day she would smile and chew her hands like it was the best ride in the world but Jordyn wasn't going for it tonight. I finished my glass of wine and took Jordyn from Bishop just before Saint returned in his boxers to take Jordyn from me. He was clearly rushing because he was barely dry. The moment Jordan was in his arms she laid on his chest and placed her knuckle in her mouth. Saint went back into the bedroom with Jordyn and I collapsed on the couch. Although Saint told me that it wasn't my fault, I couldn't help but to feel guilty.

"What's your baby daddy's name?" Bishop interrupted the silence I was enjoying.

"Jermaine Thomas."

"What does he do for a living?"

"I honestly don't know, he used to do construction. He disappeared when I was pregnant and then popped back up when his mammy told him she saw me at the hospital with Saint. Although Saint says it's not my fault, it kind of is. There were a few things I never told Saint," I confessed, staring at my white toes in my fuzzy slippers.

"Like what?" Saint questioned, holding a sleeping Jordyn in his arms.

I took a deep breath and told Saint and Bishop about Jermaine popping up at the hospital, the scene he caused and getting arrested, and then calling me from jail. Saint got up and carried Jordyn into the nursery without uttering a word once I was finished with the missing details.

"I know all that I need to know now. I'm out bruh." Bishop raised his left fist and Saint gently tapped his right fist against it. That was something they always did before departing and I swear it was an adorable sight. Bishop stepped over and gave me a side hug before walking to the door.

Saint locked up behind him and set the alarm before walking past me and down the hallway. I stood up and silently trailed behind him. He had work in the morning and I didn't want to make things worse tonight but the silent treatment was already killing me. Since the day I met Saint, our friendship was blissful and when we moved to a romantic relationship last week, things became down right enchanting. I was used to rubbing his back when he got off work, experiencing endless cuddles before bed or sharing some form of intimacy, but it looked like I wouldn't receive any of that this evening. Saint pulled the comforter back and slid into bed and I silently followed suit.

"Why wouldn't you tell me?" Saint questioned, pulling me into his chest from behind. I was so used to being discarded in life that Saint's display of love and affection at this moment caught me completely off guard.

"Jermaine showed up at the hospital the same day they sent me back for the PICC line and I was already in my head about that. Plus we barely knew each other back then, I didn't want to boggle you down with my issues when you had your own."

"Ava, we are locked in for life now. You should've told me what happened in the hospital when he reached out so I could've had all of the information before dropping y'all off. I'm never going to try to control your life, but I'm always going to do what I can to make things easier for you. I would've suggested meeting at a park or something. Don't ever go somewhere that you know you won't be respected because that's going to put me in a situation to come out of character."

"I'm sorry, I promise I'm going to work on my communication skills," I spun around and kissed Saint's lips before burying my head into his chest.

"Don't hold shit back from me, Ava, we are a team," Saint lifted my chin and I gazed into his dark brown eyes with a smile on my face.

"I won't," I confirmed.

Trailing my head underneath the cover until I was eye level with his dick. It was already hard, I felt it poking against my thigh when I turned around and pecked his lips. Grasping it firmly, I sucked it into my mouth then pulled it out to spit on the head. Saint pulled the covers off of me and I looked up at him before slurping him into my mouth. His hands gently massaged my scalp like they did every time I gave him head and I loved it. The sensation always made one of my eyes twitch and encouraged me to go harder.

"Fuck bae." His words were encouragement and I used both hands to perform the pepper grinder motion until I milked him of every last drop and sent him to sleep. We had a long ass day.

# CHAPTER TWENTY-THREE

## Kalesha

### *Three Months Later*

The echoing sounds of items colliding with the walls caught me off guard because Jibri was excited about going to spend the night with Gideon at Gabby's house this evening. Exiting my office, I rushed into his bedroom and he was tearing the place apart.

"Jibri, it's okay, let's calm down," I pleaded with him as he ran around the room throwing things. Slowly entering the room, Jibri waved his index finger in the air and dropped down to the floor.

"Mommy, TeeTee... I don't see TeeTee," he explained, waving his index finger around harder.

Jibri was currently calming down and I was so happy about that because this was his second meltdown today and that stopped me from making money during the lunch hour for UberEats and DoorDash, plus it stifled my ability to complete the party favors that were to be delivered tomorrow. Although we were off track today, Jibri showed tremendous progress in the behavior department on the average day. However, TeeTee and his favorite shoes were still definitely triggers for Jibri.

TeeTee was Jibri's stuffed dinosaur that my parents gave him when he was a newborn. From the moment he could carry an item he was fixated on that stuffed dinosaur. Jibri adored that thing, his first words weren't mom, dad, or anything similar, they were TeeTee and he was referring to his stuffed dinosaur.

"It's okay Jibri, TeeTee is in the dryer because she was dirty," I assured him, entering the room to close his blinds, they were barely open but Jibri was clearly tired after his emotional outburst.

Remaining calm, I sat in the middle of the floor about two scoots away from Jibri and allowed him to calm down in the quiet room. After a meltdown Jibri would take some time before he was prepared to talk and I allowed him to process everything free of judgment. Hell, I needed that thirty minute break as well after the day we had. After twenty minutes, Jibri stood up and I followed suit. "Let's pick up the toys and we will grab TeeTee out of the dryer," I coerced.

"Okay," Jibri nodded, rubbing his tired eyes. The room wasn't terrible and I took those few minutes to discuss the meltdown.

"Jibri, the next time you can't find something, you should look calmly and ask me if I know where it is instead of destroying the room looking for it."

"I'm sowwy," he commented and I wrapped him up in a hug. My baby was tired and this meltdown was probably less intense because of that. I planted a kiss on his forehead and smiled at him.

"I love you and we are going to remember the rules next time, right?"

"Yes mommy," he nodded his head rapidly, waving his index finger in the air.

"Can we get TeeTee so I can take a nap?"

"I'll grab TeeTee, you climb in the bed," I directed before exiting the room.

By the time I returned, Jibri's light snores filled the room. I sat his dinosaur on the bed next to him and pulled out my phone to order a shipment of stuffed animals before another meltdown occurred. Jibri's meltdowns were a lot less frequent than they used to be and that was largely due to prevention, learning his triggers and avoiding those situations. TeeTee was always a trigger for him and that was his last dinosaur on hand. He would lose his mind if it was lost or damaged. Jibri went through about four dinosaurs a year and I don't think he had any idea that I would change them out when they got a little worn.

After finalizing my purchase I sat on the couch and a FaceTime call from Gabby came through my phone. Jibri used up all of my little patience and I desperately needed to relax. Answering the FaceTime call from Gabby, I laid back on the couch and observed her surroundings and knew she was parked somewhere.

"Ohhhhhh, you a nasty bitch!" Gabby grumbled into the phone.

"What?" I puzzled, tilting my head to the side.

"You went out on a date with Bishop and didn't tell me. I know you are trying to hide the fact that you bussed that pussy open for him. It must've been on the first night too! How was it? I've seen that print on a few occasions when we take the boys to play ball and if I wasn't happily married—" Gabby drilled me while complimenting my man simultaneously. Shaking my head, I realized I mentally referred to Bishop as *my man* and sat up on the couch.

It was clear that Bishop was smitten when he left me in his apartment to go bail his brother out of jail. If it wasn't such a pleasant experience I would've taken my ass home but the view, skillful tongue, and the size of his dick had me ready for more. A part of me wanted to take my ass home and curl up in my own bed but the view in his apartment mixed with the ambiance made it inviting. I showered, threw on a pair of his basketball shorts, ate my food, and fell asleep until he woke me up with a trail of soft kisses down my neck.

Since that day I have spent all of my spare time with Bishop and it was quite the experience. I was a pleaser and Bishop clearly was too, sex between us was like a competition, seeing who could make the other cum harder or faster. We had a repeat of our date to Rocco Tacos last night and actually ate the food and enjoyed each other's company. I promise I planned to enjoy dinner and Bishop's company then take my ass home. Then Bishop's fine ass changed my entire thought process because when he wasn't talking shit, everything about him turned me on. As soon as I spotted him dressed in the black Valentino track shorts with the matching black shirt my mouth watered. I loved a black ass man dressed in black, it did something to me every time. Low key, I wondered if Gabby told his ass that too.

"Yes, we went on a date and my plans went from innocent to down-right filthy once I got that liquor in me. You know I was in my third year of abstinence and needed the relief, I'm not ashamed to admit it. As cocky as Bishop was, I had a feeling he would live up to the hype."

Closing my eyes, my mind drifted back to last night when my parents came over to have ice cream and a movie with Jibri before they left town for a week-long vacation in the Bahamas. I slid right out of here and went to Bishop's house for a quickie. That man must've had cocaine laced dick because I was addicted to it, sitting in the middle of this couch having withdrawals.

"Hoe, I know that look, you over there daydreaming about that dick," Gabby stuck her tongue out.

"And was," I cackled lowly, making sure that I didn't disturb Jibri. The break I was enjoying was much needed. "How did you know anyways?"

I eyed her and then the passenger seat of her car came open and Gideon's bobble head popped into the camera frame. "We will see you guys on Monday, Ms. Mitchell," Gabby waved towards the passenger door. She was clearly picking Gideon up from school and his handsome self was just two years older than Jibri. Their bond was super strong and Gideon was also amazingly smart. He understood Jibri's challenges, never made him uncomfortable, and was always a great friend. His heart was enormous and it was a testament of the amazing parenting that Gabby and Herc put into their son.

"Heyyyy, Ms. Kalesha, where is Jibri?" Gideon waved into the phone.

"He's taking a nap right now."

"Oh no, was it a rough day?" Gabby queried.

I nodded my head and Gideon's little voice was going again before I could utter another word. "I need to come homeschool with you and Jibri, Ms. Kalesha."

"What makes you say that?" I inquired.

"I'm tireddddddddd of waking up at seven o'clock in the morning already and school just started like two months ago. Jibri told me he gets to sleep in everyday."

"I wouldn't say Jibri gets to sleep in, but we do start our day a little later now since he is homeschooling. It allows him to feel well rested and definitely aids in the success of our homeschooling plan. He still has to work very hard though, it's not a walk in the park."

"I'm tryin' to be well-rested too," Gideon huffed.

"Boy, put on your seat belt, talking about wanting to homeschool so you can be well-rested. I can push your bedtime up to eight o'clock instead of nine if you're exhausted throughout the day at school," Gabby smirked, reaching over to rub his head.

"No ma, school is good. I'm rested," Gideon giggled.

"Good, Jibri is coming for a sleepover and I grabbed a new Lego set for us to work on tonight when dad gets off of work."

"Yesssss! Sleepover, Legos, and pizza, please?" Gideon begged in the cutest voice.

"If you clean up that room good," Gabby offered, popping an Airpod in her head. "Now back to you, Ms. Kalesha, what were we saying?"

"I wasn't saying shit, you were about to tell me how you knew something went down between me and Bishop."

"Oh, that nigga is an Instagram whore. Motha fucka usually only posts thirst traps but he posted some pretty ass floral arrangements, all featuring pink roses. The same flowers I told him were your favorite."

"Ms. Kalesha, who you dating? I need to approve of him," Gideon interjected, popping his head over into the camera screen again. His adult teeth were growing in so his big teeth invading the screen while minding my business was truly comical.

"Girl, clearly the Airpods aren't a deterrent, Gideon steady ear hustling. I'mma text you as soon as I get home because clearly you have plans tonight. I already saw the floral arrangement homeboy picked out and don't say his name unless you want Gideon's talking ass telling Jibri your business because... girl let me text you before he starts putting two and two together."

"Alright and as soon as Jibri wakes up, we will be on the way over."

"Oh yeah, I need you to keep the boys for a few hours in the morning. I have to show a house and Herc is flying out for work in the morning. I'll still be back at noon so you can get to the event venue to set up on time. Go take a nap with Jibri and call us when you get up because I can see you falling asleep now."

"I got you." I paused to yawn before ending the call. My eyes were low after this long ass day and the sleep was much needed.

~

After Gabby came to pick Jibri up, I realized that it was too late for me to finish my work for K's Creations, meet my daily gig work quota, and fulfill my date night plans with Bishop. Re-entering my office for the first time since Jibri's initial meltdown this morning, I took a deep breath observing all of the work I needed to complete and turned my apps on before drafting a text to Bishop.

**Me: Hey handsome. Jibri had a rough day today and I have too much work to finish and I need to do a few deliveries today so I'll need to reschedule our date night.**

I was well-rested so I decided to complete the most tedious job first, the hundred custom Minnie Mouse chip bags. Plopping down in my chair I got to work. Before I knew it I completed the chip bags and moved on to the custom water bottles. In the middle of that task my phone went off and I quickly accepted the UberEats order.

Gathering my purse and keys, I exited the house and went to Burger King to grab the order. I delivered the food to a house that wasn't too far from my home and I immediately rolled my eyes. This cheap motha fucka always answered the door in a Ralph Lauren robe but didn't tip. Grabbing the food off of the passenger seat, I knocked once and his old pasty ass opened the door dressed in that same black robe.

"I might have to start ordering food more often if the delivery women are as pretty as you," he grinned.

It took everything in me not to suck my teeth because he said that corny shit every time I delivered food here. If there was a way to avoid his ass I would because he was giving me creep vibes now. I raised the food in his direction and instead of taking the shit, he posed a question. "Do you drink or smoke? I got a bar full of liquor and a few pre-rolled blunts, we can make this a good Friday night."

"No, but please take the food. I have other orders to handle."

"Come in and spend the day with me, I'll pay you for your time and you won't have to run around in the sun sweating your weave out."

"This is my hair and no thanks," I declined and he finally grabbed his food.

Something in me felt off and my free hand instinctively slid into my purse to grab my pocket mace. Thank God I did because this crazy motha fucka pulled me across his threshold. Heart beating out of my chest, I raised the hot pink device and pressed down on the red button. The strong liquid shot in his face, causing him to release the grasp he had on me. Rushing back to my car, I could still see him squirming on the floor when I sped off. I felt like I couldn't breathe as I drove and I knew I needed to calm down. My phone rang and it was Bishop. Pressing the button on my LCD display, his background noise filled the car as I burst into a fit of tears. Jibri's rough day coupled with the man's attempt to do whatever he just did pushed me into a hysterical fit.

"Bae, where you at?"

I couldn't respond because the tears had me choked up.

"Kalesha, baby, calm down and breathe. I'mma count for you, slow deep breaths. **One. Two. Three. Exhale. One. Two. Three. Exhale.** Now tell me what the fuck going on because I'm already headed to the garage with my AR in hand. Wassup, Kalesha? Where ya at?"

"I'm on my way to you. I don't want to be alone right now," I expressed.

"Stay on the phone with me. What happened?"

"I don't want to talk about it."

Bishop exhaled deeply and I knew he was probably pacing or rubbing his waves like he always did when he was frustrated. I might not have known Bishop for years, but I knew my man enough to know that he would risk his freedom to execute that man for pulling that stunt. With that in mind, I decided that I wouldn't tell Bishop and I needed to get my emotions together for him to drop the situation. I'd report the man to UberEats and his account would be blocked.

When I pulled into Bishop's parking garage fifteen minutes later he was still asking what happened to me. I eased into his second reserved parking spot and shook my head. Bishop's crazy ass was really leaned up against his Range Rover with that big ass gun perched on his left side. The moment he realized it was me pulling into the spot he disconnected the call and stared me down until the car was idle. He had my door open before I could put it in park, examining my body.

"You're not doing that bullshit anymore. Fuck that shit, focus on your business instead of making some white motha fuckas rich."

"Huh?"

"We close as fuck, you hear me Kalesha." Like a big ass brat, I rolled my eyes and poked my bottom lip out as he continued lecturing me. "I tried to allow you time to come to terms with it. I was listening to Saint and trying to be patient but nah, fuck that. If you wanna feel like I'm making decisions for you then I am."

He pulled me into his chest and I melted in his embrace, accepting the affection as he rubbed my back and kissed the top of my head. When Bishop broke our embrace, he grabbed my purse out of the car and gripped his gun before leading us towards the elevator. The silence between us was deafening because Bishop was probably right. I needed to focus on my business and building my brand because dealing with random motha fuckas who barely tipped hidden behind an app wasn't the move. My mind was running a mile a minute when we entered Bishop's place but it immediately slowed down when I observed the scene before me.

"Bishop!" I squealed.

"Oh now that big ass mouth works," he talked shit behind me.

I spun around and smothered him with kisses. Bishop's home was set up for a romantic dinner for two. When we spoke this morning he told me to get dressed in something sexy and be ready at eight but this setup was definitely more than I expected. It was simple yet thoughtful and I was ready to suck the skin off of his dick, but I controlled myself because there was a chef in the kitchen preparing the dinner.

"This is so sweet," I gushed, wrapping my arms around his neck. "Thank you."

"Anything for you my Kalesha, and I mean that," he expressed before kissing me. I stuck my tongue into his mouth and he took that as an invitation to grope my ass and I moaned into his mouth.

"Come on, chill. Ms. Marley is here to cook, not watch a porno," Bishop broke the kiss, reminding me that we weren't alone. "Ms. Marley, this is my girl Kalesha."

We exchanged pleasantries and I took a deep breath, gawking over the table again. There were two vases with pink roses on the table, small unlit tea lights strategically placed around the table, and the dishes and silverware that Bishop never used were placed in the proper position on the table. Two wine glasses were in the middle of the table and whatever Miss Mama was cooking smelled good as fuck. I clearly wouldn't be dressing in anything sexy tonight but I had a few pairs of pajamas over here that would have to do.

"I'm going to take a shower and lay down. You can come get me when you're done in here."

Bishop pecked me again and I was on my way. I took enough showers over here that I had my own loofah, soap, and other toiletries. When I exited the bathroom Bishop was seated on the bed smoking a blunt and I sat in his lap, extending my hand for the substance. After the type of day I had there was no way I could refrain from smoking tonight. Bishop eyed me but he passed the blunt without incident. After one long pull I was coughing hard as fuck. This asshole was already high and took that moment to laugh at me for a few moments before finally rubbing my back and passing me his water bottle.

"You alright? This that gas, Ion smoke that bullshit," he laughed at me.

"I'm fine. It's just been a minute," I wiped the lone tear from my left eye and took another pull, much less aggressive this time.

When I was done Bishop took the blunt from me and I didn't object because I was already feeling fuzzy on the inside. "Just what the doctor ordered," I giggled, laying my head in Bishop's lap.

"So what the fuck happened to you, yo?"

"Bishop, please don't blow my high. I told you I don't want to talk about it," I sassed.

"Fuck it then, just quit doing that bullshit."

"Bishop, it's expensive as fuck out here."

"And you got a nigga with money. I got you, just keep doing yo party shit and let me handle the rest," he exhaled then leaned down to kiss me.

I gripped the sides of his face and devoured his tongue real nasty like now that I was high. His dick hardened underneath my hand, challenging me to a duel, and I wasn't one to back down. Bishop took another pull from the blunt after breaking the kiss and I sat up, placing my lips over his to accept the weed smoke. After exhaling the smoke, I pulled my towel open and straddled Bishop's lap. His nasty ass knew what time it was because he leaned over and pulled a condom out of the nightstand and passed it to me. Good and high, he laid down on the bed with his hands behind his head and a seductive grin on his face.

Using my teeth, I tore the gold wrapper open and slid the condom over his dick. I was right behind the piece of latex, easing my pussy onto him. In this position gravity wasn't on my side but I made it work, moving slow to ensure that I could adjust to his size. With my eyes closed, I licked my bottom lip, enjoying the feeling of his dick in my guts and my hands on his chiseled chest. Bishop gripped my hips and flipped us over before I could protest, he slipped deep inside of me and kissed my lips so gently.

"Nah, you so fuckin' hard headed, I gotta show you why I run shit between us," he growled and I quickly nodded my head.

When his dick was buried inside of me Bishop could get me to do anything. My mouth made love to Bishop's as I thrust my hips forward to meet his strokes. Bishop broke our kiss and his body melted into mine as he lifted my left leg and deepened his strokes and quickened the pace. It hurt so good and my nails scratched his back while I accidentally bit his shoulder to keep from screaming out while a guest was on the opposite side of the door.

Bishop loved when I got rough and that only boosted his ego.

Fucking me harder, he released the grip he had on my leg and that hand found its way to my clit. I bit down on his shoulder as the orgasm rippled through my entire body, leaving me limp and shaking. Bishop thrust into me one final time and I felt his back stiffen before he pulled out. Relaxing in the bed, I was high, satisfied and my troubles from the day were left behind.

# CHAPTER TWENTY-FOUR

## Saint

*P*eeking out of the blinds, I saw Gigi's Benz ease into our driveway. "There go yo ride," I whispered, holding Jordyn in my arms.

Grabbing Jordyn's bag off of the couch, I exited the door before Gigi could knock. Ava was still asleep and I wanted to keep it that way until everything was in place. Today was Ava's twenty-fourth birthday and I wanted to make it special for her.

"And y'all got goddy's baby dressed in one of the outfits I bought her," Gigi bubbled with her arms outstretched for Jordyn.

Truthfully, I didn't dress her in one of the outfits they purchased on purpose. Gigi and Rambo went crazy buying Jordyn clothes and shoes that her five month old self didn't need. Jordyn only went to two places, Rambo and Gigi's house from time to time and the basketball court on occasions when I was working.

"What time should I bring her back tomorrow?" Gigi questioned, playing with Jordyn's finger.

"Whenever y'all get up and are moving around is cool. We are not leaving the house."

"Y'all not leaving the house? It's Ava's birthday, Saint," Gigi frowned her face up at me. "I know y'all are homebodies, and I love

165

y'all for that. But today is the day to step out and turn the fuck up, live a little. Y'all both act like a pair of elderly married folk."

"Man, chill on us," I laughed. Gigi and Rambo were always talking shit about the way we did things but that's just how we preferred to move.

"No, take Ava out, do something different, spice it up. There are so many costume parties going on tonight in Ybor. Take her down there. Oh and does Jordyn already have a costume for Halloween on Tuesday night?"

"Yep, she will be a basketball."

"Don't worry goddy, I'll get you a backup costume," Gigi waved me off before approaching her car.

I trailed behind her and rounded the car to place Jordyn's baby bag in the backseat while she buckled her into the carseat. By the time we were done Ms. Marley pulled into the driveway and my stomach was already rumbling. Ava requested a quiet night between the two of us and that's what I planned to give her.

"See y'all later. We won't be back until goddy runs out of breast-milk. Please do a few things that you know my wild ass would do," Gigi yelled out of the window before pausing for a moment and sticking a pink gift bag out of the window. "I almost forgot, give this to Ava. It's from me and my boys."

I grabbed the bag and she rolled up her window before reversing out of the driveway. Shaking my head, I approached Ms. Marley's car to help her with the food. She prepared everything at Bishop's crib to contain the surprise. "Hey Saint," she greeted me, opening her car door.

"Wassup Ms. Marley, thanks for coming through on short notice," I embraced her with a hug. Ms. Marley has been in my life since I was in the ninth grade. Her son was on the basketball team and she always prepared our meals before the games. Now she runs a personal chef business and I ran across her Instagram account, now here we were.

"No, thank you for booking me. Your brother asked me to prepare double so he could do something cute for his girl too. He paid the bill for both of y'all and then some," she celebrated, opening her rear driver's door. She used a heat resistant pot holder to pull two aluminum pans out of the backseat and passed them to me.

"I hope you guys enjoy it. Don't forget to post a shoutout on your social media account for ten percent off the next time you book," she chirped.

"I got you. Thank you so much Ms. Marley. Enjoy the rest of your day."

"You're welcome, baby," She waved, climbing into her Hyundai and I headed back inside to set up. The warm pans were placed into the oven that was already set to the warm setting. A text from my phone came in and it was a picture message from Bishop.

**Bishop: What other cute shit you got planned for Ava so I can do it for Kalesha too. Put a nigga on, I'm trying to have her in love too.**

The picture that accompanied the message was of his dining room setup all romantic and shit. This was nothing new for Bishop, even when I was younger, he'd buy Natalie the same shit I was buying for one of my girls and if he felt it was too juvenile, he would tell me to ask my girl what type of shit they mamas liked. I replied with three crying laughing emojis and slid my phone back into my pocket.

As soon as Ava went to sleep I decorated the dining room area. Everything was Ava's favorite color, turquoise, and I added in gold for aesthetics. A huge happy birthday banner surrounded by balloons leaned up against the back wall, the table had a turquoise table cloth with a gold runner down the middle, and I even had plates and silverware to match the theme. I went into the cabinet and pulled out Ava's favorite bottle of wine and placed it in the stainless steel wine cooler I bought her for her birthday.

I heard movement in the bedroom and quickly rushed to light the candles on my way out of the dining room. It was nearing six o'clock and the sun was setting and that helped the candles flickering set the mood. Ava was in the bathroom brushing her teeth when I made it to the room and I eased up behind her, planting a kiss on her neck. "Is Jordyn still asleep?" Ava questioned after rinsing her mouth out and placing her toothbrush in the sterilizer.

"Nah, Gigi came to pick her up for the night."

"What?" She spun around, placing her hands on the counter behind her.

"Yep, you said you wanted a quiet night in for your birthday and I'm giving you that," I explained.

"Y'all are too sweet," she bubbled, exiting the bathroom. "What's this?" She questioned, pointing at the pink gift bag on the bed.

"Oh that's from Gigi, Rambo, and the boys. She dropped it off when she came to pick up Jordyn."

Ava plopped down on the bed and pulled the gift bag into her lap. Her eyes narrowed when she looked inside. I was in such a rush to get shit together before Ava woke up that I didn't bother looking into the bag. "Oh my God, this is too much!" Ava gasped after flipping the black velvet box open. I stepped over to observe the contents and it was a gold necklace that read, *MOM* and the O in the word was an oval shaped diamond. Picking up her phone, Ava called Gigi.

"You like it huh?" Gigi and Jordyn's faces appeared on the Face-Time call.

"It's too much, Gigi," Ava teared up.

"It's not enough. You are doing an amazing job as a mother, don't ever let anyone tell you otherwise."

"Thank you."

"Now stop crying, get cute, and go hang out. I told Saint to take you to one of the costume parties going on in Ybor. Y'all too young to not be in these skreets this weekend," Gigi talked shit. "Ain't that right Jordyn?" Jordyn's big brown eyes stared back at us before she emitted a gummy smile. "See, that's my goddy! When you get older I'mma make sure you love outside like I used to. Y'all go step and I'll see y'all tomorrow. I told Saint that Jordyn isn't coming home until we run out of breast milk."

"I love y'all. We will see you tomorrow," Ava blew a kiss before ending the call. "I got a wine chiller, a necklace, and a night to relax and sip some wine for my birthday. Let's order food and watch movies. I'm not trying to be in Ybor this weekend out of all weekends, everything is super packed and motha fuckas are super drunk. No thanks."

"Alright, what do you want to eat?" I trailed Ava down the hallway and she stopped once the view of the dining room caught her attention.

"Saint!" She squealed, spinning around to jump into my arms. Her arms went around my neck and her legs wrapped around my back. I cupped her ass and got lost in her dark brown eyes.

"Happy birthday, Ava."

"Thank you so much, Saint," she teared up and took a deep breath. "You're the gift that keeps on giving."

"I guess since we are already pulling out all of the surprises, I need to give you the final one now before we eat," I advised Ava, pulling her towards the front door.

"What else could you possibly have up your sleeve?" Ava inquired once we were outside.

I walked over to my truck and opened the door. Ava followed me, watching me closely as I took a seat in the driver's seat with my legs hanging out of the truck.

"Well, I love you and want the best for you and baby girl no matter what. Since I'll be a gym owner soon, I won't always be available to drive you and Jordyn will get older and eventually do her own stuff and we will need two cars."

"Saint, I told you not to! I was saving up!" Ava glared at me but I laughed and pressed the button inside of my truck to open the garage.

The garage door slid up and Ava screamed. "Saaaaaaaaaaaaaint!!!"

Bishop had money put up for me when I got out of prison and the house we were living in was paid up for the year while I paid the utilities. That allowed me to stack my bread and purchase the white Tesla Model S for Ava. Her small frame rushed over to the car and she laid on the hood, hugging the car. I snapped a few pictures of her acting a fool before tossing her the keys.

"Lock the door, I wanna go for a ride," Ava chirped and I complied. It was her birthday and I was going to follow her lead. That smile just did something to me everytime, I was going to give Ava the world.

# CHAPTER TWENTY-FIVE

## Kalesha

*I* woke up the next morning in Bishop's bed, this man had me falling for him and the shit was alarming. Since divorcing Jibri's father I remained single. Of course I'd been on a date here and there, gave a few men my number and texted for a week or two, and even went on a couple first dates but we never made it past that stage. Most men couldn't handle a woman with a special needs child.

My schedule varied and could shift with a moment's notice due to my son's therapies, tutoring, and homeschooling. Bishop never gave me any flack about that, he always told me that he was on my time and followed through on his word. If I was available and could get away from the house, Bishop made himself available. There was even an instance when my parents and Gabby weren't answering their phones and Jibri was having a very rough day, worse than yesterday. When he went to sleep for the evening I called Bishop to vent and he came over with a bottle of wine and my favorite snacks. Although I wasn't prepared for him to come inside for fear of Jibri seeing him, Bishop didn't mind. He sat on the porch and listened to me vent while I sipped the wine. If he bought me something, which he clearly had a problem with doing quite often, he made sure he grabbed something for Jibri too. There was a tower of Lego city sets that Jibri thought came from me in our storage closet. I don't know who was spoiling Jibri more, my parents or Bishop, and he hadn't even met him yet. The thought of how Bishop would spoil Jibri once they met was over-whelming.

If that wasn't enough to have me head over heels, a few weeks ago Bishop made himself available to help me with one of my parties that was booked on short notice. My dad usually helped with the heavy lifting but my parents were out of town that weekend, they loved trav-eling now that they were retired. Not only did Bishop come through on the heavy lifting but I forgot a few imperative items at home. Bishop came to the party location, grabbed my keys, and drove all the way across town to my place to grab the missing bucket then back to the venue. It was truly refreshing to have a man by my side that supported and encouraged me the way Bishop did. I heard everything that he said about focusing on my business loud and clear and he was right. Putting more time into that would be most beneficial for my future. Plus if anything happened with Bishop, it would be nothing to go back to my gig jobs, that was the beauty of them. After my divorce, I would never be without a backup plan.

The sun creeping through blinds helped me realize what I could do to show Bishop how much I appreciated him, add a few feminine touches to this fucking condo. First item on the agenda was black out curtains for every room in the house. Sitting up in the bed, reality slapped me in the face. I had a huge event this afternoon and I never went home to finish the prep work. Jolting out of the bed, I found the shorts I wore to sleep and pulled them up my legs. My body jolted back into bed and Bishop wrapped me up in a bear hug.

"Stop Bishop, I gotta go. I can't believe you got me drunk and high when you knew I needed to go home," I giggled.

"Man that was you, got high and wanted to fuck all night. You know I'mma always let you have your way," he replied, licking on my earlobe. Pulling myself out of Bishop's grasp, I knew not to let him get started. He always woke up with his dick touching the ceiling.

"I'll pay Gabby a little something, just lay with me and relax. You need it."

"I can't. Not only do I have to go home and prepare for this party but I also agreed to babysit Gabby's son if she kept Jibri last night. I told you my parents are out of town again and Jibri was having a really rough day yesterday so I couldn't work while he occupied himself," I explained, pulling a shirt over my head.

"Man fuck that party," Bishop laid back in the bed, dick still standing tall.

"Now it's fuck that party when yesterday that's what I needed to focus on. I guess you have to use your hands because I have to go. I'm already behind schedule and I can't have people spraying my name on the internet, saying I took their money and didn't come through. I don't even know how I'm going to get all of this shit together on time," I whined on the brink of tears again as Bishop lit a blunt.

"Chill out," Bishop pleaded, approaching my side of the bed with the blunt dangling from his lips. "Do you need to hit this so you can relax?" He questioned.

"Hell no, that's just going to make me wanna lay down somewhere."

"Alright, well let me finish the blunt then I'm going to come help you with whatever you need done."

"Are you sure?" I puzzled.

"Positive," he kissed my lips then went into the bathroom to get himself together.

I almost wanted to tell him no because Jibri would eventually come home. Bishop was great, I enjoyed his company but I never brought any man around my son. Plus I was apprehensive of how Jibri would respond to me dating, it was just the two of us for the last few years. Since I really needed the help I decided to let the day play out. My reputation was on the line and I was just getting started. I walked into the bathroom and brushed my teeth at the sink next to Bishop. When we were done, I looked over at Bishop and let my guards down.

"When you get over here, remember Jibri doesn't like loud noises, there will likely be an interrogation because he's very inquisitive and you are not my boyfriend today, you are just my friend. I'm not ready to introduce that idea to Jibri until we are a sure thing," I explained.

Bishop placed the cap over his toothbrush and placed it in the holder. "We *are* a sure thing. You're going to be my wife one day but I'm following your lead today."

I smiled, believing everything that Bishop said. He was completely different from anything I'd ever encountered, even my ex-husband didn't make me feel this bubbly on the inside. An hour later we were in my office with Mary J Blige's voice filling the room. I don't know if Bishop was super high or super supportive but he was getting the job done quick as hell too. We knocked out the custom water bottles together and moved on to the treat bags.

Gabby's name flashed across the screen and there was a knock on the door moments later. "That's Gabby and the boys."

"Alright," Bishop stood from his chair where he was diligently working and followed me out of the office.

I nervously opened the door and Gabby waved at me from the car before speeding off. "Mom, whose car is that?" Jibri questioned from the porch.

"That looks like Bishop's car," Gideon noted.

"That car does belong to my friend Bishop," I confirmed, leading them inside.

"What is your fwiend Bishop doing here?"

I decided to let Jibri's mispronunciations slide since there was an unfamiliar face in his territory. "Come inside so I can make the introductions. Bishop is here to help me with the party items I have to put together today. I was a little behind schedule and needed some assistance."

Jibri entered the home, his eyes scanning for the stranger and he paused when he spotted him on the couch. "Jibri, this is my friend Bishop. Bishop, this is my son, Jibri."

"Nice to meet you, Jibri," Bishop greeted him with his hand extended in Jibri's direction.

Jibri looked at Bishop's hand and I realized I forgot to instruct him to wave. "Nice to meet you but on average, we come in contact with 840,000 gewms every thirty minutes. That's too many gewms for people to shake hands." He explained then came closer to me.

"Respect." Bishop nodded his head and Gideon walked over and dapped him up. "Wassup Gideon, where have you been? I haven't seen you at Gigi and Rambo's house in a while."

"I know man, I was just asking Ms. Kalesha to homeschool me too because I be tired waking up for school early in the morning. I don't have the energy to come over there after school."

"Jit, you should have all of the energy. Take yo butt to bed instead of being up all night."

"Bishop, I have to wake up at seven o'clock in the morning to get to school on time. What time do you wake up in the morning?"

"'Bout nine or ten," Bishop replied.

"Exactly!"

I chuckled at their interaction and I noticed Jibri relax slightly when he realized that Gideon had a rapport with Bishop. "Jibri, Bishop knows my cousins that are octuplets. Don't you?" Gideon looked between the two.

"Gideon, you know they are not octuplets," Bishop laughed.

"Then what awe they? A woman would have to be huge to carry that many babies in hew tummy at one time," Jibri pointed out.

"Gideon's aunt had two sets of triplets and a set of twins back to back. We just call them octuplets because they all look alike and are close in age," Bishop detailed.

"Do you have a pictuwe? Gideon always says this but doesn't have a pictuwe. This is interesting."

"I don't but I'll make sure I take one the next time I see them."

"Thanks," Jibri replied, then looked at me. "Mom, would you like mowe kids?"

"No thank you, you are enough for me," I leaned down and planted a kiss on Jibri's cheek and he wiped it off. "Mom, please, gewms. I have to go wash my hands now."

Jibri rushed to the bathroom and I was happy with the brief conversation they shared during that interaction.

"Gideon, you and Jibri can go in the room and play while me and Bishop finish up some work in my office," I directed.

"Yes ma'am," he rushed off to wash his hands too.

Bishop quickly snuck and kissed my lips once we were in the office and I emitted a light giggle. "See, chill, he will open up to a nigga."

"I'd have to agree but it's not because of you, it's because Gideon likes you. Jibri loves Gideon and his approval was what got him to relax."

"Ion care what it was, I'm just happy it happened."

We got back to work and Bishop packed the items into the storage tote and I got started on the Minnie Mouse centerpieces. We had two hours before I needed to leave and the pressure I felt in my chest this morning was officially gone because I knew the remaining tasks would be completed in time.

When we were finished Gideon and Jibri brought a Lego set they were working on in the room out and sat at the table while I cooked grouper nuggets and fries for lunch.

"Bishop, we can't get this piece to stick on. Can you help us?" Gideon requested.

"Yeah, I got y'all..." Bishop reached for the toy and Jibri's voice stopped him.

"Hands, please wash your hands before touching it," he requested.

"I got you, Jibri," Bishop redirected his path to the kitchen sink where he washed and dried his hands. Walking back over to the table, Jibri eyed Bishop as he effortlessly placed the Lego piece.

"See, I told you he could do it!" Gideon announced.

"Gideon, too loud," Jibri monotoned, waving his index finger in the air.

"My bad, Jibri. Come on, we can finish it in the room."

"Thank you, Bishop," Jibri spoke to him.

"You're welcome. Y'all wanna finish up out here just in case you need any additional assistance?" Bishop offered.

"Yeah, let's just stay here and Bishop can help us because my mom will be here soon. It's almost noon."

"Fine," Jibri answered, eyeing Bishop as he approached a seat at the table.

I was grinning because this was going a lot smoother than I expected. Jibri allowing Bishop to help with his Lego set was not something I could have expected. However, Gideon's approval and Bishop's openness definitely helped the process along. I finished cooking and we all ate lunch together. As promised, Gabby returned before noon and grabbed the boys, giving me and Bishop enough time to transport the items across town and set up for the party.

# CHAPTER TWENTY-SIX

## Bishop

"*N*igga, I thought we was retired but you got me outside of a nigga's house, sitting in a bucket, scoping the scene like we about to commit a murder," Rambo complained in the passenger seat of the 99 Camry. I didn't plan to kill the nigga but if things went wrong, I ain't want his ass in my new truck.

"I can handle this shit solo if you got something else to do. I thought you enjoyed stepping out of retirement when I got out a few months ago," I shrugged, my eyes glued to the front door of the house in Belmont Heights.

"Who is this nigga anyways?"

"Ava's baby daddy," I explained as the front door swung open and the nigga stepped out looking dusty as hell.

"Nah, ain't no way pretty ass Ava used to deal with that nigga," Rambo refuted.

"Somehow she did. When Ava told me the story of what happened the day Saint got locked up, she said he looked like he might've been high off something stronger than weed so maybe he didn't always look like that," I explained, placing the car in drive. "When I looked up his charges from his arrest at the hospital it said he was also charged with possession of heroin."

Jermaine slid into his mother's car and backed out of the driveway. I followed him to a trap house where he entered and walked out shortly afterwards. "Fucking junky," I mumbled, following him back to his mama's house.

"I'mma snatch him when he gets out of his mama's car," I explained.

Rambo nodded his head as I trailed the nigga two cars back. The moment he stepped out of his mother's whip I was out the car with my ski mask covering my face, gun pressed to the back of his head. "Make a noise and I'll blow yo head off yo shoulders," I snarled, snatching his tall lanky ass back to the bucket.

Rambo was in the front seat and I hopped in the backseat with Jermaine. Speeding off, our tires squealing filled the distance.

"Look, I don't have the money I owe y'all but I'mma get it," Jermaine began explaining, holding his hands up in the air, and I slapped him across the face, knocking him out cold.

When he came to, I already ran his pockets, retrieving heroin and a cell phone. This nigga was clearly a junky and owed his cousins money for stealing their stash out of their trap house. He clearly didn't plan to do right by Jordyn because I read over messages of him telling his mom to deny being in touch with him when the child support papers came and her decrepit ass was down with the bullshit. Saying, "fuck Jordyn and Ava, let that other nigga take care of them," and all types of shit.

If I wasn't starting a new chapter in life and it wouldn't look horrible for this nigga to come up missing while Saint has pending charges for knocking his ass out, there wouldn't have been a discussion. I'd toss this bitch nigga over a bridge attached to a few cinder blocks and rid the universe of another fuck nigga. The universe was on his side today though.

"Cuz, don't do this man. I told you I would pay you back, I'm looking for a job, I just need some time," Jermaine pleaded.

"Shut the fuck up!" I kicked him in the stomach and he curled up, coughing, holding his stomach and shit. "We don't want no money from yo broke ass but if you want to continue breathing, you are going to do two things. First, you're not going to cooperate in regard to the pending assault charges against Saint and second is sign over your rights to Jordyn if Ava ever asks you to."

"What?" His face crumpled up in confusion.

"You heard what the fuck I said nigga. You're a fucking junky, Jordyn deserves a father that won't disappoint her. Hell, from the way yo cousins talking in their texts, you might not even make it to do either of those things." I tossed his phone at his head. "If you don't want me to pull up, shoot you and your mama, do what the fuck I said."

"Okay man, I wasn't trying to be nobody's daddy anyways... I'll sign those papers tonight if you got 'em, just don't hurt my mama."

"I guess it's true what them hoes say, dead beat niggas love their mamas," Rambo scoffed.

"Clearly," I tossed his drugs into the water and his eyes grew to the size of saucers. Despair and anguish washed over his face in a matter of seconds watching his drug of choice crash into the water.

"Come on man, I said I'mma do everything you said. Why you had to throw that?" He teared up on the rocks above the water, before curling back up in the fetal position.

"Saint got me out here beefing with a junky," I laughed as we rushed back to the car.

"I'm just glad we didn't have to get our hands dirty. Now we can slide through the block where everybody is. It's Kelvin's birthday, you sliding through?" Rambo asked once we were back in the whip.

"Yeah, we can return the car, grab our whips, and slide through. I'm not going to be out there for long though, I gotta see Kalesha before I go to bed."

"Kalesha is a good look for you," Rambo nodded.

"I know, she is the firecracker I didn't know I needed."

For the duration of the ride my mind went back to lunch with Kalesha, Jibri, and Gideon the other day. Jibri was smart as shit and Gideon didn't make shit any better with his mouth. They were entertaining as fuck. Before I knew it, we were back at the spot. I hopped out the whip and into my Range, trailing Rambo to the block party. We parked in somebody's yard and walked down the block so we weren't blocked in by any cars.

Seemed like Kelvin had the whole city out and I was proud of my youngin'. I hit him with that work, he got that shit off, now jit had major motion. He was the man to see in these streets. They were shooting dice, playing cards, while a couple of hoes twerked on the cars in front of the house where everybody was congregating. I was about to throw some money down for the dice game when I heard someone calling my name.

"Bishop, can I holla at you for a minute?"

I turned around, knowing my ears were playing tricks on me. Ain't no way the nigga Vince was approaching me. "Unless you wanna eat through a straw again, I suggest you get the fuck away from me," I replied, looking him in the eyes.

"Ion want no problems, Bishop, but word is you the reason I can't cop shit in these streets."

"Give me the money you spent up and I'll lift the ban. If not, your name dead out here. You knew what you was getting into when you started fucking with that bitch. It ain't about her, you can have the hoe, but where the fuck is my money? The only reason you are still breathing is because she called, begging me to spare yo life, and in spite of the bullshit she pulled, we have been through too much for me to make her a widow and single mother. She was down for a nigga, helped me raise my brother and I also don't put it past her to snitch if I killed you then I gotta kill her and orphan ya kids, ya know."

"Nigga..." Vince opened his mouth to respond and I pulled my gun out, placing it beneath his chin before he realized what was transpiring.

"You wanna walk off or you want me to blow yo brains out and make me go back on the promise I made to Natalie?"

Vince huffed and stalked off. I watched his ass until a car with its headlights beaming pulled up beside him. It was Natalie, she hopped out the car spazzing on his ass, and he got in after being scolded like the lil boy he was.

"I'm out, rather be home with my woman than out in this bullshit," I told Rambo before turning to leave.

"Did I hear you say that's Natalie's husband?" Rambo asked, walking behind me.

"Yeah, why?"

"You know that's *Kalesha's* ex-husband and baby daddy, right?"

"That bitch ass nigga?" I stopped to question him and he nodded in confirmation.

"Even more of a reason to cut that bitch ass nigga off, I'm the one helping Kalesha make sure his jit straight," I shook my head and continued towards my truck.

# CHAPTER TWENTY-SEVEN

## Ava

*A*lone tear rolled down my cheek and Saint quickly kissed it away. I was trying to hold my emotions together but that was easier said than done. It was Jordyn's first Halloween, her first holiday outing, and I was an emotional wreck.

"Okay, I'm good," I used a Kleenex to wipe away the next tear to preserve my full face of makeup. In true basketball lovers' fashion, I was Lola and Saint was Bugs from the Tune Squad and Jordyn's chunky self was our Spalding basketball.

Saint reclaimed his seat on the couch with Ava in his lap. "You sure?" Saint questioned, placing Ava and her basketball costume onto the couch and coming over to me again.

"No, now you're out of position," I squealed. "I'm fine, now get back on the couch so I can set the timer on my camera."

He pecked my lips then followed my command. The camera was positioned on my ring light and this was a normal routine for us now. The ring light facilitated many photoshoots but none were as special as this one. For the first time since my father died, I felt like I had a family again. My family consisted of more than just Saint, it included Gabby, Gigi, Kalesha, Rambo, Bishop, and all of the children between them. I don't know why this photoshoot was hitting so hard but it was.

Thoughts of my father resurfaced and I wished that he was here to meet Jordyn, he would've loved her. I was a female replica of my father and Jordyn was my twin so we would've been a perfect set of triplets. Saint stood from the couch again and I allowed him to wrap me up in a hug this time.

"I'm sorry for ruining the vibes, I am just so thankful for where I am in life. Eight months ago I was at my lowest. I was homeless with no one to turn to and now I have so much love and support," I expressed and Saint rubbed my back.

"That won't ever change either," Saint declared, placing his forehead against mine. I closed my eyes, reveling in his closeness for a moment before they popped open. Leaning up to plant a kiss on Saint's lips, he cupped my lips and tried to deepen the kiss but I pushed him off.

"No, I already have to go fix my mascara real quick," I explained, rushing to the bathroom.

I returned a few minutes later with my emotions together and we snapped a few family pictures to document Jordyn's first Halloween. We packed into my new Tesla and drove to Kalesha's neighborhood in Seminole Heights. When we made it to the roundabout the police had the entrance blocked off so I kept going.

"Oh yeah, Bishop said they parked at the store around the corner. The police are letting the kids walk in the street so we are going to meet everybody around the corner store, go trick or treating for a little, then end the night at Kalesha's house. Bishop is ordering pizza."

"Okay."

I turned at the next corner and followed Saint's directions to the store where everyone was parked. We got out of the car and I smiled at all of the cute costumes. Everyone was there except for Bishop, Kalesha, and Jibri but that wasn't unexpected. They already informed us that Jibri stayed in and handed out candy on Halloween to avoid being overstimulated.

"I'm not going to lie, when Saint told me that Jordyn was going to be a basketball, I was annoyed and I bought her a cheerleader costume to match mine but seeing y'all in person is everythiiiiiiing!" Gigi celebrated.

As described, Gigi was dressed in a pink and white cheerleading costume, Rambo was dressed like a football coach, and all eight of their boys were dressed as football players. I laughed at the sentiments because everyone always joked that they had a football team. Then Gabby and Gideon rounded the car and I took a moment to admire their Woody and Andy costumes.

"Is Herc coming?" Gigi asked her sister.

"Yeah, he got off work late and is pulling in right now," Gabby replied before embracing her in a hug then making her way around to everyone else with Gideon right behind her.

Gabby's husband pulled into the parking lot and she offered a quick introduction once he exited the car dressed as Buzz Lightyear. This was my first time meeting Herc, and he was a handsome reserved gentleman, definitely not what I expected for Gabby and her rambunctious nature, but they were clearly in love from the way he greeted her with a passionate kiss.

After snapping a few pictures, we got Jordyn into her stroller and were on our way to trick or treat. Growing up, Halloween was my favorite holiday and my father took me trick or treating every year until I grew out of it and wanted to chill with my friends on that day. My dad wouldn't wear a costume but he bought me whatever costume and accessories I wanted. It was refreshing to create similar memories with my daughter now.

The men and boys took charge, knocking on doors and collecting candy for about an hour before we changed courses and headed back towards Kalesha's house. When we arrived, Gabby knocked on the door and Kalesha and Jibri opened the door, happy to see us. Jibri and Bishop were dressed in slacks and a button up shirt and Kalesha wore a black dress. Initially, I was confused about their costumes but then my eyes landed on their custom name tags. They all had name tags with *architect* in front of their names.

"Okayyyyyyy, Architect Jibri looks amazing!" Gabby bubbled.

"Gabby, too loud," Jibri mumbled, waving his index finger in the air.

He shoved the candy bowl into Kalesha's hand and backed away from the door. Gideon stepped up and made his presence known. "You know she is always loud," Gideon eyed his mother. "But look, the octu-plets are here."

I didn't know what that was about but Gideon definitely helped ease Jibri's mind and his eyes lit up.

"This is Tyrone, Jamel, Jamarion, Tyrese, Gabriel, Gage, Ralph, and Pierre," Gideon listed off their names who I could never remember. Half of them looked like Gigi and the other half resembled Rambo. My mind couldn't remember all of them but they knew my heart. Jibri stood in shock at their appearance. "Y'all, this is my best friend Jibri. He doesn't like handshakes or hugs but y'all can wave hi, you gotta wash your hands before you go in his room and if you take any toys off his shelves, you put them back."

"Go ahead and regulate shit. Ion wanna have to fuck y'all up for disturbing the peace over here," Bishop eyed the octuplets.

"Bishop, language," Jibri monotone, waving his index finger in the air.

I quickly picked up on his signal when people were doing things he didn't like.

"My bad, Jibri. Y'all come in before gnats and mosquitoes start coming in," Bishop requested and everyone entered the home.

"Since the octuplets would take up more space than my woom will allow, can we go to the backyawd?" Jibri requested.

"Yeah, that's fine. The pizza should be here in a minute," Kalesha explained.

Jordyn was knocked out in Saint's arms and Kalesha offered her a spot in her bed so she could rest comfortably. They returned a few minutes later without the baby and everybody lined up in the kitchen, taking shots while getting to know each other better. The love filling this room almost made me want to get emotional again but Saint must've sensed it and hugged me from behind. Rambo went around pouring more shots, we took them, and Kalesha's giggling caught my attention. She was leaned up on Bishop in the kitchen, furthest in the back and out of sight of the kids. They were hiding but the pure happi-ness that resided between them was hard to contain.

"Y'all scary asses better stop that kissing, here comes Jibri," Rambo announced a little too late.

Bishop glared at Rambo because the nigga said it so loud. He stepped away from Kalesha and grabbed a bottle of water from the refrigerator. "Damn nigga, use your inside voice."

"Bishop, language," Jibri appeared at the kitchen entrance. I was feeling my shot because I wasn't a real liquor drinker, I stuck to my wine and that was that, but I wondered if Jibri heard what Rambo just blurted out. My internal thoughts were answered moments later because Jibri's mouth kept going as he washed his hands in the sink.

"I know that Bishop kisses my mom and they awe dating. I saw them thwough my window outside at night twice when they thought I was asleep," Jibri blurted out and Kalesha spat her water out.

"What, Jibri?"

"I like Bishop, he is good at Legos, and he washes his hands," he replied.

I couldn't stifle my giggle because Kalesha made it clear that keeping the relationship a secret was her priority. Clearly, she didn't do a good job of that. Kalesha was speechless and I was observing the interaction because I don't even know what I would say if I was in her position.

"I am dating Bishop and he will continue to be around like he always is, but nothing will change outside of that."

"Okay," Jibri eyed her, clearly not giving a damn before grabbing a bottle of water from the refrigerator and returning to play with the boys.

"See you was doing all of that sneaking and he doesn't give a damn," Rambo broke the silence in the room.

"Boy shut up," Gigi nudged him before there was a knock on the door.

"That's the pizza," Bishop explained.

"I'll go get the kids so they can start washing their hands," Kalesha offered.

Jordyn's loud sobs came from Kalesha's bedroom and Saint eased up off me to grab the crying baby. My first Halloween as a parent was definitely one that I'd never forget.

# CHAPTER TWENTY-EIGHT

## Bishop

### Six Months Later

*K*alesha was asleep on the couch after a long day of delivering treats and various items while Jibri sat on the floor working on his *Architecture for Kids* workbook I bought him. The book was formatted to introduce children, from eight to twelve years old, to drawing and architecture. Jibri just turned seven when I purchased it for his birthday and he loved it, comprehending everything in the book, and I already knew he was going to be the architect of the family when he grew up. After Rambo's big mouth let it slip to Jibri that we were more than friends, his response shocked the shit out of everyone, especially me. Based on Kalesha's level of apprehension I was prepared for Jibri to have an entire meltdown or try to beat my ass. It was that day that I realized Kalesha's level of protectiveness hindered her ability to see Jibri's growth.

I was in the kitchen watching a video Ava sent me on TikTok to help me cook seafood paella. Although me and Kalesha still lived separately, we were always at each other's house. My guest bedroom was turned into a room for Jibri to have his own space when they were at my place. We spent more time at my place than theirs because Jibri loved the view of the city at my spot. I told Kalesha that they should just move in on multiple occasions but she wasn't ready and I was struggling to respect that. It was hard to be away from them and they didn't live a skip away. If some shit popped off I would have to fight traffic to get to them. With the population rising daily the travel time to various places that used to take ten or fifteen minutes was increasing as well.

"What are you doing?" Kalesha's sleepy voice sounded off behind me.

"Cooking dinner for my family," I explained, turning to the side to face her as I moved the rice and seafood around in the pan. When I spotted Kalesha's phone in her hand I knew she was recording me so I offered a smile.

"Whew," she shuddered, coming closer. "My man, my man, my man, my man would never leave me for dead hoes. He's in the kitchen now and will be helping me with a few deliveries this afternoon so I can be outside with my girls tonight."

Kalesha moved the camera from me to the food on the stove then she leaned up to kiss me. Our phones both chimed simultaneously and Kalesha opened whatever the message was and grinned before turning the phone to face me. Ava sent a video of Jordyn to the group chat, she was taking her first steps. Baby girl was eleven months old and trying to walk on us already. I snatched the pan off the eye and sat it in the middle of the stove before initiating a Facetime call to everyone in the groupchat. Rambo joined the call first and Gigi was right up under him. Before I could greet them, Saint answered the call and we saw Jordyn take two steps then fall. Gabby hopped on the phone moments later and caught the tail end of the event.

Once the ladies noticed Gabby and Herc were on the phone, they started singing happy birthday to her. Gabby was smiling bright as hell. "Thank you guys!" She bubbled. "Make sure y'all are at my house by ten o'clock. I want to pregame before we go out tonight."

"Oh, that's why you were all up under me today. You trying to go be a thot with your sister tonight while I'm home with these jits. Naw, make sure you call up the nanny," Rambo mugged Gigi.

"Boy, shut the fuck up. The nanny will be here because Ava and

Saint are dropping off Jordyn too. We know you can't handle them and the baby."

"Where the fuck you going tonight, Saint?" Rambo quizzed.

"None of your business," Ava chimed in.

"Right, we will see you at ten sis, that's all that matters!"

"Period," Kalesha added.

"Man, get out the camera with all that shit, we are here for Jordyn. Hey mama, you over there taking steps without Unc there to see?" I yelled into the phone.

"Bishop, volume," Jibri waved his index finger in the air while Gabby, Herc, Gigi, and Rambo cheered baby girl on too.

"My bad, Jibri, I'm a little excited. Jordyn took her first steps today," I explained, lowering my tone. Jibri no longer said *too loud*, jit moved on to a one word response when people were noisy around him, *volume*.

"Let me see," Jibri monotoned, entering the kitchen. I flipped the phone around and he waited patiently as Ava stood Jordyn up again. She took three steps, this time clapping her hands before falling. "Thw... thwr... three steps and a hand clap, impressive," he nodded his head and I was over the moon hearing Jibri correct his own pronunciation. "Very good, Bishop, my mom is up so you can ask her about my report from my speech therapist now."

"What about it?" Kalesha questioned.

"What did his monthly report from his speech therapist say?"

"He is progressing and they are working on new goals," Kalesha detailed.

"Bet, I promised Jibri that he could go to Walmart to buy that new Lego spider man lair set if he earned a positive report for the month."

"Bishop," Kalesha rolled her eyes and folded her arms across her chest. I knew she was about to talk shit but I didn't give a damn, my word was my bond. "Come talk to me in the room."

"Go get your shoes while I talk to your mom in the room," I advised Jibri.

"Bishop, I told you that you can't keep doing that type of stuff. I don't want Jibri getting used to that."

I wrapped my arms around Kalesha and pulled her close. "No Kalesha, I told you that I'm here, I'm not going no fuckin' where. *You* are the one who needs to remember what I told you. Relax and accept that Jibri will be rewarded for his strides for the rest of his life. Once he finishes that architect book, I'm buying him some big dumb shit."

Kalesha shook her head and Gabby's voice sounded off in the room. "Go 'head Bishop, get my friend together."

I almost forgot they were on the phone.

"I'm glad y'all are still on the phone. Ava and Saint, meet us at the Target on Dale Mabry so I can buy Jordyn some stuff too. Baby girl needs one of those push walkers now to help build her strength and I bought her a few things when we took Jibri shopping for new shoes last week."

"Alright, we will see y'all there," Saint announced before disconnecting the call and everyone offered their salutations as well.

Since I could remember I was always a giver and spoiling the people in my life was a part of my personality. I pecked Kalesha on the lips again and slapped her on the ass. "Go grab your shoes or are you staying here?"

She smirked and slipped her feet into her Tory Burch slides before exiting the room. We piled into my truck and drove to the Target as directed. Before we started shopping, Jibri and Kalesha always had to stop at the cafe for Icees and then we were on our way to the toy aisle. Jibri was lost gazing at the sea of toys as Kalesha and I stood back and observed. Choosing a new Lego set was probably the most difficult decision Jibri had to make in life and he didn't take it lightly.

"I have to use the bathroom," Kalesha announced, sitting her big ass Icee cup in the cupholder.

Jibri had his index finger in the air, waving it from side to side as he scanned the various Lego sets in front of him while having an internal debate verbally. That wasn't out of the norm for Jibri, he always discussed the pros and cons aloud before deciding on a new item and I gave him space to do his thing. Stepping out of the aisle, I scanned the end cap where the board games were held. Grabbing a Jenga set, I placed it in the cart and looked over at Jibri. Just that fast I noticed what appeared to be a pair of teenage boys on the aisle. One of them was standing behind Jibri mocking his hand gestures while the other one covered his mouth with laughter. My blood instantly boiled after seeing that shit, all common sense went out of the window. Releasing the grip on the cart, I marched over in their direction. When they saw me approaching their eyes got big and instantly straightened up.

"Do that shit again motha fucka so I can drop both of y'all on your shit and send y'all to get yo bitch ass daddies so I can fuck them up to."

"Bishop, volume and language," Jibri eyed me with embarrassment while waving his index finger in the air.

If it wasn't for Jibri, I would've fucked them up but I didn't want to scare him. Taking a deep breath like we preached to Jibri when he had a meltdown, I gathered myself to speak without elevating my voice. "Get on before I..." my voice trailed off because I got mad again and they scrambled off of the aisle.

His innocence was the only thing that saved their asses and spared me a new mugshot today. I fully understood why Kalesha was so protective of Jibri, the world wasn't kind and I was going to always act a fool behind them. When Kalesha told me about the incidents that he went through during his year in kindergarten, that shit broke my heart. It was alright now, Jibri was warming up to Gigi and Rambo's boys and he always had his best friend Gideon.

"I'm going to get this one," Jibri announced.

"Just slip both of them in the cart, I saw you were having a hard time choosing so we will get both."

"Okay," he shrugged, placing the Lego sets in the cart.

"Look who I found at the entrance," Kalesha bubbled, pushing Jordyn onto the aisle in her stroller with Ava and Saint right behind her. "What's wrong?" Kalesha questioned, parking Jordyn's stroller next to me. I guess I wasn't doing a good job of hiding the residual anger from those boys I almost dropped on their heads.

"Nothing," I lied as another little boy and his mom walked onto the aisle.

Still annoyed, I didn't pay them any attention until the little boy walked over and greeted Jibri. "Hello, can I grab one of those behind you?" he waved. Jibri stepped closer to us, allowing the other boy space to access the Lego sets he was interested in.

"Oh my God, he looks like Saint," Ava pointed out.

The boy's mother glanced in our direction and scanned our faces, looking for the person Ava was referring to. Her eyes traveled from Ava to Kalesha then stopped on me. When our eyes connected, horror instantly spread across her face. She grabbed her son's arm and yanked him off the aisle. "Why are we leaving? I was supposed to get a new Lego set," the boy whined.

"Interesting," Jibri noted, watching their interaction. "Are we ready to check out?"

"Yeah, let's go," I ordered, ready to get the fuck up out of here but nobody moved. Today couldn't get any worse.

# SAINT

Ava glared at me like I was the reason for the woman damn near drag-
ging her son off of the aisle but I didn't even know her. The nasty look
Kalesha gave Bishop let me know that she caught the same thing I did.
The strange woman's demeanor was relaxed as she looked at us until
her eyes connected with Bishop. I never met that woman a day in my
life but it was evident that Bishop had.

"Do you know her?" Ava inquired, giving me the side eye.

"Nah and don't even let your mind go where it's going," I replied.

"How do you know her, Bishop?" Kalesha quizzed.

"Come on, let's check out," Bishop suggested, ignoring her
question.

"But Bishop, we were also supposed to buy a walker for Jordyn,"
Jibri reminded him and all eyes went to my brother.

I didn't know what was going on but my crew was about to head
out. Bishop pushed the cart down the aisle and we all trailed behind
him until we ran into another stranger wearing my face at the end of
the aisle. My interests were piqued now. This motha fucka looked like
we could be identical twins, from the same womb and nut sac. Bishop's
jaw tightened and I noticed how tight his grasp was on the cart. He
stood there seething and tight lipped, knowing he possessed the

answers to everyone's questions. I was about to ask him what the fuck but the stranger spoke up before me.

"I don't want to cause any commotion but my name is Lamont and I debated on whether or not I should follow my wife's request and leave the store without approaching y'all, but I couldn't miss this opportunity. I feel like the universe put us both in this store at the same time for a reason. Saint, we are brothers. Bishop told me to stay away from you if I valued my life but I don't feel like that's his place anymore, you're old enough to make your own decisions now," he spoke, eyes locked on me before turning to address Bishop. "The statute of limitations is up so I ain't scared of none of that shit you were talking about before. If you gone do something then do it but Saint deserves to know the truth."

I instantly felt like I was transported to the twilight zone after hearing what Lamont had to say. Me and my brother had different fathers, mom was married to Bishop's dad before he was killed in an accident on the oil rig he was working on. Then my mom met my dad at a Mary J. Blige concert and they engaged in a long distance relationship until she found out that he was married and didn't live in Miami like he told her but instead lived in Lakeland. When my mom confronted him about all of his lies and dropped the pregnancy announcement on him, he told her to get an abortion.

After that conversation he cut my mom off, changed his phone number, and disappeared. I never met my father a day in my life. The story my mom and Bishop told me was all I had. On many occasions I wondered where he was, how he was, what type of man he was, and how he could abandon an innocent child, but I never would've thought Bishop would hinder a relationship between my paternal family if they were reaching out.

"Why would you do that? If you found out I had another brother, why didn't you tell me?" I questioned Bishop, my anger rising with each word.

"Kalesha and Ava, y'all take the kids and go checkout," Bishop requested. Ava looked at me and I nodded my head while Kalesha took the cart from Bishop and grabbed a hold of Jibri's hand. Ava pushed

Jordyn off the aisle with Kalesha and Jibri right behind her. Once they turned the corner Bishop refocused his attention on me.

"Saint, I didn't say shit because yo bitch ass daddy only reached out to make amends because he was dying. Then this pussy..." Bishop's voice trailed off and I knew he was fighting off the rage building within. "*He* is *the reason* you went to prison! I didn't connect the dots until yo pops popped up at my house looking for you. Pussy nigga didn't even realize that you were still in prison because they threw the book at you! He figured they would go easy on you since you were a basketball prospect and just turned eighteen. As soon as I saw Lamont, I knew. This nigga was the wannabe gangsta that did that bullshit that got you locked up and his daddy helped him set you up. So I lost my mind, pissed with myself for not thinking about the other son your father had with his wife. I was in the process of killing these niggas with my bare hands when the police spun the block. Somebody called the police on me because I lost my mind on them in broad daylight in front of a bunch of witnesses. That's what got me locked up. Lamont and y'all bitch ass daddy!"

Lamont didn't refute Bishop's claims, I didn't know the nigga but I spent eight years around criminals so I *knew* a guilty motha fucka when I saw one. My temper got the best of me and I punched Lamont in his jaw and he fell back into the toys behind him. I didn't let up, eight years of pent up aggression was released on one of the two people who deserved it. Thoughts of my promising future that was snatched away from me, the time I lost with my brother, being surrounded by men I didn't know, hardening myself to ensure that I could survive in prison. Bishop wrapped his arms around me and pulled me off Lamont. I felt my mind tuning back into reality, I blacked out thinking about every-thing I'd been through. When I came to, I snapped at Bishop next.

"Get the fuck off of me, nigga! I'm grown as fuck Bishop, you don't get to keep this type of shit from me." I pushed Bishop's ass into a shelf and looked down at Lamont's bloodied face before storming off the aisle in search of Ava and Jordyn, it was time for me to go.

"Come on Ava," I gripped her hand once I spotted them in the self-checkout line. She pushed Jordyn's stroller in the direction I led them to and we were gone.

"What happened?" Ava pried once we were outside and she noticed the blood on my shirt.

"I'll tell you when we get home. Just get the baby into her car seat so I can put her stroller in the trunk," I requested, using my key fob to unlock the doors and pop the trunk.

Bishop's name flashed across my phone and I ignored that shit. I needed time to myself to think and I didn't want to speak to anybody that wasn't Ava and Jordyn until further notice.

# CHAPTER TWENTY-NINE

## Kalesha

*B*ishop was tight jawed from the moment he found me and Jibri at the self-checkout lanes. I was thankful that we already paid for our items because Bishop damn near ran us out of there. We stopped at his condo to drop off the items we purchased from Target, grab the treats and party favors that I needed to deliver today, and packed Jibri, Gabby, Herc, and Gideon some of the seafood paella Bishop cooked. He was silent throughout the entire ordeal and I couldn't wait to drop Jibri off and figure out what was going on with him. The way Saint stormed out of Target, I knew it was something serious. About forty minutes later I exited Gabby's house and climbed into Bishop's truck.

"Ion wanna talk about it right now," Bishop stated as soon as the door closed behind me.

"Well can you at least tell me if you're okay?" I pried.

"I'm straight, I just want to get this event over with so I can go home and smoke," he grumbled.

I relaxed in my seat and enjoyed the ride, thankful that the two events we were about to hit only required minimal work, a few balloon centerpieces and treat tables, and then we were on our way. Halfway through the second party setup I texted Gabby and asked if Jibri could stay there since he was spending the night anyways and she agreed. When the party was over, Bishop was happy to drive straight home.

As Bishop previously mentioned, he rolled up a blunt and sat on the balcony smoking it while I went to take a shower. The questions continued to swirl around in my head until I exited the shower and was hit with a shocking text. It was my ex-husband. After no contact after all of these years the dead beat had the audacity to text me. I unlocked my phone, prepared to delete his message thread and block his number, but the preview of the message caught my attention.

**Dead Beat: So you started fuckin' my wife's ex nigga? Trash ass bitch. Fuck both of you hoes since y'all in love with that nigga Bishop, he can take care of y'all hoes and these kids.**

Squinting my eyes at the phone, I wasn't sure what the hell he was talking about and my pettiness kicked in on a thousand due to his audacity. I didn't even know the nigga was remarried or how he knew I was dealing with Bishop. Then I remembered the video I posted on my Instagram earlier. I guess the dead beat was still watching my Instagram account. Due to the nature of my business my page was public and I never went through who was viewing my stories.

**Me: Fuck you bitch! For a nigga who doesn't take care of Jibri you always find a way to mind my business. Who I'm fucking and who helps me with Jibri hasn't been your concern since you walked out on him and started running from child support. You have two other kids under three by two other women and I hear you take care of those kids while neglecting Jibri so why are we even any of your concern?**

I blocked his number and continued drying off in the bathroom. After dressing in an oversized shirt for the moment, I joined Bishop on the balcony.

"Is what Vincent said true?" I inquired, placing my phone on Bishop's lap while standing in front of him.

His ears perked up at the mention of Vincent's name, it was definitely true. "Yeah, Vince is married to my ex but I didn't know until the other day. I ran into him while me and Rambo were out and he made the connection," Bishop explained before taking another pull from the blunt.

"Why didn't you tell me?" I questioned out of curiosity.

"It didn't matter," Bishop shrugged. "You said y'all don't have any contact so none of that shit matters, the only thing that's important is the fact that I love you," Bishop expressed, gripping my waist.

Those three words scared the shit out of me and Vincent texting me didn't make shit any better. Things between us were perfect but my last relationship left me scarred and I never thought I'd say those words again. Similarly, my relationship with Vincent started on a high note as well, now look at us. Mortal enemies, I wouldn't piss on him to put out a fire.

"Vince and Natalie are the past and not a part of our future. That nigga don't even take care of his jit, so why it matter what he say? Why that nigga even got access to you?"

"He's still his father, Bishop." I explained.

"You still got feelings for the nigga? Don't you? That's why you worried about the bullshit he texting you and still allowing him access to you when he clearly doesn't deserve it! My love doesn't just extend to you Kalesha, I love your son too. If you gone pull some flaw shit and run back to that nigga to make y'all family work, spare me the bullshit and let me know now. I have seen too many homies go through it."

"It's not like that Bishop," I sighed. "I don't care for him in that way but I've left the door open in case he wanted to step up to the plate."

"Everybody doesn't deserve access to you and I'mma keep shit real with you. The nigga been talking big shit because I put out the word that he's dead out here in these streets. Now he finding this shit out, tender dick nigga gone come at my top and I might have to lay him down."

Bishop stood up to leave the balcony and I trailed behind him. "Where are you going?" I queried, watching him grab his keys off of the coffee table.

"I need a minute to clear my head," he explained.

On the average day, I would've put up a fight but I let Bishop go today. I needed some time to myself to clear my mind as well. There was an unspoken issue between us and I noticed it as soon as those three words left Bishop's mouth. He was bothered by my lack of response and I couldn't say I blamed him. I loved Bishop, how could I not after the way he treated me and Jibri? I was working on my business full time, growing my brand, and had all of the tools at my disposal thanks to Bishop. He was smart, caring, funny, and freaky as hell, just like me. At the same time, I was terrified of laying my feelings out and getting hurt again. Entering the bedroom, I went into Bishop's nightstand and pulled out a blunt and sac of weed to roll up. In the midst of preparing my mental relief, I drafted a text to the groupchat with the ladies.

**Me: Today was crazy. Are we still sliding tonight?**

**Gabby: What happened?**

**Ava: Some crazy stuff but I'm still down if y'all are. Let's just have fun and worry about the drama tomorrow.**

**Me: I'm with it.**

**GiGi sent a voice clip.** *I love outside I ain't never coming home nigga!*

**Me: (crying laughing emoji) I'll see y'all at ten.**

I placed my phone down on the bed and lit the blunt, leaning back in the bed to stare at the ceiling. While watching the blades on Bishop's ceiling fan spin, I had a come to Jesus moment with myself.

# BISHOP

I would never ask Kalesha to leave my crib but I needed a moment to myself and a few shots after everything that popped off today. The fact that Kalesha didn't reciprocate my love wasn't lost on me but the look in Saint's eye when he told me to get the fuck off of him was what crushed me. I called Saint while I rolled my blunt but he didn't answer. Out of concern, I texted Ava and she told me that Saint was fine, taking a shower but wants to be left alone. He needed space and I was going to give it to him but that shit was killing me already. Saint always followed my lead, we were never on bad terms so this shit was fucking with me and it had only been a few hours.

Walking along Twiggs street, I was happy as fuck to live downtown today. I could literally walk to a restaurant and bar and didn't have to worry about driving home. I wandered into an Irish pub and sat at the bar, ordering two shots of Hennessy that I tossed back before ordering a third and fourth. While waiting for my shots, I thought about everything that led up to this situation with Saint.

He asked about his father on a few occasions growing up but I never had any answers. I could've used my resources to find the nigga when Saint was younger but that was something I planned to do after he graduated high school. Then he went to prison and I didn't give a fuck about that shit, my only concern was getting him out early. Next thing I know, the pussy nigga was rolling up my driveway in a wheelchair looking for Saint.

Throughout my thirty-six years on earth I'd done a lot of wild shit, but I was always meticulous when it came to handling a motha fucka that crossed me. That day I couldn't hold my composure, I reacted without thinking and paid for that shit with two years of my life. Throwing back the third and fourth shots when the bartender returned, I thought about the irony of the situation in its totality. Those sneaky motha fuckas got me and Saint sent up the road effortlessly. I couldn't even take the shit to trial, because the dashcam footage was irrefutable. Instead of wasting my money on a trial we opted for reducing the charges and a light sentence.

I wasn't purposely hiding what happened from Saint, it honestly never came up. Saint was on a path of elevation when he was released from prison and I didn't want that type of information to bring him down. I wouldn't say that Saint's father was a sore spot for him, but it was definitely perturbing for anyone who didn't know their father. The bitch nigga died before I started my two year sentence so he couldn't meet the weak motha fucka and I told Lamont to stay the fuck away from Saint if he valued his life.

A pair of soft hands brushed across my shoulder and my reflexes kicked in, I gripped them tightly, ready to tell the culprit to get the fuck on until I heard Kalesha's voice.

"Ouch Bishop," she squealed, snatching her hand away from me.

I instantly softened up when I realized it was Kalesha. She climbed onto the stool next to me and I pulled it closer, damn near placing her in my lap. Taking her hand into mine, I brought it to my lips and smothered it in kisses before moving to her lips. She sucked on my tongue and I pulled her into my lap.

"I love you, Bishop. Your words scared me earlier, they caught me off guard but I've felt that shit in my chest for a minute now. I'm just scared to get hurt again," Kalesha expressed, breaking the kiss. I pulled her into me and kissed her passionately until she fought her way out of my grasp.

"I love you too, Kalesha. You got my word that I'll never do anything to hurt you, I promise to work at this shit because I want it forever." She blushed, staring up at me. "Let's go back to the crib so I can give you some of this loving dick," I suggested, admiring the lil romper shit she had on.

"No, it's Gabby's birthday, remember? We are going out."

I gripped her waist and kissed her neck then down to her clavicle bone. She pushed my head away and giggled, cupping my face in her hands. "I love you, Bishop."

"I love you too," I replied, pecking her lips gently. "Don't get nobody fucked up out there tonight."

"I won't," she chuckled, pulling out of my grasp.

"Hol' up, let me close my tab then I'll walk you to your car," I offered and she paused to wait for me as I pulled out two hundred dollar bills and sat them on the bar.

Hand in hand, we walked back to Kalesha's car in the garage of my building. She snuggled up into me and I loved the feeling. I was going to convince Kalesha to stay home with me but the women called talking shit, telling her to hurry up, and she rushed off to be with them. As soon as she bent the corner in the parking garage I called Rambo.

"Yooooooo," he answered.

"Your girl left the house looking like a thot?"

He exhaled deeply so I knew he was smoking a blunt. "Now that I think about it, I don't know. When we got off the phone she asked me to do a few things around the house then put that pussy on me and I fell asleep. Her ass was being slick huh?"

"Definitely," I laughed at his silly ass. "Is she sharing her location with you?"

"Always," he confirmed. "I know they are going out somewhere in Tampa so I'mma get dressed and slide through."

"Bet."

I ended the call and took the elevator up to my apartment to get dressed. The half smoked blunt Kalesha was working on sat in the ashtray and I knew she was leaving the club early with me for sure now. When she got that weed in her system she damn near turned into a succubus and I loved it.

Around midnight we found them in Ybor at King's. I should've known that's where Gigi would take the girls because she was cool with the owner's wife. Me and Rambo shook it up with the bouncers before entering the club. This was the first time I noticed the ten year age gap between me and Kalesha. Clubs weren't my scene but I trusted the owner here and Kalesha was in attendance so I slid through. Rambo led the way through the crowded club as *TRX* by Rob49 sounded off. He clearly knew his way around because we were in their section within a matter of seconds.

Kalesha and Gigi were standing on the couch pouring Patron into Ava and Gabby's mouths, oblivious to our presence until they were done.

"Bae," Kalesha bubbled, jumping off of the couch and into my arms. I caught her ass and she crashed her lips into mine. She was only with the girls for a good hour and a half and my baby was lit. I tasted the liquor on her tongue as it swirled around in my mouth.

"What the fuck are they doing here? It's my birthday and they are about to ruin the vibes," Gabby complained. "It used to be Rambo popping up, now it's Rambo and Bishop."

Kalesha broke our kiss and slid out of my grasp before turning to Gabby and embracing her in a hug. Saint slid into the section and hugged the ladies, I wanted to address him but now was not the time. Kalesha maneuvered her way in front of me and I wrapped my arm around her abdomen, pulling her closer to me. Saint slid behind Ava and Gabby started talking shit again. "Not you too Saint, you didn't give me the crazy crash the party vibes like your brother and Rambo."

"Naw, I didn't crash the party, Ava invited me and bought the outfit," Saint laughed and Ava nudged him.

Gabby gasped and clasped her chest. "You invited him?" Gabby quizzed as Saint pulled Ava out of the section, guilt written all over her face. The nigga clearly wasn't fucking with me right now and I couldn't wait for us to fix this shit.

Refocusing my attention on Kalesha, I leaned down and whispered in her ear. "What is it going to take for you to love me like Ava loves Saint? I want you to buy me an outfit and invite me to the girls night too."

"Boy hush, I prefer the stalking method, make you work for it," she flirted.

"I can definitely do that for you," I confirmed, nibbling on her ear.

Gabby stood to the side with her face frowned up and I felt bad for her. She was texting away on her phone, clearly pissed off at our presence and I felt bad. Next time we crashed the party we were going to invite Herc along for the right. Lowkey, the nigga was a square ass nigga and probably wouldn't slide but I'd extend the invite. In an effort to not make Gabby feel like the third wheel, I released my grip on Kalesha and sent her to dance with her best friend. Just being in the same vicinity, laying eyes on my girl was good enough for me.

# CHAPTER THIRTY
## Saint

**Two Weeks Later**

*L*amont Dandridge's name was etched into my brain and I hated that shit because I wanted nothing to do with him. Growing up, I always wondered about my father, where he was and if the details Bishop and my mom gave me were true. The older I got, the less I found myself thinking about the nigga. I had my brother, Natalie, and Bishop in my corner, supporting my dreams and ensuring that I was loved and cared for. Growing up, I traveled, domestically and internationally, went to the best basketball skills camps, and experienced shit most people twice my age hadn't, all before I graduated from high school. Unfortunately, Lamont Dandridge and *his* father Justin Dandridge put an end to all of that shit. Changed my life for good. Now I could add an eight year prison stint to my list of rare accomplishments at a young age.

I hadn't said two words to Bishop since that day at Target. He reached out to me on multiple occasions and even dropped off a folder to Ava while I was at work. It contained all of my father's information with a note from Bishop attached.

*My intentions weren't to hide anything from you, I only wanted to protect*

*you from additional heart ache. That wasn't my place, I should've told you
when I got out and allowed you to move accordingly.*

The contents of that folder exposed all of Justin's bullshit. He was a
serial cheater and moved his family around to keep his infidelities a
secret but he was an excellent father to Lamont. Attended every
school event, put him through college, and was an active grandfather.
When Justin met my mom, he lived in Jacksonville and then relocated
to the central Florida area when his wife got sick with cancer so they
could be closer to her family. The basketball championship being held
in Lakeland was the perfect opportunity for Justin to do what he did.
Everyone who was into Florida basketball knew where I would be that
night so it was the perfect opportunity.

No matter how hard I tried to push those thoughts to the back of
my mind, they popped up in the forefront, sending anger through my
entire body. Anger hadn't consumed me like this since my first six
months in prison, it was damn near suffocating. I despised everything
and everyone for what I was going through during those first six
months in prison and now that rage was targeted at a dead man and
Lamont.

My stopwatch sounded off, pulling me out of my head. I took a sip
of water and shook those daunting thoughts off. I glanced up at the
boys on the basketball court and an immediate sense of accomplish-
ment took over me. The four boys and two girls I was working with
this afternoon had no basketball experience prior to working with me
and now they were handling the basketball while performing the v-
dribble cross then putting the ball through their legs like pros.

"Alright, we only have five minutes left so we are going to finish
today with some layup drills. Y'all start off with right hand layups,
make sure you get one or two dribbles in and hit it off that backboard.
I wanna see ten apiece. Five regular layups then five scoop layups. If we
have time we will switch to the left hand layups!"

"Yes coach!" They replied in unison.

Being referred to as *coach* would never get old to me. We finished
up ten minutes later and their parents were already waiting for them in
the parking lot. I chopped it up with a few of them for a brief moment
before hopping in my truck and taking off. I usually stuck around to

run up the court and shoot around for a few minutes after the boys left but the resentment filling my veins called for me to see my mother. Something I hadn't done since I got home.

I stopped at Publix and grabbed a bouquet of sunflowers, my mom always had an infatuation with them. Pulling up to the cemetery I spotted Bishop already there, cleaning off the headstones. I wasn't surprised to see Bishop there, mom was buried next to his dad and he visited them once a month. Deciding to end the feud, I exited my truck and walked across the grass. Bishop already placed a fresh set of sunflowers in the holder attached to her headstone and I sat down on the grass and placed mine flat in front.

"The lawyer called earlier, he said you didn't answer but they are dropping the assault charges," Bishop interrupted the silence.

"That's what's up," I nodded.

"Yeah, I'm happy you came out here to see her."

"Had to, I knew she would bring me peace, just like when we were kids."

I placed my hands over my lips and then touched her headstone and closed my eyes. "Ma, I wish you were here to see how good life is. I'm a gym owner, training lil boys and girls to play basketball. The system didn't break me, it made me stronger though, that's for sure. If you were still here I know that you would love Ava and Jordyn. You'd be spoiling baby girl rotten but Bishop does that enough for everybody."

"Aye, lil mama got my heart," Bishop chimed in. I looked to my left where Bishop stood with his hand placed over his heart.

"I love you, ma, and I miss you like crazy."

Bishop sat next to me and we remained in complete silence for a few minutes before I finally decided to speak again. "If ma was here, she would be on our asses for not speaking. She hated when we used to beef with each other."

"Yeah man, always told us to leave that for the niggas in the street," Bishop confirmed with a smile on his face.

"I love you, bro," I wrapped my arm around his neck and he did the same.

"I love you too, Saint. I've apologized a million times and I'm willing to go a million more. I'd never do anything to intentionally hurt you."

"I wish you would've told me but I get it. As angry as I am now to find out the truth, I probably would've done some reckless shit and extended my prison sentence," I assured him. "You've always done what you thought was best for me."

"That won't ever change," he rubbed my head like we were jits again.

We'd never be too old to share these moments, I was my brother's keeper. Another ten minutes passed and we got up to leave the cemetery.

"Now that we are back on speaking terms, me and Kalesha are throwing Jordyn's birthday party next month. It's not up for debate. I know Ava told Kalesha she wanted to do something small and intimate and that's cool but we are going all out for her," Bishop explained.

"Just take it up with Ava," I caved. Embracing Bishop in a hug before hopping in my truck. When I got home Ava and Jordyn were in the kitchen. Jordyn was in her high chair eating the banana chunks Ava cut up for her. I smiled at the chicken frying on the stove. Ava cooked extremely well to have learned everything on the internet and her fried chicken made me fall deeper in love.

"Go shower so we can eat. I'm not trying to eat with you all sweaty tonight," Ava complained, pulling Jordyn out of her high chair. Baby girl was rubbing her eyes, signaling that she was about to knock out soon. I pecked Ava's lips and rushed to take a shower, a nigga was ready to smash this food.

When I got out of the shower Ava was in the kitchen sipping her red wine while listening to Summer Walker. That was her go to music selection once Jordyn went to sleep. Ava strutted over to me and I wrapped my arms around her swaying from side to side. She melted into my embrace and I kissed the top of her head. I swear that visit to my mom's grave was just what the doctors ordered. My mom would want to see me happy and thriving, not allowing the past to dictate my future.

"I'm happy to see you are in a good mood and it can't just be the chicken," Ava purred as I planted a kiss on her neck.

"Yeah, I talked to Bishop, I went to the graveyard to see my mom and I'm feeling like a new man now," I explained.

"I'm so happy because you and Bishop beefing is some shit I don't ever want to see again."

"I could never beef with my brother," I replied.

"Well let me rephrase it, y'all not being on speaking terms was hard for everyone. You came to the club on Gabby's birthday and we barely interacted with him. He hasn't seen Jordyn in two weeks and I just didn't like the feeling."

"Me either, it won't happen again."

"Good, let me make your plate before I have to clock in," Ava bubbled.

I watched her move around in the kitchen and everything about her was perfect, she was handcrafted just for me. Although I had to eat dinner alone because Ava had to clock in for work, I enjoyed my time in solitude. When I was done eating, I cleaned the kitchen up so Ava could go to sleep when she was done taking calls in three and a half hours, a nigga was counting down because I couldn't go to sleep without her.

While cleaning the kitchen, I decided to call Lamont, that would be the last step on my journey of healing. I rinsed the sink out and went into my bedroom and retrieved the envelope with Justin and Lamont's information. Pulling my phone off of the dresser, I dialed Lamont's number and sat down on the bed. The phone rang twice. "Hello," Lamont answered, sounding slightly groggy. I looked at the time to ensure that it wasn't too late. It was only nine o'clock so I proceeded.

"Wassup, this is Saint."

Lamont cleared his throat and I heard movement in his background. "Hey, I... ugh... wasn't expecting to hear that. What's up?"

"Can you meet up to hold this conversation face to face?"

"I actually don't live in the area anymore, we were only in town for that weekend because my wife's sister was having a baby," he explained.

I hated hearing that but it might've been a blessing in disguise. If I met with Lamont in person I might not have been able to control my anger. After beating that last charge I didn't need anything throwing me off track.

"That's cool, I'll keep this brief. That asswhooping I gave you, you deserved that plus more. You ruined my future and got to live your life uninterrupted after the bullshit you did. I should've been on somebody's court balling, instead I'm eighteen years old, green to any street shit, and thrown into prison. I've seen niggas get shanked, gang fights, showering with a bunch of grown ass men, eating slop, and all types of shit that you should've experienced."

I paused for a moment to calm my anger before continuing. "Based on your age you were twenty years old, old enough to know better but young enough that I could see how your father influenced you. I place most of the blame on Justin, the man who didn't raise me and then decided my life was worth less than yours for a second time. I know you've reached out but I don't know in what world you think there could be room for us to move on like one big happy family. How could you expect me to look you in the eyes at family functions or a cordial event?"

"I don't..."

"That was a rhetorical question," I cut him off. "I've thought about revenge and all that good shit but I couldn't do that to your son. I have a daughter that I will go to the end of the earth for and I know how it feels to grow up without parents so I'm going to extend you the grace that I wish you and Justin extended to me and leave you the fuck alone. I can't take you away from your son, your family, your future. Due to your actions, I still have obstacles like having my record expunged to overcome before I can reach my full potential."

"For what it's worth, I'm sorry about what happened and if I could go back, I swear I would have accepted the consequences like a man."

"If only it was that simple. Stay the fuck away from me from this day forward, allow me to leave the past behind me," I requested and ended the call.

Placing the phone down on the nightstand, I pulled out *Animal* by K'Wan and used reading as my therapy while I waited for Ava to get off of work. I was leaving the past behind me, my future was too bright to dwell on the past.

~

Since seeing Lamont in Target two weeks ago I finally felt the anger diminish. I was back to myself and our conversation last night freed me from that anger he fueled in me again. A notification on my Facebook page caught my attention, it was that dreaded name. Lamont Dandridge again. I felt my blood boiling at the audacity of this nigga to find me on social media and tag me in a post. Sliding off the couch where Ava and Jordyn were knocked out, I opened the message, prepared to read everything except what my eyes landed on.

**Lamont Dandridge tagged you in a post.**

**About eight years ago I was young and wilding the fuck out. My dad was cheating on my mom while she was dying of cancer. I lost all respect for the man and was rebelling hard. Dropped out of college, posted up on the block, smoking weed and popping pills. Then I got a girl pregnant and started hanging with jack boys as a way to make money to handle my responsibilities. That resulted in me committing a home invasion when there was someone home. We tussled over the gun, I got the upper hand and let off a shot by mistake before leaving. The man was in the hospital, my physical description and car were on the news, and I tucked my tail, informing my father of what happened. He said he would handle it and took the gun. A few weeks later Saint Carmichael was arrested and I knew my father framed him. When I confronted him, he told me that Saint was barely eighteen and his brother had the type of money to get him off. At twenty years old, I was immature as hell and moved on with my life. My mother was dying and I had a child on the way. I didn't want to be away from my mother or child and I also didn't want to break my mom's heart by exposing a child born through the duration of their marriage. An eighteen year secret my father hid from everyone.**

**I'm older and wiser now and I would like to apologize to Saint for the role I played in the situation. I understand if you**

**never want to speak to me again but I wanted to publicly clear your name and take responsibility for my actions.**

I appreciated Lamont for clearing my name publicly, to the best of his ability, but it was still *fuck that nigga*. Turning my phone off, I knew my social media pages were about to blow up and if the post went viral, the media would likely pick it up. All I wanted to do was nap with my girls though, I reclaimed my spot on the couch and joined them in a mid-afternoon nap.

# EPILOGUE

## Bishop

### *Two Years Later*

"*U*ghhh, I want to know what it is," Kalesha complained in the passenger seat with the blind folds on.

"You will see," Jibri assured her.

Two crazy ass years in prison led to the last two blissful years with Kalesha and Jibri so I wouldn't change shit about my journey to this day. Kalesha was the one for me and that big ass engagement ring resting on her finger proved that. We were still living apart until we were married and I was cool with that, I told her we would take things slow and we definitely did that. I allowed her to have her time to keep her space but that shit was about to come to an end.

I was enjoying retirement and you might as well say I was Kalesha's full-time employee because she worked a nigga like a slave every fucking weekend. Her business picked up and I helped out more. If shit kept going the way it was going Kalesha was going to have to hire an employee for real once college football started up again because I was going to be at the crib watching the games on Saturday.

Glancing in the rearview mirror I saw the excitement on Jibri's face as he sat in the backseat, fidgeting with his fingers. The surprise we had in store for his mother was a joint effort and we knew it would catch her off guard. At eight years old, Jibri earned his stripes in the architect game and helped me and the actual architects design the house I was having built from the ground up for our family. Jibri was engaged, offering opinions, and picked out every design involving his room and homeschool area. When we pulled up at the construction site I popped the trunk and allowed Jibri out of the truck while Kalesha waited impatiently.

"Don't take that blind fold off either! Let us get set up first."

"I'm not but y'all need to come on. I need to be in on the surprise," Kalesha sassed.

I met Jibri at the trunk and pulled out the blueprints and three hard hats.

"This is exciting," Jibri bounced around.

I closed the trunk and we sauntered over to the front of the truck. Jibri stood back while I opened the door and helped Kalesha out. Slowly guiding her steps to the front of the truck, Jibri stood in front of the foundation with the blueprints in his hand. Positioning myself behind Kalesha, I slid her blind folds off and Jibri waved the blueprint in the air, hopping up and down.

"Surprise," I hummed.

"Mom, Bishop let me design our new house. It might not look like much now but let me show you the plans," Jibri explained, rushing over with the blueprint in hand. He slapped it on the hood of the truck and ran down the key elements of our future home. I could listen to Jibri go on all day every day. Jit made so many strides in the last two years and I couldn't be prouder. In addition to architecture, Jibri was also interested in interior design now, thanks to this process. He became obsessed with picking out things for his room and home school space. That led me to purchasing a subscription for Architectural Design magazine and he read those things cover to cover as soon as they arrived in the mail. Whatever Jibri decided on when he grew up, he was going to be great and just like I did with Saint, I was going to make sure that he had the tools to thrive in his niche.

# KALESHA

Jibri was clearly excited about this entire ordeal because his mouth was going a mile a minute as he reviewed the plans for our future home. Nothing about Bishop surprised me anymore. I don't think a man could get better than Bishop Carmichael. He loved, cherished, and supported me in every way possible and next month we would make things official and tie the knot. My parents loved Bishop, Jibri loved him, and more importantly, I was head over heels in love with him.

Just take this moment for instance, he took the time to incorporate Jibri in the plans for building our new home. It was clear from Jibri's speech that it wasn't a gesture for vanity purposes either. Jibri was reading off square footage details and a bunch of other things I knew nothing about but architecture was Jibri's thing so he knew what the fuck was going on and that was enough for me.

"You two are amazing," I teared up, allowing a few tears to fall. They dripped onto the blueprint and Jibri quickly snatched them away from me.

"Mom, you'll ruin them," he complained, rolling the blue prints up and placing them into a long tube.

"I'm sorry," I chuckled, wiping away my tears. "I am just so excited to see what you and Bishop have in store for me and this house. It sounds amazing."

I hugged Jibri then kissed his cheek and he immediately wiped it away. Turning to Bishop, I wrapped my arms around his neck and he placed his hands on my waist. "Gross, I'll be in the car," Jibri monotoned.

I chuckled and leaned up to kiss Bishop and he sucked on my tongue for a brief moment. Our kisses were known to get nasty but we had to keep it PG since Jibri was here but when we got home tonight, I was popping this pussy on a handstand to show my appreciation.

"Jibri said they will be done in nine months, is that really possible?"

"Give or take a month as long as there aren't any major delays or screw ups," Bishop explained.

"I can't wait to see the final product, I'm going to let you and Jibri do y'all thing. I should've known something was up when Jibri started reading those interior design magazines."

"Yeah, I said I would hire someone but my boy wants to design his bedroom and homeschool space himself. Whatever he wants he gets, just like his mama," Bishop confirmed before pecking my lips again.

"Let me get Jibri out of the car so we can take a picture," I bubbled.

Bishop nodded and I went to retrieve my son. He hated pictures so I was prepared for a fight. "Come on Jibri, I want to take a picture in front of the foundation to add to our scrapbook."

"Okay," Jibri confirmed, shocking the shit out of me.

If he wasn't going to put up a fight I wasn't going to question him. "Bishop, you said I could have a hundred dollar Roblox card if I took the picture so come on."

I glared at Bishop and he shrugged his shoulders. "Come on Jibri, that's supposed to stay between me and you. Now yo mama gone try to tell me not to give it to you and we gotta do the whole song and dance we always do."

"My apologies, I'll remember next time. Her antics are getting old and I need new skins," Jibri stated, standing in front of the foundation next to his mom. Pulling my phone out, I decided to let Jibri and Bishop's antics slide today and take my pictures while I could. Jibri looked at the camera, smile nowhere in sight, but me and Bishop were smiling hard enough for him too. I was just happy he didn't downright refuse to take a picture like he usually did. I snapped a few selfies and stopped when an unsaved number started calling me.

"Hello," I quickly answered.

My business was booming and I wasn't leaving any coins on the table. Bishop took care of me and Jibri, we didn't want for anything but I would never stop chasing my own bag.

"Hey Kalesha, this is Natalie, Vince's wife. I'm not trying to call you on no drama shit but I was wondering if you've heard from him because he disappeared like six months ago and I haven't heard from him. Do you know how I can get in touch with his parents?"

I pulled the phone away from my face and squinted my eyes at it, knowing that my ears had to be playing tricks on me. Saying Vincent's name was like saying Candy Man five times in the mirror for me. His delusional ass hadn't been in touch to mind my business or check on his son since that day I posted Bishop on my Instagram story two years ago. I heard Natalie sniffling on the phone and that added to the unbelievable factor.

The evil bitch in me wanted to laugh at Natalie's sad ass. Natalie thought she was doing her big one, laying up with a young nigga who didn't take care of the child we shared while they were living like one big happy family with her newborn and another child he had with some other chick after abandoning Jibri. The empath in me would never do that though. I couldn't laugh at another woman's pain after going through the same exact thing.

"Who is that?" Bishop pried.

His voice made the situation even worse because I quickly remembered that Bishop was in a relationship with Natalie until she fumbled him. Oh how the tables turn. I raised my finger and found the words to answer Natalie's question. "I don't know where Vince is and he never fucked with his parents like that. He hasn't helped with Jibri in years and doesn't even bother to check on him."

"Okay, ummm... sorry to bother you," Natalie sniffled.

"Yeah," I ended the awkward call.

"Who was that?"

"It was Natalie, she was looking for Vince like I talk to his ass," I shrugged. "She said he disappeared on her six months ago. That's his MO, and he is probably already onto his next victim."

"See she should've let me kill the nigga when I had the opportunity."

"Bishop," I chastised him.

"What? At least that way all of y'all could've gotten some death benefits off his ass."

"Please relax and get us to the basketball game on time tonight," I pleaded. "Rambo and Gigi can't come because the boys got sick and Gabby and Herc are out of town so Ava will be by herself with the girls."

"I got us, we will be on time this time," Bishop assured me.

# SAINT

Swaggering over to the front of the locker room, I was on an indescribable high. After everything I'd been through I came out on top. My name was free and clear thanks to Lamont's confession, my record was expunged and Bishop's lawyers sued the fuck out of the police department for the eight years they stole from me. I didn't even give a fuck about the money, my freedom and ability to live out my new dream was most important for me.

However, I wasn't about to leave a penny on the table. I collected my settlement money and put it to good use, creating Saint's Legal Clinic, a nonprofit aiming to help those from impoverished backgrounds who found themselves facing legal trouble. Whether they committed the crime or were proclaiming their innocence, the mission of my foundation was to ensure that they had the best legal defense.

"Alright, alright. Y'all settle down and listen up," I spoke up, commanding the attention of everyone in the locker room.

The voices ceased and all eyes were on me. A team of dedicated young men from my alma mater stared back at me, waiting for a few motivating words. After my record was expunged, I was offered the coaching position at the same high school I never had the pleasure of graduating from due to my incarceration. I obtained my high school diploma and a bachelors in exercise science while locked up and after my record was cleared they came in handy when I applied for the open position this year.

It was truly humbling to be in the position I was in after everything I'd endured in life. We were gearing up for the FHSAA state championship basketball finals and this was a full circle moment. After everything I'd been through, I never could've guessed that I would end up coaching in that game and my boys had a real chance at winning for the first time since I led our team to victory.

"Tonight is the night that we put Tampa High on the map! Y'all have worked hard throughout this entire season to get to this point. I need y'all to push yourselves to the limits tonight. We've faced tough opponents in the past and came out on top, we need to do that shit one last time. This is your opportunity to show those recruiters what you are truly capable of. Leave everything on that court tonight and I know we will come out with the dub. Believe in your abilities and lean on each other while on that court so they can't stop us. Let's get out there and ball!"

"Let's get out there and ball!" They screamed in unison.

We exited the locker room and I spotted Bishop, Kalesha, Jibri, Ava, and Jordyn near the doors. Bishop was dapping my players up, patting them on their heads, and offering words of encouragement. I don't know who was more excited about my position as the head coach for Tampa Bay High, me or Bishop. I worked with an AAU team during the summer but now those boys were his as much as they were mine. Jibri attended the games but couldn't take the loud crowds so he had on a pair of noise canceling headphones. He peeled them off at the sight of me and offered a slight smirk. "Good luck, Saint. I was just reviewing your opponents' stats on the ride over and I'm positive you have this in the bag," he assured me, turning his iPad around so I could view the screen.

"Thanks, Jibri. I'm confident in my boys as well." I smiled at Jibri and he placed his headphones back over his ears.

"Y'all got this shit in the bag," Bishop dapped me up.

"I hope so. Don't be out here embarrassing me tonight man," I laughed.

"I already told him to watch his mouth, it's your big night, I got him. You just worry about those boys," Kalesha assured me.

"Thanks, sis," I expressed.

Finally reaching my favorite girls at the end of the line of people, my wife's beautiful face was exactly what I needed to help calm my nerves before stepping onto the court. Our one year old daughter Savanna sat perched on Ava's hip with her hands extended in my direction. I pecked Ava's lips and took my baby girl from her arms.

We had a small wedding ceremony on the anniversary of the day we met. That day was no longer a date we looked back on with despair, it was now a momentous date on our calendars. After we were married I started the process of adopting Jordyn and Jermaine was so strung out on drugs that he happily signed his rights over. Watching Ava go through a second HG pregnancy wasn't as hard as the first because we knew what to expect and how to address her symptoms. It was still rough and I got a vasectomy because I never wanted to see her go through that shit again, two kids was enough for me. I needed my wife present, happy, and healthy.

"Let that angst go. You poured your all into those boys and they are going to do what needs to be done," Ava encouraged me and I received it.

Jordyn was almost three years old and stood next to her mother giving me a look that said I better pick her up too. She didn't have to speak, that was Jordyn's usual face when I picked Savanna up. Scooping Jordyn off the ground, I held both of my daughters in my arms and kissed their cheeks, causing them to giggle.

"Ball da da." Savanna bubbled.

"Yep, daddy is about to go out here and win a basketball game. Y'all be good while I'm on the court," I kissed their cheeks again and handed Savanna back to Ava before placing Jordyn on the floor.

"Alright, I gotta get out there," I explained. Kissing Ava again before trailing my boys to the court.

# AVA

"I knew Saint and them boys was gone fuck 'em up," Bishop cheered from his seat in the stands.

There were only five seconds left and Saint's boys were up by five points. It was impossible for their opponents to come back from that type of deficit, especially when they weren't in possession of the ball. The game was being played as a formality at this point. Cam, the point guard for Tampa Bay High, pushed the ball up the court and shot a nice layup, increasing their lead to seven points just before the buzzer sounded off.

Saint's boys were up by seven points and officially the state champs. I grabbed both of my daughters' hands and rushed onto the basketball court to celebrate with my husband. It was easy to get to Saint because we always sat right behind his team. My husband's eyes connected with mine and he rushed over in our direction. We hugged and I pecked his lips repeatedly. Bishop's overly excited ass scooped both of the girls from the floor and bounced them up and down in his arms. They giggled with excitement, loving all of their Uncle Bishop's wild antics.

"Y'all daddy got two state championship titles under his belt now! One as a coach and one as a player!"

I was thankful that he kept that statement age appropriate because

Bishop's mouth was unfiltered all night, embarrassing the shit out of me throughout the entire game, even Kalesha couldn't put a muzzle on his ass.

"Congratulations, Saint," Bishop celebrated and I could see the tears he was fighting back. "Alright, let me get off that soft shit. You did the motha fuckin' thang!"

Bishop placed the girls back down on the floor and Saint's boys crowded around them. "Go celebrate with the team," I encouraged Saint.

His boys were in the middle of the basketball court chanting his name, Coach Saint! I rocked an enormous grin thinking about all of the obstacles I overcame and how they led me to Saint and the prosperous life we lived now. I co-owned *Saint's Fitness*, while attending school to obtain my bachelor's degree in business management, my family was happy, and I couldn't ask for anything else. The celebration in the gym lasted for at least an hour, I lost track of time. Then Saint spent a great amount of time speaking with coaches, staff from the high school, and anybody else who wanted to smile in his face after winning the championship game. I loved all of this for my husband, nobody deserved it more than him. Not just because he spent time in prison for a crime he didn't commit either, Saint was genuinely an amazing person.

When we finally exited the gym the parking lot was practically empty but Bishop was waiting with a bottle of champagne in hand. He popped the top, sending the champagne everywhere.

"I couldn't present my gift to you after your high school win but I can get it right this time!" He announced, passing Saint a large envelope.

"What the fuck is in here, Bishop? You do realize I'm grown as fuck with my own money, right?"

"That won't ever stop me from doing the shit I do, nigga," Bishop celebrated, drinking the champagne from the bottle.

I laughed at his antics but peered into his truck that was parked only a few feet away to ensure that Kalesha was driving home because Bishop was on one. Saint opened the envelope and pulled out a key fob.

"You never made it home for me to give you that Tahoe ten years ago after winning the state championship and I'm past my two year upgrade on the truck. Let me have this moment," Bishop choked out and I was no more good. I could feel his emotions seeping out as his voice cracked. "Congratulations, Saint! Don't try to give it back either, it's yours and you're taking it."

Bishop clicked the button on the key fob and the alarm to a brand new Chevy Tahoe sitting behind his Range caught my attention. Saint loved his truck and probably would've continued driving the other one because he didn't care about materialistic things. The fact that Bishop stuck to Saint's simple nature instead of going all out like I know he wanted to really stuck out to me.

"I love you, Bishop," Saint hugged his brother and Bishop reciprocated.

There was nothing like brotherly love.

# THE END!

I truly hope that you guys enjoyed this beautifully chaotic love story. It was different for me to write but I loved every moment of it and I hope you did as well. Thank you for supporting and please don't forget to leave your honest feedback!
Join my mailing list or my readers group to stay up to date.

**Mailing list:** https://bit.ly/2RTP3EV
**Readers Group: Kee's Book Bees**

# FOLLOW ME ON SOCIAL MEDIA

Instagram: https://instagram.com/authorlakia
Facebook: https://www.facebook.com/AuthorLakia
Facebook: https://www.facebook.com/kiab9o
TikTok: https://www.tiktok.com/@authorlakia

Join me in my Facebook group for giveaways, book discussions and a few laughs and gags! Maybe a few sneak peeks in the future.https://www.facebook.com/groups/keesbookbees
Or search Kee's Book Bees

# ALSO BY LAKIA

Surviving A Dope Boy: A Hood Love Story (1-3)

When A Savage Is After Your Heart: An Urban Standalone

When A Savage Wants Your Heart: An Urban Standalone

Trapped In A Hood Love Affair (1-2)

Tales From The Hood: Tampa Edition

The Street Legend Who Stole My Heart

My Christmas Bae In Tampa

The Wife of a Miami Boy (1-2)

Fallin For A Gold Mouth Boss

Married To A Gold Mouth Boss

Summertime With A Tampa Thug

From Bae To Wifey (1-2)

Wifed Up By A Miami Millionaire

A Boss For The Holidays: Titus & Burgundy

Miami Hood Dreams (1-2)

A Week With A Kingpin

Something About His Love

Craving A Rich Thug (1-3)

Risking It All For A Rich Thug

Summertime With A Kingpin

Enticed By A Down South Boss

A Gangsta And His Girl (1-2)

Soul Of My Soul 1-2

Wrapped Up With A Kingpin For The Holidays

New Year, New Plug

Caught Up In A Hitta's World

The Rise Of A Gold Mouth Boss

A Cold Summer With My Hitta

Soul Of Fire

Sweet Licks (1-3)

Riding The Storm With A Street King

Running Off On My Baby Daddy At Christmas Time

Crushing On The Plug Next Door (1-2)

Love Headlines

Gone Off His Thug Kisses (1-2)

Made in the USA
Monee, IL
03 October 2023